# 3 AM

---

*By*

**Peter Samuel**

# **Contents**

# The Ghostly Curse of Dubh Artach Castleo

# Chapter 1 - Leaving the City, Finding the0 Dream

Percival Somerville was a shrewd stockbroker on the London Stock Exchange floor. He had a special gift for knowing when to buy and when to sell his clients' stocks and shares, which earned them—and him—a great deal of money over the years. Not all deals worked out, however, but with other trades, he soon recovered what he had lost. A lot of people put their trust in Percy. This was the shortened name he had been given; his friends called him Perse. He also had a reputation for being calm and level-headed when the need arose. But as the years rolled by, he was becoming fed up with the rat race in the city. The swinging 1960s were not his scene. He preferred jazz and classical music. Some of the modern music was fine, but there were other bands that, in his opinion, should never have reached the top of their game. Noise and more noise seemed to be their genre for success—along with makeup.

Percy had accumulated a small fortune. It could have been more had his divorced wife not taken a large chunk of it. He had brokered a deal with her: he was allowed to keep the mansion in Surrey, the holiday cottage in Devon, and the apartment on Bayswater Road, London, which saved him the long drive home after a day of haggling on the Stock Exchange floor. His Silver Shadow Rolls-Royce was bought after the divorce and did not enter the negotiations. All in all, Percy was satisfied with the settlement. Even though it was his money that had given her the luxury she had become accustomed to—until she ran off with her accountant—Percy smiled, knowing that the large settlement she had received would be long gone, or at least seriously reduced. Avril was always a big spender.

It was the weekend. With no Stock Exchange dealings, Percy drove south to Surrey. While studying the *Times* property section, his eye fell upon a specific advert: *Scottish Estate in need of investment. Offers begin at £220,000.* Percy wanted out of the hassle. It was 1968. He had had enough, and now was the time to pack it all in. This Scottish estate could be the answer to his dream. He wrote down the telephone number of the Scottish Crown Office.

On Monday morning, he telephoned his solicitor, Brian Dimitri. "Brian, I want you to drop what you're doing and submit a price." He gave the solicitor the details and the offer. "Let's start with what they're asking, then increase it if necessary. I want that estate, no matter what it costs." He paused. "Within reason, Brian. You know the drill. Let me know if it gets out of hand."

Percy sat in his office waiting patiently for the call. It was nearly two hours before the solicitor got back to him. "Sorry it took so long, Perse. There was a bit of haggling to be done. However, I can now say that you are the owner of a two-hundred-square-mile estate called Acharacle in the region of Lochaber in the western Highlands of Scotland. Sanna Lodge needs a lot of work, as do the two farms, a gamekeeper's cottage, a water bailiff's cottage, and six holiday cottages. Two need renovation work. The four in the village of Kilchoan need only cosmetic repairs, nothing serious. You have a Land Rover and a Ford Consul Saloon car. Here are the two bricks on top of the chimney, my friend: the Acharacle Estate comes with a title—'Laird of Acharacle'—which has its own tartan. There is a castle with its very own ghost. I won't even hazard trying to pronounce its name, but it stands on an island of volcanic rock known locally as the Black Rock Castle."

Percy interrupted him. "How much, Brian? How much has this cost me?"

"£230,000, Perse, and an estate of that size is worth every penny. Knowing you, you'll recoup that within four or five years." The solicitor paused. "There is one thing, Perse: this is not business. I want you to guarantee a free week's fishing and shooting for me and my friends when you get the cottages renovated and the estate up and running." He paused again. "The Scottish Crown Office will fax through the documents for your signature. I think it would be wise to get the cheque off to them sooner rather than later. Meanwhile, I'll get to work on the details. Congratulations, Perse— that was some scoop."

The telephone purred as the solicitor ended the call. Percy leapt to his feet and jumped into the air. It was something he had never done before—show his emotions. He usually liked to keep things close to his chest. Now that the estate purchase had been settled, it was time to realise his own assets. A keen American buyer had submitted a price of $360,000 for the Surrey mansion. This still left him with the London flat on Bayswater Road. The holiday cottage in Devon took longer to sell, but now Percy Somerville had working capital of £425,000 after his cheque to the Scottish Crown Office had been accepted and cleared. He toyed with the idea of driving to Scotland but decided instead to pack his suitcases with fine ornaments and photographs, which would be transported with the Silver Shadow Rolls-Royce on a low loader.

It was time to think about a going-away party. Christmas and New Year were fast approaching. He could hold a New Year's celebration. That is what he did. His friends from the London Stock Exchange were invited. Some fair-weather friends insisted on joining the party. How could he refuse? They had worked alongside him for years. The invitations were sent out, but like every New Year's bash, there were the gate-crashers. Percy didn't mind too much—so long as they behaved themselves. The security company did its job well when any drunk stepped out of line.

There was one member of the press who started to ask awkward questions. "This is all rather sudden, Mr Somerville. A stockbroker making a quick exit to the Highland heather. I take it all exchange dealings are above board?" Percy smiled. "Yes, Dora, I can say with sincerity that things are fine and on the level. My middle name is 'Squeaky Clean', and if I ever hear that your newspaper has printed anything to the contrary, I'll sue you and your paper, no matter what it costs. Now, be a good girl and make sure your glass is charged. It's nearly that time." He walked away to join his other guests, leaving Dora standing with her notepad and pencil.

The bells tolled, bringing in the beginning of 1969. There was plenty of backslapping, handshaking, and well-wishing as the New Year party got into full swing. Not that Percy overindulged in alcohol. A couple of champagne flutes made his head spin. But it did take a little time to get over the celebration and have the mansion cleaned for the American buyer.

He boarded the steam train at Euston station. Two large steam engines were pulling sixteen carriages: a buffet restaurant carriage, a mail carriage and the guard's, twelve carriages with six sleeping compartments each, and four first- and second-class carriages. Percy was shown to his sleeping compartment by his carriage attendant. There wasn't much room, but it was comfortable: two bunk beds and a small toilet. There was also a seat where he could sit at a small table and watch the world slip by. He decided the compartment would be used mainly for sleeping on the twelve-hour journey to Fort William in the Scottish Highlands.

The Caledonian Express made its way out of the city before gathering speed. There were limited station stops as the *Flying Scotsman* headed north. Percy enjoyed a scrumptious three-course meal in the spotless buffet car, then relaxed with coffee and a mint. He enjoyed talking with other passengers who were travelling north for different reasons.

It was time for bed. His bunk had been turned down for the night and his pyjamas laid out. He lay awake for a while, listening to the clickety-clack of the train crossing the points. He fell into a deep sleep until he got his alarm call the next morning. He was handed a lemon tea with a biscuit.

"The breakfast buffet is open, sir. If you would like your breakfast served in your compartment, just press the attendant bell and I'll come back to take your order." Percy thanked him for the wake-up call but said he would rather eat in the restaurant car. He sat drinking his lemon tea in his dressing gown, watching painted stations whistle by.

There was the occasional sound of the steam engine's whistle as it approached stations and level crossings—a sign marked with a large *W* giving the leading engine driver his instruction to sound the whistle to warn of the express train's approach. It was obvious to Percy that they had crossed the border. He made his way to the restaurant car for breakfast, and a fine breakfast it was. He spoke to the attendant in the corridor.

"Where are we now, Garry?"

"We've just left the town of Callander and are about to begin the steep climb over Glen Ogle. Our next scheduled stop will be Crianlarich, then our last stop will be Tyndrum Upper, before we begin to climb again over the steep gradient to Rannoch Moor, one thousand two hundred and twenty feet above sea level. Watch out for the wild deer. The scenery is spectacular, with the snow-covered mountains of Glen Coe in the distance. The moor itself is especially striking on a clear morning such as this. Stand in the corridor and you'll be able to see the mountain of Schiehallion, known as the Fairy Mountain in Perthshire. But the best scenery can be observed from your compartment."

"I know you're busy, Garry, but are we on time? How long before we reach our destination?"

"Yes, we're on time and should pull into Fort William at 8:00 a.m."

The Caledonian Sleeper from London entered Fort William station two minutes ahead of schedule. The steam engines shuddered to a halt, glad to be relieved of the strenuous work. The attendant pointed Percy to the exit and the taxi rank, and he was tipped accordingly. The taxi driver got out and opened the boot, where he placed Percy's small suitcase and briefcase.

"Where to, sir?" he asked amiably.

"The village hotel of Kilchoan on the Ardnamurchan peninsula."

The taxi driver was pleased to be getting such a long drive, which meant a large fare.

"You have a choice of routes, sir. We can take the Road to the Isles and turn off at the head of Loch Eil, or we can drive down the A82 to the Ardgour ferry, where we take a short crossing to the village, then onward to the Lochaber district and your destination."

"Which route would you suggest, driver?" Percy asked suspiciously.

"It's as broad as it's long, sir, but I would suggest the ferry. It's not expensive, and the Loch Eil route can be busy with animals at this time of the morning."

"Ah, you mean wild deer?"

"No, sir, sheep and cattle."

"The ferry it is, Eddie."

There wasn't much to see as they travelled the eight miles to the ferry, but once they crossed to the other side, a vista of mountains in Glencoe stretched behind them. The Strath of Appin, across the Firth of Lorn, amazed Percy the Englishman.

"That area is where the famous Appin murder took place, mentioned in Robert Louis Stevenson's novel *Kidnapped*."

This meant nothing to the illiterate Londoner. However, he marvelled at the scenery.

"Coming into view ahead of us is the Island of Lismore. The Gaelic spelling means 'large garden', where many species of tropical plants grow in abundance. It has a ferry link to the town of Oban. Also ahead, at the tip of the island, we have the Lismore Lighthouse. Then look across to the Isle of Mull and the mountain of Ben More. We'll continue up the Sound of Mull, bypassing the town of Lochaline, world famous for its sand used in glassblowing and all kinds of glass." Eddie then sat silent for a while, concentrating on the narrow single-track road with passing places—an original part of the General Wade project of roadbuilding to transfer troops to the wild, unsettled Highlands of Scotland.

"Not long now, sir—twenty minutes or so should see you safely deposited at your hotel."

Percy watched as Eddie carried his belongings up to the hotel reception. He paid the fare and tipped him for making the journey seem shorter with his touristic information. He tapped the bell on the reception desk and stood waiting. After a delay, a woman appeared.

"Sorry, I was upstairs making the beds."

"Sign here, please. How long are you staying?" she asked bluntly.

"Indefinitely, until my lodge is renovated," he replied in the same tone.

"Good lord, you must be the new Laird of Acharacle. I'm Rosemary. Your sea-view room is ready for you, sir." Her attitude had changed at the drop of a hat.

# Chapter 2 - Settling In & Stirring the Waters

"If I'm going to be staying here for a while, I think we can drop the 'sir' and just call me Percy, or Perse. Now, I've had a long journey, so if you show me to my room, I'd be very much obliged." He followed the receptionist-cum-chambermaid upstairs and walked to the window to admire the view.

"Just one thing, Rosemary. I need a taxi to pick me up at 7:30 p.m. to take me out to the estate lodge." He could see she was struggling with the twenty-four-hour clock. "7:30 tonight, Rosemary."

She nodded and said, "We don't have a taxi as such, sir, but Mr MacDonald, the builder, uses his Land Rover to transfer people from the pub and croft to croft."

"That will do fine until I get my own vehicles serviced," he replied, watching her close the door.

After hanging up his few garments, Percy decided to take a walk around the village and make a note of his assets, especially the six holiday cottages. He found it strange that three of them were occupied, but he left questions for later when he was settled into running the Acharacle Estate. Now seemed a good time to locate the village mechanic. He stumbled upon a small garage where a mechanic was working under a Ford Transit van. The man pulled himself out from below on his duckboard.

"Fergus MacLennan. Can I help you?" he asked, wiping his oily hands on a rag.

"Percy Somerville. I've just arrived in the village. I need two vehicles serviced that are apparently garaged at Sanna Lodge, and I wonder if you can help get them back on the road. I understand they've been lying dormant for some time."

"Ah, you must be the new laird everyone is talking about." Fergus paused. "I need to get this vehicle repaired and tested today, so if tomorrow morning suits you, let's say 8:30. Only on one condition—you put down a deposit for the work to be carried out. Cash, if you don't mind."

"You make it sound as if you don't trust me, Mr MacLennan."

"I don't. The last laird buggered off, leaving a trail of debt in his wake. I was one of the unfortunate ones caught, and it nearly put me under. I'll never be caught again. That's the deal, sir."

"Agreed, Fergus. Make out a bill for any parts used, and I'll pay that up front as well."

Percy had seen what he wanted to see. A quick nap before dinner would freshen him up for the night drive out to Sanna Lodge. The bed was comfortable, and he enjoyed an afternoon nap. The timing was perfect, as he was the first guest in the dining room. A pretty waitress approached to take his dinner order. He read her lapel badge.

"Home-made Scotch broth with steak and kidney pie, Rebecca, followed by custard and pears. Coffee to finish, thank you."

"Coffee is served in the lounge, sir."

"I wish people would stop calling me 'sir'. Percy or Perse would suffice—Mr Somerville, if it's business."

Rebecca giggled with embarrassment. "We're not allowed to call guests by their first name, Mr Somerville, but I'll remember that when I'm not at work."

She was about to walk away, but turned back. "Is it true you've booked Duncan MacDonald to take you to Sanna Lodge tonight? Don't accept his price. He has a habit of overcharging tourists and strangers."

"Thanks for the warning, Rebecca. Forewarned is forearmed. I'll keep that in mind."

"My husband has a car you could use during the day, free of charge. Or I could drive you to and from the lodge as long as it's after 9:30 a.m. and we're back before 3:00 p.m. I have a child at primary school."

"I just might take you up on that offer, Rebecca. I'd pay you for your time and petrol expenses." He paused. "Dash it all, I'll meet you at the school tomorrow morning, and you can do your chauffeuring."

"Please don't come to the school, Mr Somerville. People in this village have vicious tongues, so I'll pick you up at the pier. It's normally quiet at that time of the morning."

"The pier it is, Rebecca."

After his dinner, he had coffee in the lounge while he sat waiting for the builder. He looked at his watch time after time. It was 8:05 p.m. when Duncan MacDonald arrived. Percy followed him out to the noisy Land Rover.

"One thing I think we should get straight, Mr MacDonald. If I book a time for transport, I expect the person who is driving to be on time. It's a little important fad of mine."

"Aye, but I think you'll find things a little different up here in the Highlands, Mr Somerville. When the Lord made time, he made plenty of it. Now let's get going. I have another hire to attend to."

There was no conversation on the short journey out to the lodge.

"That'll be £6 and 10 shillings," the builder said, getting out of the vehicle.

"For a two-mile journey, MacDonald, you'll have to think again," Percy retorted.

"You're going back to Kilchoan later, I take it? That's the return fare."

"It's still too much. I'll walk back. I'll pay you £2 and 10 shillings for taking me here. Take it or leave it."

"Call it four quid and I'll pick you up at eleven."

"That's more like the price, Mr MacDonald—and don't be late."

The builder held out his hand for payment, but Percy laughed. "You'll be paid after you drop me at the hotel later tonight." Duncan MacDonald was livid as he charged up the lodge veranda steps and unlocked the lodge door.

"Is that the estate door keys you have on the keyring, Mr MacDonald?"

"Yes, and the castle key is the big one."

"I think as the Laird of Acharacle, owner of the estate, I should have these, Mr MacDonald."

"I'm the hereditary keeper of Dubh Artach Castle. My family have a duty to carry out inspections from time to time. We've been keepers of the castle for generations."

"Well, as the owner, I'm now relieving you and your family of those onerous duties, Mr MacDonald." Percy felt the heavy key ring thrust against his chest.

"A word of warning, Mr bloody laird, sir. Be careful when you visit the castle—especially at night. There are things that happen in the Highlands that are beyond your wildest imagination."

Percy listened to the builder crunch the gearbox and drive off. He walked into what could only be described as a fuggy, damp smell. He shone his torch at the damaged ceilings caused by water ingress; there was a lot of damage on the first floor as well. This was going to take a lot of repairs. One thing he noticed was how it stayed light in those parts of the Highlands long after town and city lights would have been switched on.

The panoramic view looking out to the dark shapes of the Inner and Outer Hebrides was truly spectacular. He looked down at Sanna Beach, where the water broke gently onto the sand. Sanna Point jutted out as if pointing to some distant shore. He shone his torch around the bedroom before inspecting the old-style cast-iron bathrooms and toilets, taking notes as he walked around the building.

Stepping outside, he discovered the garages and across the courtyard were stables from a bygone era. He noted that the garages attached to the lodge could be converted into a dining room-cum-ballroom accessible from the lodge. The garages could link the staff quarters above to the stables, which could be converted into estate offices. He could visualise in his mind's eye how it would look when finished. If the existing garages were extended upwards, they would provide extra bedrooms accessible from the upstairs lodge.

He walked back indoors. The kitchen didn't look too bad, and the laundry, with its old-fashioned round boiling tub, could be stripped and fitted with modern machinery to service the lodge and holiday cottages. How the time seemed to fly. Percy secured the lodge when he heard the approaching Land Rover. He looked at his watch—11:45 p.m. The builder was late again. Percy wondered if MacDonald had thrown the teddy out of the pram.

He waited until they had reached the hotel. "I've a good mind to deduct a pound because you were late again," he said, handing the builder the four pounds.

"Don't call me again, Somerville. You'll need to find another fool to take you to and from the lodge. But I will give you a piece of friendly advice—tread carefully when you visit the castle. You would not be the first Laird of Acharacle to disappear under suspicious circumstances." The builder crunched the gearbox and drove off.

A cold shiver ran up Percy's spine. Not that he was afraid of the so-called Grey Lady ghost that apparently haunted Dubh Artach Castle, but it was the way the builder had put it across, making it sound like a warning. He hadn't realised how late it was when he finally got to bed. The light at night was confusing him.

It made no difference to Percy—he was awake and up at his normal time. The only difference was that he did not have to make the horrendous drive from Surrey to London. After breakfast and ablutions, he walked down to the pier to meet Rebecca. She arrived as promised and drove tentatively up the track to Sanna Lodge. Percy made a note: *Urgent...Road repairs.* It was mostly small talk on the short journey, though Percy told her what MacDonald was going to charge him.

"Robbing sod," was her response.

"I'll unlock the lodge, then show you the damage inside. Then I'll wait for the mechanic who is going to work on the cars in the garage."

"Is Fergus MacLennan coming here this morning? One of the biggest village gossips, and friendly with my husband. I need to go, Percy. I just hope I don't pass him on the way back. I'll pick you up at 2:30 p.m."

"Listen, Rebecca, there is no need for all this subterfuge. I'll explain to Fergus the reason why you're here, and you can tell your husband tonight the reason I'll need you for a day or two until I have my own transport. It's perfectly harmless."

She switched off the car engine and followed him indoors.

"Is there any coal, peat, or logs, Perse? I'll light some fires and open the windows. This will help get rid of the dampness."

"I noticed the bunkers at the rear have plenty of fuel. I'll help carry the coal upstairs."

"I know Fergus smokes, so he should have matches or a lighter. I'll leave you to do the asking. I don't want him casting aspersions."

"Relax—you just concentrate on setting the fires ready to light. I'll do the asking and explaining."

The mechanic soon arrived and handed Percy a box of Swan Vestas matches, which he passed on to Rebecca. They went to the garages at the rear.

"Is that Somerled MacLeod's car in the driveway?" the mechanic asked, raising his eyebrows.

"Yes, she's helping while you get the vehicles serviced. Nothing more, Fergus—just in case you happen to mention it to her husband."

"Ah, so he doesn't know what she's up to. Watch her, Mr Somerville—she's a cunning little vixen. Now, did you bring the cash?"

"Yes, I have the cash, but let's see what you think needs done."

He unlocked the doors. The Ford Mark II Consul, registration KWG 32, was covered in dust, but when he rubbed his finger lightly along the roof, it gleamed with a black polished surface. The mechanic assessed what he would need to do.

"I'll top up the oil and water on both vehicles. However, I notice that the handbrakes on each vehicle are in the on position, which means they are probably seized. I would suggest that when I take the wheels off, it would be wise to replace the brake shoes. Both batteries are flat, but I'll give them a charge to see if their cells are still working, which I doubt due to the time they've been idle. That means new batteries, which I'll order today. Note that one will need to be a heavy-duty for the Land Rover."

"So, how long do you estimate before they are up and running?" Percy asked hopefully.

"Two days for the Consul and the same for the Land Rover. They both should be available by Friday. £60 should cover my time. I'll give you the battery invoices and price when I get them from my Fort William supplier."

Percy nodded while counting out the cash—he wanted to keep the mechanic sweet. He was pleased to see smoke coming out of the chimneys; Rebecca had been busy. He went inside.

"Do me a favour, Rebecca. Take an inventory of what we should keep and what we should dump. I can then start to think about the renovation project."

"At a glance, the bedding is ruined with mould. Some of the furniture is completely ruined, but we can wash and iron the velvet curtains and cushion covers. The dust covers protected the lounge furniture, so most items can be sponged down, and that goes for the carpets as well. A carpet cleaner could have them looking as good as new. It might be worth considering getting rid of the old twin fireclay sinks in the kitchen. Apart from that, all the kitchen needs is a good spring clean. The laundry room is a different matter—it needs gutted."

"I've taken a note of that, so I think I'll open some windows."

"While you are doing that, I'll start to take down the curtains. Most of the items can be stored in the stables when the renovation work gets underway."

Percy appreciated her help. "I'm going to need transport for a couple of days, Rebecca, so tell your husband about the extra days I'll need you while using the car."

He went out to the garage and was pleased to hear the Consul engine purring like a cat.

"You'll need new batteries, Mr Somerville. The existing ones are not holding the charge."

"I'll leave that in your capable hands, Fergus." Percy walked across to the stables and unlocked the doors. There were five stalls in all—plenty of room to store furniture in the dry conditions.

He went back indoors and topped up the fires, then replenished the baskets with peat and logs. The coal scuttles took slightly longer. He noticed that the mechanic had left, which made him look at his watch. He gasped.

"Rebecca, let's shut the windows and place the fire guards in position. It's time to collect Lorna from school."

On the journey back, they talked about what they would do tomorrow.

"I want to get a look at the two holiday cottages on the estate. There are also two farms I need to look at, so make sure you have plenty of petrol in the car."

She dropped him at the edge of the village.

"Remember to discuss our arrangement with your husband, Rebecca. It's important he knows before hearing it from a third party."

He watched her drive away to school. The night was much the same as before—dinner, a walk, then bed.

The next morning, he had a light breakfast and then sat with his coffee in the lounge. He noticed there was no sign of Rebecca in the dining room. He glanced through the two telephone directories from the phone booth in the hall, looking for companies to carry out the renovation work. He would also need a surveyor to get his plans into the planning department stage.

He found what he was looking for—an Inverness company, A. Dean and Sons, which had every trade within the construction company. He also took note of a surveyor's telephone number from Fort William, Connan Lamont, by name. He telephoned the free-post office engineers from the hotel booth to have the Sanna Lodge telephone reconnected.

"Friday," he was told bluntly. That would give him time to go over other parts of the Acharacle Estate that had slipped his mind.

There were other important estate matters to be dealt with. The most important one was income. Of all the businesses that had premises on the estate, none were paying any rent. This was something that would need to be rectified A.S.A.P. He took a note of it.

It was time to wander down to the pier and await Rebecca. She seemed apprehensive when he stepped into the car.

"My husband wants to speak to you tonight, Percy. He sets out for the fishing grounds at 7:00 p.m. each weekday. He said he'll meet you at the pier at 6:00 p.m." She paused. "Please be careful, Perse. Somerled can be a devil when in one of his moods."

"You leave Somerled to me, Rebecca. Now let's make our way to the holiday cottages first, then we'll drive out to the farms as planned."

The road to the cottages was much the same as the road to Sanna Lodge. He could kill two birds with one stone when it came to road repairs. They drew up at the first cottage. The interior was in good shape—a touch of paint here and there would smarten the place up. There was no dampness or water ingress, just the stale smell of being empty for so long. Rebecca commented on the bedding and curtains that would need laundering. Percy looked up to the roof and inspected the gutters and downpipes, which were all intact.

The second holiday cottage needed repair. Slates were missing, which caused water ingress and severe dampness. This one would need much more than a lick of paint to put right. Percy stood taking notes.

They drove out to the first farm where they found devastation. The farmhouse roof had collapsed, the barn had practically blown away, and the byre roof was missing. Percy walked to the nearby fields. Nothing that a good farmer could not put right.

The second farm lay eight miles further from the lodge. It was in reasonable condition except for the barn. The corrugated iron fluttered in the breeze, but nothing serious that couldn't be fixed.

"Right, Rebecca, take me back to Sanna Lodge. I want to see how Fergus is getting on with the Ford Consul."

"Does that mean you won't be needing me any more, Perse?"

"Not if Fergus MacLennan has done his job."

"And here is me thinking you wanted the pleasure of my company because you fancied me."

"That will never happen, Rebecca. You've probably heard the proverb, 'Once bitten, twice shy.' Well, that applies to me. I love my business—that is the only companionship I need. Now let's get back."

He turned her face towards him. "What's this bruising on your cheek, Rebecca?"

"I walked into a cupboard door," she said with the hint of a tear.

"And here's me thinking it was a slap. Silly me." Percy hesitated. "I think the sooner I have a word with that husband of yours, the better. However, there is a request you can consider. I need to start staffing the estate. I offer you the job as estate secretary. I need to employ an estate manager, a gamekeeper, and a water bailiff, and that is only the start."

"Why not employ those who worked on the estate before—if they're available, that is?"

Percy shook his head. "A new broom sweeps clean, Rebecca; I don't want to knock away the old habits from previous employees."

"I'll talk your proposition over with my husband tonight. He can give you our answer when you meet."

The drive back was filled with Percy's dreams of the estate, which would include Dubh Artach Castle.

"You'd do well to stay clear of that godforsaken place, Perse. Everyone in Lochaber knows its reputation."

"Ghost stories around a log fire at Christmas are for the tourists—something to be told with a glass of port in one hand and a mince pie in the other. But I will keep it in mind to be included in the guided tours when I turn my attention to the castle."

"Tell me, Perse, how do you propose to get to and from the castle?"

"Gosh, I never thought of that. I suppose I could purchase a boat, then learn how to steer the damned thing." He smiled.

"Perhaps Somerled could help you there. He has a pleasure boat that takes tourists and locals over to Mull on a Saturday afternoon, and two short trips to Seal Island on the Sunday. However, that will be between you and him."

They arrived at the lodge to find the Consul parked in the courtyard. Fergus was busy working on the Land Rover.

"Just give the engine a chance to settle in. There's plenty of oil in the engine, but when the parts start moving fast, it could create a problem. I've fitted trade plates that allow you to use the car on a public highway until you get it taxed and insured. Not that Willie Dempster, the sergeant, bothers too much, unless you step out of line—if you get my drift. I'll M.O.T. the car next week."

Percy was over the moon. Now he could explore the other parts of the estate. He sat typing a letter while Rebecca continued with her chores. When finished, it read:

"A meeting for all business personnel and crofters from the villages of Kilchoan and Acharacle will be held in Kilchoan village hall on 14 February 1969 at 8:00 p.m. and in Acharacle village hall on 15 February 1969 at 8:00 p.m.

On the agenda will be the back payment of rent, the future payment of rent, and the signing of a new lease agreement. Please do not dismiss this.

It is of the utmost importance that these documents are rectified by the Acharacle Estate.

Signed, Percy Somerville (Laird of Acharacle)."

Percy signed the letters. He would set out later to put each in the parish notice boards of the villages.

After Rebecca had gone, he drove out to view the Ardnamurchan Peninsula. There was so much scope and opportunity for investment. A caravan park could be placed on the large swathe of level land. Then there were three tiers that sloped down to a sandy cove, ideal for installing static caravans. On the fourth level would be a security barrier, a site office with a shop attached, men's and women's toilet blocks with showers, and a small laundry room. Percy took several notes while trying to work out the best approach and road system. He could leave that to the surveyors. He looked at the stunning view that would be a big attraction when the photographs were advertised in the right magazines and newspapers.

He drove out to the Ardnamurchan Lighthouse and stood on the slipway, looking out to his castle. He had great plans for Dubh Artach Castle in the future. There were two vacant lighthouse keepers' cottages, their curtains tightly drawn. He tried the doors, but both were locked. Taking one last look at the castle, he turned and went to meet with Somerled MacLeod.

He parked the Consul in the hotel car park and walked down to the pier. Somerled appeared with his crew of three, fists clenched, spoiling for a fight with the Englishman.

"So, you're the English arsehole who has been pestering my wife."

As he approached Percy, he took a wild swing at the Laird's jaw. Percy had boxed at college and had once been a champion of his London boxing club. He avoided the attempted blow with ease. Egged on by his crew, someone shouted, "Kill the English toad!"

Inspired and full of rage, Somerled lunged again, but once more failed to connect. Percy decided it was time to protect himself. He struck the advancing fisherman with two rapid blows to the chin and an uppercut that floored him. Turning to the surprised crew, he said,

"Do any of you want the same medicine? If not, lift your skipper onto the bench seat; it'll give him a chance to recover before I talk to him about business."

A crew member caught Somerled by the arm. "Come on, get up, ye big eedgit, the Englishman just wants tae talk business." Somerled was placed on the bench.

"I have a business proposition for you, MacLeod. I also have one that concerns your wife. The proposition can make you a lot of money. Let me make it perfectly clear—the only interest I have in your wife is strictly business, nothing more." He paused while Somerled rubbed his chin.

"I need a boatman when the time comes to visit the castle. Your wife has been offered the job as estate secretary—no strings attached. Think it over, and let's agree on a price. I know there are restrictions because of your job, but I'm sure we could work something out. Let Rebecca know both your decisions about the estate job by breakfast tomorrow. She can give me your answer and the price for the hire of your pleasure boat then. Keep it in mind, Somerled, that a lot of money can be made. One more thing: if Rebecca comes to work with a bruised face again, I will not be responsible for my actions. It just won't be a broken nose or a jawbone you'll be nursing." Percy left the dazed skipper to recover.

Dinner at the hotel was a sombre affair. How the fracas with Somerled had spread so quickly, he had no idea, but Rebecca approached his table in a pensive mood to take his order. She touched briefly on her husband's bruises, which suggested that Somerled had already gone home to discuss his propositions.

"I've accepted your offer to become estate secretary on condition that my hours are 9:30 a.m. to 2:30 p.m., Monday to

Friday, with no lunch break. I can work Saturdays if I can bring my daughter, Lorna, to the lodge until you have the stables renovated into estate offices. I can also pass this message from my husband: he can take you out to the castle after 6:00 p.m. He will wait on the other side until the tide turns, but no later than 9:00 p.m. The cost for Saturday is £25. On Sunday, he can take you out at 9:00 a.m. and return for you at 6:00 p.m. The price for that is £40. These days and timings will depend on the tides and the weather." She hesitated. "There is one stipulation he insists on—he will not set foot on the Black Rock or enter Dubh Artach Castle, no matter what." She paused again. "If you accept the price, then I can pass the message back to my husband. Now about me—when do I start?"

"Excellent, Rebecca, I accept your husband's offer, and as for you, I think we can say you've started. You'll be paid for five hours' work plus petrol expenses. I'm sure a tea break at eleven will fortify you until you go home. If you're required to work Saturdays, you'll be paid time and a half until 12:00 noon and double time from then until you finish. I have no objections to Lorna joining you on Saturday or any other day, which could include school holidays."

Rebecca smiled and took his order.

The telephone had been reconnected to the lodge. Percy expressed his wish that an extension to the stables should be installed. The engineer told him it would need to be carried overhead and that a pole would have to be erected to support the line.

"Just get the pole erected and the line taken across until the renovation work is completed."

Percy now felt that things were moving fast regarding the Acharacle Estate.

The meetings held at both village halls were rowdy and noisy debates. Percy raised his hands on both occasions, appealing for calm. At one point in the Acharacle village meeting, he considered abandoning it when fighting broke out at the rear of the hall. Some agreed that a compromise could be reached, while others were adamant they would not pay the excessive rent proposed. On both occasions, Percy managed to subdue the crowded halls, but it was the village of Kilchoan that proved most rebellious.

"I want to make it clear that I have no intention of letting any business in the villages go under. However, I think it is fair to say that if you have business premises, then you must pay rent."

This brought more threats and waving fists. Percy took a sip of water, allowing the bedlam to subside.

"My proposals as Laird are to date your rent from 5 April this year. That gives you a chance to organise and restructure your business charges, and it also gives my surveyor the chance to take measurements. That is how your rent will be assessed and charged." He held up his hand. "I have the legal right to backdate the rent charges to 20 November 1968, the date I bought and took over the estate." He paused.

"My solicitor and I now know that no rent has been paid since the last Laird left or disappeared. However, that is no concern of mine. That is the affair of the Scottish Crown Office, which I have no intention of becoming embroiled in. The Acharacle Estate wants to start afresh, and that is why I have given you time to organise your business." Percy waved a paper in the air. "This is a copy of the new lease you'll sign when your rent is assessed."

"And if we refuse to sign, Englishman?"

"Then, ladies and gentlemen, it will be out of my hands when the legal process begins."

"You mean eviction, don't you? Just like the Highland Clearances."

"It's a nasty word I don't use. That is why I urge you not to bury your head in the sand. Talk to me, discuss your problem with me in the strictest confidence, and I'm sure we can come to some agreement."

There were more shouts of defiance until Percy raised his hand once again.

"Ladies and gentlemen, consider what has been said tonight. I now bring this meeting to a close."

There were those who lingered about the halls looking for trouble, but they were swiftly dealt with by a contingent of police brought in from Fort William, who suspected these meetings would not end peaceably.

However, progress was made when a surveyor was employed to measure the various business premises. It was now all hands to the pumps—not that the estate was a sinking ship; far from it. The estate employees had been interviewed and appointed. Niel-Iain Morrison, the river and Loch Mundle water bailiff, reported to David Semple, the estate manager, that the loch would need to be restocked with brown and rainbow trout. The gamekeeper, Rory MacGilvray, added that a deer cull would be necessary due to the unchecked growth of the herds over the years. The month of January seemed to fly by.

Percy left much of the organising to his estate manager, but he referred to his notepad and telephoned the Dean Construction

Company. A meeting was arranged for Monday morning, and he also wanted the surveyor present to get an idea of his plans. At a loose end as the weekend approached, he sent a message to Somerled MacLeod that he would need his boat on Saturday to take him out to the castle. After spending Saturday night in Dubh Artach Castle, he would be ferried back to the mainland on Sunday.

Percy was excited at the prospect of his first visit to the castle. He packed a sleeping bag, matches, candles and a storm lantern into his kitbag, and in another he packed food, milk and water, despite Rebecca's warnings. On Saturday, he went to the post office and newsagents for a newspaper and label ties.

The huddle of gossiping women nudged each other and began whispering when he entered the shop.

"Watch out, ladies, here comes the ghost buster," Catriona MacDonald said viciously. The crones and women giggled and laughed. Catriona made him wait while she packed a box of food items onto the shelves.

"Yes?" she said officiously.

Percy handed her the newspaper and labels, then took his change.

"I notice your father hasn't submitted all his premises for rent, Catriona. Tell him he has until Friday before I take legal action."

Percy knew it was petty and something he should have discussed with the builder personally, but her obnoxious behaviour provoked him to lash out. It certainly sparked a serious debate among the gossip mongers.

# Chapter 3 - First Crossing to Dubh Artach

He climbed into the Land Rover and drove out to the lighthouse slipway. He watched as Somerled MacLeod came round the tip of the Ardnamurchan Peninsula from the Sound of Mull and berthed the pleasure craft at the slipway. Percy loaded the two rucksacks onto the boat.

"Are you sure you want to be doing this, Somerville?" the boatman said loudly.

"I'm all prepared. What about you, Somerled?" There was no response as the boat was put astern, zig-zagging its way out to the castle.

"Why the deviations, Somerled?" Percy asked amiably.

"Underwater pinnacles that can rip through any craft," Somerled shouted from the tiller.

He carefully drew the boat against the landing stage with its slippery, green, slimy steps. Percy threw the two rucksacks onto the platform above and grabbed the handrail to prevent himself from falling into the water as he struggled up the slime-covered steps.

"I'll pick you up tomorrow at 7:00 p.m. Don't be late," the boatman said with contempt as he maneuvered the boat back into the channel.

Percy stood on the concrete platform, not knowing what to expect. He had an uncanny feeling that someone was watching him. Looking up at the barred windows of the east curtain wall on the first and second floors, he lifted his rucksacks and walked slowly up to the castle door of solid oak studded with copper. To his surprise, the lock turned easily.

He stepped into the cobbled tunnel entrance, paying attention to the spiked portcullis gate supported by a thick rope above him. Walking up the sloping tunnel, the entrance opened out into a large courtyard. He put down the rucksacks and marvelled at the sheer size of the castle, running jubilantly round the central water well, turning and turning until he felt dizzy.

"What a wonderful place!" he said loudly, listening to his echo bounce off the surrounding curtain walls of his castle. Enough of this hilarity, he thought, as he went to inspect the ground-floor rooms. The first, which would once have been the guardroom, bore signs of later use as an office: papers were strewn across the floor, and feather quills with dried ink sat in their wells. The kitchens were next, followed by the western passage with stone steps leading upwards to the next level. Each ground-floor corridor had the same arrangement. He noticed plenty of coal, logs and peat blocks in the storage huts across the courtyard, which meant he would at least be warm. Leaving one haversack of food, milk and water on the kitchen table, he pressed on.

Climbing the narrow spiral stone steps linking the east corridor with the northern corridor of the first floor, Percy resolved to examine one level at a time. He placed his other haversack in the northern corridor and opened a door that revealed what was clearly once the dining room. A dumb waiter linked the kitchens below, carrying food up and dirty dishes down. Running his finger along the length of the large polished oak table, Percy thought of the Ford Consul. The faded dust marks suggested a large candelabra had once stood at each end and the centre of the table. Ten high-backed chairs remained in place, and a large pine cupboard stood against the wall, once filled with table covers, napkins and tableware. The drawers and cupboards were empty, and dust marks on the walls showed where pictures or paintings had once hung. Looking through the barred windows, he saw the heathland stretching north.

Stepping back into the corridor, Percy thought he heard a door banging, but was distracted by the paintings and tapestries that still decorated the walls. The corridor windows gave ample light without him needing the storm lantern. Opening a central door, he found a primitive excuse for a toilet—a wooden bench with a circular hole through which waste would drop into the water below. He closed the door and moved on.

He was amazed when the next door revealed a vast library, its walls lined floor-to-ceiling with bookshelves. Percy made a note in his pad, but didn't waste time scrutinising the many objects and paintings still on display. On the second floor, below the battlements, he noticed tell-tale marks where furniture and paintings had been stripped out, likely sold by the Scottish Crown Office to recoup costs during the estate's dereliction. There were no ornaments or candle holders left in the bedrooms.

After walking the second floor, he climbed onto the battlements where replicas of cast-iron cannons stood. Steps led up to embrasures where arrows and muskets would once have been fired. As the light began to fade, he decided he had seen enough and searched for a place to sleep. A mattress in the first-floor east wing suited him; he lay out his sleeping bag in preparation for a good night's rest.

He lit a fire in the large black kitchen range, heating tinned soup, boiling vegetables and potatoes, and frying a large steak. Sitting with his coffee, he went over everything he had seen. Then came that damned door banging on the second floor again.

Taking the labelled keys, he climbed wearily back upstairs, locking every door after checking the rooms again and leaving the keys in their locks before returning to the warmth of the kitchen. Tomorrow, he would label and mark every door in the castle.

He had second thoughts about sleeping upstairs and dragged the mattress and sleeping bag down to the kitchen, placing them on one of the tables near the fire. It made sense to stay warm. While folding the mattress, he thought he heard a noise like a child crying—two children crying. Percy shook his head, dismissing it as imagination.

Getting the mattress down the north-eastern spiral steps was awkward, but with much tugging and pulling, he managed it. He returned upstairs for his sleeping bag, and while all was quiet, he decided to walk the corridor once more. Unlocking the south-eastern door, he shone his storm lantern inside. The room appeared normal: a single bed, a large dressing table with two chairs, and pictures on the walls. The rotating beam of the lighthouse lit the space at intervals. Percy shook his head at his own actions—inspecting noises indeed! This was an old castle; creaks and groans in the wind were to be expected. Grabbing his sleeping bag, he returned to the kitchen, poured himself another coffee, and thought over the work ahead of him.

It was an uncomfortable night on the hard table, though the warmth of the kitchen helped. He tossed and turned, searching for a comfortable position. Well after midnight, he snuffed out the candles. The last thing he remembered was a door slamming shut.

He slept late into Sunday morning, waking to the peal of village church bells. He had not meant to sleep in; there was much to do. After a quick breakfast, he began labelling and marking each door key, tying on labels and attaching them to his large keyring. Soon every door—room, and corridor stairwell alike, was locked, marked and labelled. Two keys remained. One, unlabelled, he assumed belonged to the dungeons, which he had yet to find. The other was clearly the main door key.

Feeling inquisitive, he returned to the second floor to investigate the faulty end-room door. It was swinging to and fro on its hinges, though the lock was in the locked position. *How could this be?* he wondered, knowing there must be a logical explanation. Still, he pressed on with his inventory—the purpose of his visit. Unlocking the mechanism, he closed the door firmly, locked it again, and left the labelled key in the door like the others.

The ground and first floors were easy to list. The south corridor above the tool sheds and fuel storage huts would have been used by the defenders and perhaps the staff of the castle, with small rooms lining the corridor. The eastern corridor rooms he could remember from last night's episode. The dining room took a little more time as he entered each object into his notepad, while the library would take a great deal of time and effort to catalogue, so he could wait. The west corridor was much like the eastern one, the only difference being the two rooms facing out to the Hebrides, which had a spectacular panoramic view.

When he finished, it was back to the second floor. This was where much of his time would be spent, taking inventory notes and imagining what the renovated rooms would look like. He felt a pang of hunger, so he descended to the kitchens for tea and biscuits. When he finished his snack, he shut down the black range stove fire and oven. He placed the filled rucksacks at the tunnel entrance in preparation for Somerled MacLeod's return; the sleeping bag could stay. It was time to get on with his chores.

With it still being bright outside, he lost track of time. "Struth!" he said with concern. His time was nearly up before he would be left stranded on the black rock of Dubh Artach Castle. There was no time for hesitation. He hurried down the spiral stairs to the tunnel exit, lifted the rucksacks and stepped out, locking the castle door behind him before standing breathless on the platform. He handed the rucksacks to the agitated boatman.

"Another two minutes and you were left, Somerville. I'm not prepared to put me and my boat at risk because of your whims," Somerled said as he guided the boat out into the channel.

"Well, did you find what you were looking for? I must hand it to you, Somerville. Spending a night in the castle would boggle the minds of the entire Western imagination. Did you shake hands with the 'Grey Lady'?" He went into fits of laughter.

"I achieved part of my aim, but as for the ghost, well, as I've said, that is a story for the tourists."

Percy was looking back at the castle while speaking. He had a profound feeling that someone was watching him. However, he dismissed the thought as Somerled opened the throttle to increase speed. They glided alongside the slipway in minutes. Percy watched the boatman go astern and then head off to the Sound of Mull, £65 richer.

# Chapter 4 - Secrets, Skeletons, and the Sting

He threw the rucksacks into the Land Rover and drove to the hotel, where he finally sat down to a proper cooked meal and later slept soundly in a comfortable bed.

Monday morning arrived like any other, except for the meeting arranged with the surveyor and the boss of the Inverness construction company. Both were already waiting when he arrived.

"Sorry, gentlemen, I thought I said 9:00 a.m."

"You did, Mr. Somerville, but 'the early bird catches the worm.' That's why we're here a bit early," Mr. Dean replied as he stepped forward to shake the Laird's hand. Percy noticed Dean's firm grip: a man used to sealing deals this way.

"I hope you don't mind, but I've sent my roofer up onto the roof. Briefly, from down here it looks in a sorry state, but Jimmy will give us a report on the condition of the slates and the leadwork."

It was the surveyor's turn to speak. "The dormer windows look as if they might need some attention or even full replacement, but we'll hear what Jimmy has to say when he comes down." He paused thoughtfully.

"You also mentioned remedial work needed on two farmhouses and six holiday cottages. I think our prime concern should be to get the Sanna Lodge project up and running. The other work can be completed by the winter. What do you think, Mr. Somerville?"

"I agree, Mr. Lamont; however, it is imperative that work also begins on the stable conversions. We desperately need offices for the estate to run smoothly."

Andrew Dean spoke up. "That won't be a problem. We'll draft in more of our workforce to prevent any delay on the lodge renovations."

"Excellent, Alistair. Now, we can take a look at my proposals while the slater checks the roof."

After they walked around the lodge, Percy pointed out exactly what he required. The surveyor and contractor both agreed the work was going to be a real challenge. Worse news came when Jimmy returned from the roof.

"Due to the weather, the slats have become badly worn. It'll be better to strip the whole roof and re-slate or tile it. Much of the leadwork needs replacing, as do the dormer windows." He paused grimly.

"While you were looking around the complex, I went into the attic. I'm afraid the news isn't good. With so much water ingress, the supporting beams have rotted in several places. The timber covering will need to be replaced. I'm honestly surprised the roof hasn't collapsed into the lodge."

Percy sighed. "So, the roof must be our priority." He paused before adding, "I need a price for the lodge and the conversions, Andrew. However, I think we can safely say that you have the contract we've discussed. When pricing, don't forget there's going to be a very large renovation later in the year; plus, of course, the cosmetic work on the other estate buildings."

"We can have our machinery brought down mid-week, and our workforce can start next Monday—a week today, in fact." Alistair Dean smiled as he shook Percy's hand.

"How does that suit you, sir?"

"That suits me fine, Alistair. And stop calling me 'sir.'"

The surveyor looked concerned once Alistair Dean had left.

"You're leaving yourself wide open to inflated pricing, Mr. Somerville. Having no priced contract signed and sealed is a dangerous game. It could cost you dearly."

"I really do thank you for your concern, Conan. But as a stockbroker in my early days, I knew when to take calculated risks. I don't believe I'm taking one with Dean Construction, or with you, for that matter. I'll certainly study the prices very carefully, just as I will your bill. However," Percy leaned forward, lowering his voice slightly, "I think Alistair Dean is a sly old fox. Right now, on his way back to Inverness, he'll be thinking about the big picture, not just the cosmetic repairs, but the renovation of Dubh Artach Castle in the future. That, my dear Conan, is the real prize."

Percy paused again, then continued.

"The next time you and I meet, I want you to bring your theodolite. I'm planning to install a caravan park on some spare rough ground. It has three tiers below the area where I plan to put in static caravans. I've estimated ten on each tier, with the final ten at the caravan park level. That'll give the estate forty statistics, bringing in steady income. On the caravan park itself, there'll be an office, a small shop, toilet and shower blocks, and a modest laundry. So, when you come over next week, bring a helper with you."

He hesitated before adding, "There's one more thing. I conducted a reconnaissance of the castle over the weekend. I have an idea of what's required, but it'll be your submission to the planning department that counts. That's why we need to get out to the castle before winter sets in. Hopefully, by that time I'll have my own boat, but I already have a plan B in place should the need arise."

"Yes, I can understand your urgency, Mr. Somerville, but like the Sanna Lodge project, everything I submit in the plans will be inspected and will need to be passed by the planning authority. They'll even send their own clerk of works to oversee Dean's construction. That, sir, could take time."

"I understand that Rome wasn't built in a day, but I must have income coming into the estate offices by spring 1970. If we can get the six holiday cottages renovated by winter, I might be able to fill them for the Christmas and New Year holiday period. It would be a start." He hesitated again.

"While we're talking about income, there's another job you can do in the meantime. I have a list of businesses in the villages of Kilchoan and Acharacle. Those premises need to be measured to determine the square footage of each, for which the businesses will pay rent. This must be completed and sent to the hotel reception by the middle of March - earlier if possible. Any later is no good. Can you handle that?"

"Yes, though it might mean bringing in another surveyor. I'm sure I'll have it done within the time allocated. May I ask why the hotel reception?"

Percy smiled. "Much as I have faith in you and Dean Construction, I don't think we can wave a magic wand and have Sanna Lodge and the offices finished in time, do you?"

Percy considered that January had, in some ways, been a very productive month despite the winter weather.

"Perhaps after you've surveyed and forwarded the plans for the caravan park and static site, we could go out to the castle and stay the night. There are so many ideas I want to put forward. We could renovate one floor at a time. However, there's a problem with the ferrying. Somerled MacLeod can only take us out on Saturday night. He said he'd wait for us, but it leaves us little time to go over my proposals. Sunday is different; we could spend all day from 9:00 a.m. until 6:00 p.m., which might be better."

"If I can stop you right there, Mr. Somerville," Conan interrupted. "Some of us have a home life. It might not be much, but what my wife and the children have, we try to cling to. Therefore, weekends are a no-go."

Percy nodded. "I understand, Conan. Perhaps that can wait until I get my own boat. Then we can all go together; that includes Dean Construction as well." The thought of arriving at the castle by his own boat gave Percy a flicker of pride.

"I have another construction job in mind. I intend to install a new landing platform and steps at the castle, but that involves a marine company from Glasgow, which reminds me, I must phone them." He took out his notepad and wrote it down.

"I've arranged for a local crofter to plough the heathland for the proposed caravan park. He's agreed to plough it, scatter grass seed, and then roll it. That will give the roots time to establish and grow for next spring and summer."

Conan Lamont, the surveyor, smiled. "You won't allow the grass to grow under your feet, Percy. I wish I had half your energy."

"Just get those plans for the Sanna Lodge complex pushed through. We don't need planning permission to renew the roof, but the extensions and renovations could give us a headache."

"I'll do my best, Percy. For now, though, I have another client to attend to." Percy watched the surveyor drive away.

Now, he had an important message for the office staff. "Sanna Lodge is now out of bounds. The roof is unstable and could collapse at any time. In the meantime, we'll have a temporary telephone line taken across to the stables. We can all pitch in by giving each stable a good cleaning; then we'll install desks and filing cabinets. I intend to start advertising the holiday cottages for the coming summer, autumn, and Christmas holidays. That's something you can handle, David. The sooner we start advertising, the sooner people will hear about the Acharacle Estate complex."

Percy and two locals began emptying the lodge of furniture and other belongings. Most were stored in the end stables that would not be needed, while the rest were placed in the spare garage. It took hard work, sweat, and no shortage of frustration before the lodge was finally ready for the joiners and roofers.

Work had begun as promised by Dean Construction. Their workforce arrived on-site promptly at 8:00 a.m. on Monday, bringing with them the hum of machinery and the sharp smell of fresh timber and tar. It didn't take the roofers long to strip the old slats from the lodge roof, their steady rhythm of hammering and prying echoing across the quiet estate. By midday, broken shards of slate lay piled against the walls, and the joiners had begun lifting away the rotting timbers beneath. By the end of the working day, the roof supports were completely stripped, exposing the skeletal frame of Sanna Lodge against the pale spring sky.

Alistair Dean supervised the work personally, moving between teams with an air of calm authority. He advised Percy that it would be far better to re-roof with tiles rather than slats. Percy hesitated; the lodge had always had a distinctive, traditional look, and he had wanted to preserve its original charm.

"Tiles will last longer, Percy," Alistair explained patiently, running a hand over a section of exposed beam. "You'd be waiting months to source the right slats, and that would stall every other part of the project."

After weighing the options, Percy reluctantly agreed, settling on a muted grey tile that would complement the lodge's stonework without compromising its dignity.

By Wednesday, the work was well underway. The joiners had started laying the new timber boards, fixing them carefully into place, while rolls of waterproof tar felt were unspooled across the roof to protect it from the unpredictable Highland weather. Freshly constructed dormer windows leaned against a wall, waiting to be installed, and plumbers bustled about fitting new leadwork. Inside, the double-glazing firm had already replaced all the first-floor windows and was gradually working its way down to the ground floor. The transformation was striking. By Friday afternoon, Sanna Lodge was finally wind- and waterproof, its new roof gleaming faintly beneath the spring sun.

Alistair Dean approached Percy as the last of the scaffolding creaked under a departing roofer.

"Do you want us to start on the electrical and plumbing work on Monday, Mr. Somerville?"

"We'll need planning permission for interior work, Alistair."

Dean frowned. "Who told you that? You only need planning permission for extensions, major alterations, or taking the roofline around the courtyard, and for converting the stables into offices. But stripping out an existing bathroom and replacing it? That's straightforward. Same with renewing the pipework and electrics. No permission required."

He pulled out a folder. "All I need from you is the colour scheme for the bathroom suites. I'll bring our painter and decorator on Monday, and the two of you can go through wallpaper patterns and paint samples together. If we move quickly, there's a fair chance we can have the lodge interiors finished by the end of the month."

Dean paused, lowering his voice slightly. "There's one more thing I meant to raise earlier, and it slipped my mind. With the lodge being so far from the nearest fire service—I believe the closest one is in Lochaline—I strongly suggest we install fire reels in the corridors and a hydrant outside. We can fit the reels flush into the walls so they won't be an eyesore. Better safe than sorry."

Percy hesitated, watching Dean carefully. Was this another way for the man to add more work to his company's contract? Yet, after considering the lodge's isolated location, he agreed. Safety had to come first, and he gave the go-ahead.

Despite the extras, Percy was delighted with the speed and efficiency of the work. For the first time in months, he could picture himself living at Sanna Lodge. It filled him with a quiet sense of achievement and renewed energy.

***

A few days later, on a bright, early spring morning, Percy drove down to the Ardnamurchan lighthouse. A cool sea breeze carried the scent of salt and heather as he stepped out of the Land Rover. He wanted another look at the vacant lighthouse keepers' cottages now that the lighthouse had been fully automated. Walking around them, he examined the slate roofs and gutters with a critical eye. They seemed to be in reasonable condition, though a few areas of flashing would need attention. He could already imagine these cottages as charming holiday lets, their windows facing the restless sea.

His gaze drifted across the narrow channel to Dubh Artach Castle, its weathered silhouette rising starkly against the horizon. How he wished he already had a boat; he could have crossed the strip of water in minutes on such a fine, still morning. That, along with inquiring about purchasing the cottages if they were up for sale, would be his next priority.

The boat, at least, was easy to arrange. A small boating company in Oban had exactly what he was looking for. Its owner, Douglas, came from a family with a long history of operating boat trips and sales, and he couldn't have been more helpful. They agreed on a price quickly, and Douglas promised to tow the boat up the Sound of Mull to Kilchoan. He would also teach Percy the basics of handling it during their sail round to the Ardnamurchan boathouse.

Saturday morning arrived crisp and clear, the sunlight glinting off the calm waters. As promised, Douglas and his father arrived with the sleek pleasure craft in tow, its varnished hull gleaming in the light.

"Dad will wait here while we sail around the peninsula to your boathouse," Douglas said, unfastening the moorings. "Will it be a long walk back to the village?"

"No," Percy replied. "I've arranged for my estate manager to pick us up once the boat's berthed safely."

Douglas nodded, then began his instructions patiently, as though speaking to someone entirely new to the sea. "This is the start button, but before you press it, make sure the forward or astern lever is in neutral and the throttle is closed. Think of her much like a car. Keep the fuel tank filled with diesel, ensure the batteries are charged, and remember: the tiller is your steering wheel, the throttle is your accelerator, and astern mode is effectively your brake."

He paused to let Percy absorb the information. "Most important of all is the throttle control. That lever manages the speed, and the forward-astern handle determines direction. Always give a short pause when switching between them; otherwise, the engine fights itself."

Douglas grinned. "Tell me, Mr. Somerville, have you ever handled a boat before?"

"Yes, Douglas," Percy replied dryly. "Plenty of times—in my bath and at the boating pond as a boy."

Douglas roared with laughter. "Well, there's no time like the present to learn properly."

As they moved away from the pier, Percy followed Douglas's guidance carefully, the tiller shifting under his hands. At first, his movements were jerky, but as the boat glided into open water, he began to relax, adjusting course smoothly as Douglas pointed out landmarks along the Ardnamurchan channel. Before long, they reached the boathouse, where Douglas took over to berth the craft neatly, ensuring no scratches or damage.

After securing the boat, Douglas handed Percy a business card.

"Any problems, just call that number and ask for me. We provide free after-sales servicing for a year."

Percy watched as Douglas and his father drove away with the towing craft disappearing into the Sound of Mull. For the first time, he felt a sense of independence. Owning a boat meant freedom; the castle was no longer an untouchable island on the horizon but an attainable part of his vision.

Later that afternoon, Percy joined David MacLean, his estate manager, at the heathland recently ploughed and rolled for the proposed caravan park. Fresh grass seed lay scattered across the dark earth, and the faint smell of damp soil lingered in the air.

"A fine job, if I might say so, boss," David said, gesturing toward the wide, levelled ground. "Have you ever thought about turning that corner over there into a campsite for tents? It's not a big area, but tents don't take up much space. It could bring in a little extra income."

"Well thought of, David. Let's do it while we still have the tractor, plough, and roller available. Speak to Morag the crofter and explain what's needed."

David hesitated before adding, "And the purchase of a boat, boss… don't you think that's a bit extravagant?"

"Not at all," Percy replied firmly. "The boat gives me independence. I can reach the castle when I need to without relying on ferries or favours. My priority now is to get the marine surveyor from Aqua Marine out to the castle steps to start planning the new landing stage and steps. He's coming up from Glasgow on Monday, just as work begins on the lodge interior. I'm sorry you're all having to manage in those cramped stables for now, but things can only get better."

That evening, Percy sat at his desk, going over the estate's income and expenditure figures. For the first time in months, the numbers looked promising. Business rents were due next month, several of the holiday cottages were already booked, and plans for the caravan park were progressing steadily. For the first time, Percy allowed himself to feel cautiously optimistic. The estate was beginning to turn a corner, and the future—though still fragile—finally seemed within reach.

A handful of businesses had refused to pay what they called the "extortionate" rent charges. Their letters now sat neatly stacked on Percy's desk, ready to be answered. They would each receive a formal notice stating that if payment was not made by the **5th of April, 1969**, the matter would be handed over to the Acharacle Estate's solicitor without further discussion. Percy folded the letters carefully, his expression unreadable.

There was no more to be said on that subject.

Still, other decisions loomed. The choice of bathroom suites and wallpaper for the Sanna Lodge bedrooms and lounge could not be delayed any longer. Percy spent the rest of Saturday and most of Sunday in his hotel room, browsing catalogues that littered the table and floor around him. He studied each page intently, tracing patterns with his fingertips and trying to picture how they would look in the finished rooms. In quiet moments, he found himself imagining the lodge restored to its full glory—roaring fireplaces, gleaming floors, sunlight pouring through new windows.

Once his mind was made up, he marked each catalogue with small stickers, carefully noting his selections in a well-thumbed notepad. It gave him an unexpected sense of control amid the whirlwind of projects.

***

Monday promised to be an especially busy day. Percy met with Alistair Dean, the head of Dean Construction, handing over his final choices for bathroom suites and wallpaper. Dean received them with obvious relief and gratitude, promising his decorators would begin preparations immediately.

The site was already alive with activity. Joiners, plumbers, and electricians had started ripping up floorboards to lay copper pipes, drainage channels, and new electrical cables. Sparks of sunlight flashed from tool edges, and the sound of hammering echoed through the estate. Percy stood for a moment, hands in his pockets, watching the organised chaos unfold.

Yet even amid the progress, another concern weighed on his mind. The wall charts for the holiday cottages were filling up quickly, and bookings for the first row of static caravans for the **1970 season** were already coming in. Foundations for those caravans hadn't even been started, nor had the units been purchased. Still, he reassured himself: everything regarding the cottages would be ready in time for the coming summer school holidays.

He glanced at his notepad. "What's next?" he murmured under his breath.

The answer was the Aqua Marine surveyor. Percy checked his watch; there was still half an hour before their scheduled meeting at the slipway. This would be his first real test as a boatman, and he wasn't about to fail it.

***

Percy Somerville was never one to refuse a challenge. He had carefully written down the instructions Douglas had given him during their sailing lesson. Taking a deep breath, he untied the bow rope, double-checked the lever positions, and glanced at the tiller before flipping the switch and pressing the start button.

The small engine coughed, then settled into a steady hum. Tentatively, he manoeuvred the boat out of the boathouse, his movements slow and deliberate, recalling Douglas's advice about astern movement and throttle speed. Once in the channel, Percy allowed the craft to drift before switching into forward gear and easing the revs. The boat moved smoothly toward the slipway, sunlight dancing on the rippling water.

It took several attempts—and one brief, embarrassing moment where he gently grounded the boat on a shingled beach—before he managed to draw the craft alongside the slipway. Luckily, the incoming tide soon refloated her, and Percy laughed quietly to himself. It was a valuable lesson learned just in time for the arrival of the Aqua Marine surveyor.

***

Mr. Simpson, the surveyor, was a brisk, no-nonsense man, carrying a well-worn measuring tape and a notebook tucked under his arm. Percy piloted the boat towards the castle's crumbling landing steps, their green slime glistening in the morning light.

"A wise decision, Mr. Somerville," Simpson remarked as he inspected the worn stones. "This landing stage and these steps are an accident waiting to happen, especially at low tide."

"Speaking of tides, Mr. Simpson," Percy replied, tying the stern rope to the iron handrail, "I'd like to be across the channel before the tide turns."

"This won't take long," Simpson assured him. "A few quick measurements, and we'll be away."

As the man climbed up the slick steps, Percy instinctively glanced toward the castle. That unsettling gut feeling returned—as though unseen eyes were watching him from behind the barred windows. He shook it off, holding the measuring tape steady while Simpson jotted down numbers and sketched diagrams.

"The water here's beautifully clear," Simpson commented. "That'll make things easier for our divers when they handle the underwater welding." He snapped his notebook shut and climbed back into the boat.

"You've got yourself a fine castle, Mr. Somerville," he said with a wry smile. "Though I can't say I'd care to spend a night here, not when darkness falls."

Simpson outlined the next steps briskly: a quote would be sent by the end of the week, and if accepted, work could begin the following Monday. They'd need lodging for two engineers, two labourers, and two divers.

"There's no bed and breakfast nearby, and the hotel's usually fully booked this time of year," Percy admitted after a pause. "But I can arrange bedding in the castle kitchens—it's warm enough down there—and hire a cook to handle your men's meals. Just let me know how many will be coming."

"Perfect," Simpson replied. "We'll prefabricate most of the platform and stairs at our workshop, but we'll need your boat to transfer the assembled pieces to the castle steps."

"Very well, Mr. Simpson. I'll leave the details in your capable hands," Percy said, pushing the throttle gently astern.

As they turned away, Percy's gaze was drawn irresistibly to the central first-floor window. For an instant—he was almost certain—he saw a pale woman's face shift in the shadows behind the bars. His grip faltered, and the boat veered slightly.

"Are you all right, Mr. Somerville?" Simpson asked, steadying himself. "I've got my own boat on Loch Lomond; I can take the helm if you'd like."

Percy shook his head quickly. "Just a lapse in concentration. Got this boat only on Saturday."

Simpson raised an eyebrow but said nothing more.

A cold sense of foreboding ran down Percy's spine, settling like a weight on his chest. By the time they returned to the slipway and Simpson disembarked, Percy was relieved to watch the man drive away. He stood for a moment in the stern, staring across the water at the brooding castle before returning the boat to its boathouse berth.

***

Back onshore, Percy made his way to the proposed caravan park where Morag, the crofter, was finishing her work. She had just scattered the last of the grass seed and was rolling the soil smooth when she spotted him.

"Almost finished, Mr. Somerville," she called, hopping down from the tractor. "Would you like to pay me now?"

Percy smiled. He appreciated Morag's directness; she never wasted words. Handing her the agreed sum along with a £20 bonus, he thanked her for fitting the work in at such short notice.

From there, Percy returned to the temporary office. David, the estate manager, was nowhere to be seen, and Rebecca would be busy collecting Lorna from primary school. Left alone, he decided to ring the Northern Lighthouse Board Headquarters in Edinburgh.

"Can I speak to someone about purchasing an empty property?" he asked.

"Hold, please," came the reply. "I'll transfer you to our property section."

After a long wait, a brisk voice answered. "Reg Fraser. How can I help?"

Percy explained his interest in the two empty cottages on the Ardnamurchan peninsula.

"They've been on the market for some time," Fraser said after pulling up the file. "Since the light was automated, in fact. We struggled to sell them because of the constant glare of the lighthouse. They were shelved, but technically they're still available."

"And the asking price?" Percy asked, sensing an opportunity.

"Seventeen thousand pounds each, but the board would be willing to negotiate."

Percy hid his excitement. "Perhaps we could arrange a meeting to discuss the matter further," he said evenly.

Fraser checked his diary. "I have a slot at 3:00 p.m. on Friday. Does that suit you?"

"Perfect, Mr. Fraser. Until Friday, then."

After ending the call, Percy leaned back in his chair, allowing himself a moment of quiet satisfaction. The cottages were worth a trip to Edinburgh. With careful negotiation, this could become a very favourable deal indeed.

It had been a long time since Percy had taken a proper break, and he decided to make the most of the opportunity. He reserved a room at the North British Hotel, conveniently close to Waverley Station, and booked a first-class train compartment. His plan was simple: drive to Fort William on Friday, catch the early train to Glasgow Queen Street, and change for Edinburgh Waverley. Business first, and perhaps, for once, a little leisure afterwards.

He had no intention of telling the estate office he would be away over the weekend, nor did he plan on revealing why he was going to Edinburgh. By mid-morning, such news would have spread around the entire village like wildfire, and Percy preferred to keep his business private.

On Friday, he left the hotel car park early, the morning air still cool and damp with a hint of salt from the sea. It was a pleasant drive around the head of Loch Eil, the rising sun throwing streaks of gold across the water. He parked his Ford Consul neatly in the station car park and boarded the train, feeling a twinge of anticipation mixed with quiet determination.

He remembered parts of the journey vividly. Ben Nevis, the highest mountain in the British Isles, loomed majestically above them, its peaks still capped with lingering snow as the steam locomotive chugged steadily towards Tyndrum Station, where the overnight express from London had stopped. There was a timeless serenity in watching the landscape unfold, each mile carrying him closer to the business ahead.

However, Percy was slightly surprised when the train stopped at an unfamiliar station on Rannoch Moor. He lowered his newspaper briefly, then buried his head back into it as the commotion settled down. That was when his compartment door slid open.

"In here, Archie; this will do," said a blond-haired woman, struggling to hoist her heavy luggage onto the netted rack above Percy's head.

"Let me help you with that," Percy offered, rising quickly, eager to bring some order to his quiet surroundings.

"You're so kind, thank you." She turned to the young boy with her. "Right, Archie, please sit down there, and not a word out of you." Handing him a colouring book and crayons, she finally settled into her seat after they introduced themselves.

The journey continued in companionable silence until the ticket collector slid open the compartment door. "Tickets, please." He clipped Percy's ticket briskly, then frowned as he examined Mhairi and Archie's.

"I'm sorry, madam, but these are third-class tickets, and this is a first-class carriage. I'm afraid you'll have to move or pay the balance."

Mhairi Lawson stood sharply, her voice edged with indignation. "Damn class distinctions in this day and age! I can't afford the first-class fare, so come on, Archie; we must move."

Percy raised a hand calmly. "I'm sure we can avoid the lady and her son having to move. If I cover their travel expenses to Edinburgh and back, I trust British Rail will accept that?"

The ticket collector's expression soured. It was clear he disliked the extra work.

"I have friends in British Rail, London," Percy added evenly, "who would not take kindly to hearing you refused a perfectly valid solution."

The collector hesitated, then grudgingly calculated the fare difference. He handed Mhairi the updated tickets and left, muttering under his breath as he closed the door behind him.

"How can we ever thank you, Mr. Somerville?" Mhairi said softly, her composure returning.

"Think nothing of it, Mrs. Lawson. Now I can enjoy you and Archie's company all the way to Edinburgh."

"Miss Lawson," she corrected firmly, though without explanation.

Percy smiled apologetically. "That's typical of me, Mhairi— always so presumptuous. I apologise profusely."

They both smiled, and the ice was broken. Soon, the train rolled into Glasgow, and they transferred together onto the Edinburgh train. Conversation blossomed, not intimate but comfortable, and Percy found himself drawn to Mhairi's warmth and resilience.

"I have a problem to sort out for next year," she confided as the train rattled eastward. "The Rannoch Primary School, where I teach, is closing after Christmas. That means I'll be out of a job and out of my tied house. There are always adverts for teachers in Glasgow, though, and since I trained at the Teachers' Training College in Jordanhill, I may have a slight advantage."

Percy's mind was already turning two to the dozen. "I own an estate in the West Highlands, and we're forever taking on extra staff as the estate expands. I could arrange for you to help in the estate office. It comes with a good wage, self-contained living accommodation, and free weekends unless you're needed during peak holiday lets. Archie could even be enrolled at the local primary school, a minibus collects and drops the children daily. And if he wanted, he could help me around the estate on Saturdays." He hesitated, then added warmly, "In fact, why not come for Christmas and New Year?"

"This sounds too good to be true, Mr. Somerville. It could be the answer to our problems," Mhairi admitted, her voice carrying both hope and caution.

"Think about it, Mhairi. Here… take my calling card. You can also phone the Acharacle Estate office directly. But," he smiled, "the offer stands if you drop the 'Mr. Somerville' and call me Percy."

Archie, who had been quietly colouring, suddenly looked up eagerly. "Please, Mum, can we?"

Mhairi smiled faintly, stroking her son's hair. "Let's wait and see how your Aunt Isa is doing first." She turned back to Percy. "We're visiting my sister in the hospital—nothing serious, but they want to keep her overnight for observation. I suppose if we see her in the evenings, there's no harm in meeting up during the day. What hotel are you staying in?"

Percy handed her his estate card, scribbling the North British Hotel's number on the back. "I wait with bated breath, Mhairi," he said lightly, then turned to Archie with a wink. "Make sure your mum calls that number, son."

As the train pulled into Waverley Station, the journey felt over far too quickly. They shared a brief, warm hug before parting ways.

Mhairi and Archie disappeared into a waiting taxi, leaving Percy wondering if he would ever see them again.

He walked up to the large hotel towering above the railway station, signed in, and was shown to his room. After freshening up, he hailed a taxi near the Lighthouse Board offices and managed a quick snack and a coffee beforehand.

Inside the offices, he was met by Mr. Simpson, who led him down a long corridor to a spacious boardroom where four men were already seated around an oval table. After introductions, questions were exchanged with quiet professionalism.

"There are certain stipulations we must clarify, Mr. Somerville," began the chairman. "As you know, the Ardnamurchan Lighthouse is critical to keeping the shipping lanes safe. If, at any time in the future, we require lighthouse keepers again, we will reserve the right to buy back the cottages at today's agreed price without contest."

Percy nodded thoughtfully, his expression unreadable as the chairman continued.

"You would also be responsible for the condition of each cottage, as well as removing any graffiti from the lighthouse building. Furthermore, the slipway, though seldom used by lighthouse supply ships nowadays, must remain in safe condition and accessible should we require it."

Percy folded his hands calmly on the table. "Agreed."

"Then the price for both cottages stands at £17,000, which we believe is fair."

Percy rose slowly, fixing the board with a measured gaze. "Gentlemen, you're forgetting several things. These cottages are badly run down and have been sitting on the market for quite some time. They are difficult to access, and, more importantly, the slipway in question is, in fact, part of the Acharacle Estate. I own it." He paused deliberately, letting the information settle. "A charge could very well be applied for its use."

The members shifted uncomfortably.

"I'm afraid your price is far too extortionate for the estate to consider," Percy added smoothly, gathering his notes. "We have other commitments that directly support employment and growth in the area."

He began packing his papers into his briefcase when murmurs broke out among the board. Chairs scraped, voices dropped into hurried whispers, and the atmosphere shifted.

"£14,000 for the two," the chairman finally said. "That is our final offer."

Percy extended his hand, his expression composed but inwardly triumphant. "Agreed. I might just manage to catch the bank before it closes, or, if you prefer, I can write a guaranteed cheque now."

"We've already checked your credibility, Mr. Somerville," the chairman replied with a faint smile. "Your cheque to the Northern Lighthouse Board will suffice."

The formalities were completed swiftly. Mr. Simpson handed Percy the two cottage keys with a satisfied nod.

"Glad to have done business with you, Mr. Somerville."

Percy turned the keys over in his palm thoughtfully before asking one last question, his tone casual but probing. "One thing: irrelevant to the sale, of course. Has anyone ever been given the keys on approval? Just to inspect the property before buying?"

"No, not to my knowledge. Our method of any sale is this." Mr. Simpson paused for effect. "If, unlike you, Mr. Somerville, an interested party wanted to view any of our properties, then a colleague or I would accompany them and ensure the property was securely locked after the inspection. Is there a reason you ask, sir?"

"No reason, Mr. Simpson. I just don't want any duplicate keys flying about out there."

Percy walked out of the offices in a jubilant mood. "All in all, a good day's trading," he thought to himself, echoing what he used to say when the London Stock Exchange closed for the day. Now it was back to the hotel for a celebratory drink.

***

Saturday morning brought good news over breakfast; Mhairi and Archie would join him at 10:00 a.m. He shaved carefully, chose fresh attire, and was downstairs when they arrived just before ten. Archie hugged him around the waist before handing him a detailed sketch of the three of them on the train, along with a comically grumpy ticket inspector. Percy was genuinely touched.

"This is wonderful work, Archie. You've a real eye for detail," Percy said warmly. "I'll leave this behind the reception desk so it doesn't get damaged and collect it later."

He turned to Mhairi. "How is your sister doing?"

"She's getting tests done this afternoon, which gives us a free day," she replied.

"And tomorrow?" Percy asked quickly, hope edging his voice.

"I'm afraid tomorrow's out, Perse. We'll be visiting her in the afternoon and evening."

Percy caught the look of disappointment on Archie's face.

"Never mind," he said kindly. "Let's be thankful for small mercies like today. So, let's make the most of it."

And they did.

They began with a visit to Edinburgh Castle, wandering through grand halls and stone battlements as Archie peppered Percy with endless questions about kings and battles. After a quick fast-food lunch, they strolled down the Royal Mile to the distant tunes of bagpipes, passing shop windows bursting with tartan scarves, kilts, and souvenirs. Percy bought three Glengarry hats, insisting they each wear one proudly.

From there, they walked to Holyrood House, the Queen's royal residence, before taking a bus tour around Arthur's Seat and through the elegant streets of the New Town, passing the former home of Robert Louis Stevenson, the author whose tales Percy had loved as a boy. Later, they climbed the winding stairs of the Scott Monument on Princes Street, pausing halfway to take in sweeping views of the city below. The day was crammed with sights, sounds, and laughter, and before they knew it, evening had fallen.

They rounded it off with dinner at the North British Hotel. Midway through the meal, Archie's head drooped forward and fell straight into his soup, fast asleep.

Mhairi flushed red and shook the boy's shoulder. "You stupid little tyke, look at the mess you've made of the hotel tableware!"

Percy raised a hand gently. "Dennis," he said to the waiter, "please change this cloth and bring the boy another plate of soup." He smiled reassuringly at Mhairi. "Accidents happen, Mhairi. It's been an exhausting day for all of us. I nearly nodded off myself earlier, so don't worry about it."

Mhairi sighed, embarrassed, but said nothing.

"I've got an idea," Percy said thoughtfully. "Why don't I arrange a room here for you and Archie tonight? No need to traipse back to your sister's flat at this hour. This place is large enough to have adjoining rooms available."

"That's kind of you, Perse," she admitted. "I must confess, I didn't relish the thought of catching the late bus to the suburbs."

"Leave it to me," Percy said with quiet finality. "That way, we can have a relaxing Sunday morning before you head to the hospital."

***

The next morning, after a hearty Scottish breakfast, they sat reading the Sunday papers until Percy summoned a cab for them. There were hugs—plenty of them—especially from Archie.

"Promise you'll consider my offer to spend Christmas at Sanna Lodge?" Percy asked, crouching to meet the boy's eyes.

Mhairi smiled. "We talked it over last night and decided to accept your offer, Perse."

"Fantastic," he said, beaming. "You won't regret it."

The taxi arrived almost immediately. There were more hugs and quick goodbyes, and then they were gone far too soon. Percy felt like a fish out of water without them. He collected Archie's sketch from the reception desk, took the lift to his room, and tucked it carefully into his briefcase alongside his business papers before packing his small suitcase.

He paid the hotel bill and walked down to Waverley Station in high spirits. Catching the midday train back to Glasgow, he made his connection to Fort William and drove his Ford Consul homeward. The journey through the Highlands, framed by rolling hills and shimmering lochs, reminded him of why he had chosen this life over London.

Reaching the Kilchoan Hotel, he dropped his briefcase and case onto a chair, climbed into bed, and was asleep within minutes.

****

By the next morning, refreshed and showered, he made his way to the estate office, only to be met by an irate secretary.

"There was a search party out looking for you, Percy Somerville!" Mrs. MacLeod's voice was sharp. "It was called off when your car was found in the Fort William station car park. After a police investigation, they discovered you'd purchased a return ticket to Edinburgh. Would you care to explain yourself… and why all the secrecy?"

"I took a well-deserved break away from the estate," Percy said evenly. "And I don't need to remind you, Mrs. MacLeod, that I'm your boss. I don't owe you—or anyone else—an explanation. Now, let's get back to business."

"One day, two nights," she muttered. "I don't believe you. You're up to something, Mr. Somerville."

Percy ignored her and turned to the estate manager.

"The booking charts look healthy. I think 1970 could be a very good year for the estate." He pointed to a blank section on the board. "This static caravan area needs to be started. We can lay the concrete foundations with six eyelets ready for the go-ahead from the planners. If we're refused planning permission, we can always re-turf the foundations."

"Why the steel eyelets, boss? They'd need ripping out," the manager asked.

"They'll secure the statics against whatever the weather throws at them," Percy explained. "I've got a meeting with the surveyor this morning. I'll be at the proposed caravan park, then maybe I'll head to the castle. If anyone's looking for me, Rebecca, you know where I'll be."

After watching tradesmen arrive from Inverness, Percy drove his Land Rover to the caravan park site, where the surveyor and his assistant were waiting.

"We've already taken several readings for the static caravans," the surveyor reported. "There's not much levelling to do, just a bit near the embankments at the far end. You're right; we can fit ten statics comfortably, with plenty of space for parking beside each one."

He hesitated. "I'd rather wait until the planning—"

"I'm not prepared to wait while the planning department debates what I should and shouldn't do," Percy interrupted firmly.

"We'll start laying the concrete foundations with six steel eyelets each, just as discussed. Now, let's focus on the road layout and the buildings to be erected."

They walked around the large site, Percy pointing towards a freshly levelled area. "We'll need a path here for my new idea. This section's perfect for campers' tents."

***

After leaving the surveyor, Percy drove over to the two lighthouse cottages. Unlocking the first door, he froze.

Inside, the cottage was crammed from floor to ceiling. Paintings and tapestries leaned against the walls. Silver candelabras, cutlery, and ornate crockery were stacked haphazardly alongside antique furniture and odd trinkets. It was an Aladdin's cave - a treasure hoard hidden in plain sight.

Percy's breath caught. He edged through the narrow passageway, then locked the door again before heading to the second cottage. It was much the same: piles of valuable objects stacked wherever space allowed, with a small cleared corner seemingly ready to receive more loot.

The implication struck him hard; this was stolen property. It had to be.

He hurriedly locked the second door and glanced around nervously. Thank God he hadn't told the office staff about the purchase; no one knew these cottages were now his, and he intended to keep it that way until he learned who was behind this. But he also realised something else: there had to be more than one person involved.

"How did they manage to transport all this from Dubh Artach Castle?" he wondered grimly. Somerled MacLeod came immediately to mind. He had the kind of boat capable of hauling furniture discreetly, though other pleasure craft owners on Mull could also be suspects.

His thoughts were interrupted by a voice behind him.

"I hear you've got yourself a boat, Somerville. Thought I'd take a look at what you've bought."

Percy turned slowly. "I'm afraid you're out of luck, Mr. MacDonald. I left the boathouse keys at the office."

It was a lie, and Percy knew it.

MacDonald folded his arms. "Can't understand why you bought a boat you can't even steer, Somerville. Seems like putting the cart before the horse."

"I'll just have to learn like every other mariner," Percy replied calmly. "Perhaps Somerled MacLeod might help me out with that."

Percy did not tell him that he had already managed to take the pleasure craft to the castle and back without mishap, apart from gently beaching it on the shingles beside the slipway. He smiled inwardly, pleased at having pulled the wool over the builder's eyes.

"I'll need to learn quickly," he said lightly. "I have Aqua engineers coming to fit a new landing stage and steps sometime next week. They want me to ferry the men and parts to the Black Rock."

Percy paused, thoughtful. "I just might attempt the crossing this week if I can find the time. And I was planning to visit the castle at the weekend to organise their sleeping accommodation and take out the necessary food and water. Wish me luck."

Duncan MacDonald laughed heartily. "I'd suggest you wear a life jacket and keep a lifebelt handy. I just hope your boat's well insured." He gave a knowing grin before heading up the road and disappearing.

Percy knew he had planted a seed in the builder's mind. Duncan MacDonald would tell his daughter, who ran the post office, and she would tell the local gossipmongers. Soon, Percy's weekend visit to Dubh Artach Castle—and his plans to replace the steps and landing stage, though not yet confirmed—would spread like wildfire. He could almost hear the whispers forming already.

He glanced across at the castle, momentarily dismissing what he thought he had seen: a pale, greenish, shell-like face at the central window. He put it down to a trick of the light, a figment of his imagination. Yet, deep down, the fleeting image left a strange unease in his chest, one he couldn't quite shake.

He didn't unlock the boathouse door, just in case MacDonald returned unexpectedly. Instead, he counted his blessings for having locked the cottage before the builder's sudden appearance during working hours.

With that in mind, he drove back to the office. There, he noticed a faxed price quotation from Aqua Marine. Seeing no one around, he lifted the telephone and called to confirm.

"We can start the work next Monday, as our marine surveyor mentioned," the voice on the other end assured him. "Our workforce is prepared to sleep in the castle for the few days it'll take to carry out the work. How does that suit you, Mr. Somerville?"

"Excellent," Percy replied, satisfaction edging his tone. "I'll have their bedding and food taken out this week. I'll also be on hand during the day to ferry them out with the parts and anything else they require. Thank you for your swift reply."

Everything felt as though it was falling into place. Still, the renovation of the castle wouldn't begin until every other project on the Acharacle Estate was complete, probably by early spring or summer of 1970. The caravan park and the static caravan foundations remained his priority.

***

It was a busy week for Percy. He ferried food and bedding out to the castle, arranging everything meticulously. The first-floor dining room had been set up as a dormitory with single beds and mattresses moved from the south wing. All this, he did without interruption—or so he liked to believe—from the so-called ghostly figure of the Grey Lady.

Yet, each time he arrived and left via the slippery steps of the castle, he could not shake the feeling of being watched. Often, he would pause in the stern, gaze fixed on the first-floor central window, half-expecting to see a shadow flicker past or a pale face materialise. But it never happened.

By Friday, everything was ready for the Aqua Marine engineers. Percy was fully prepared for their arrival next Monday—and equally determined for his personal trip to Dubh Artach Castle that Friday night. He was resolved to put an end to this ridiculous ghost story once and for all.

***

What Percy didn't know was that unrest was brewing in the office. Nothing serious yet, but if left unchecked, it could fester into rebellion—perhaps even a strike.

The estate manager shook his head, addressing the estate secretary with growing frustration.

"This boss of ours doesn't know when to stop. He has five projects underway already, and now he's adding Dubh Artach Castle to the list. The whole estate's turning into a building site. Do you know what he's talking about now?"

Rebecca stopped typing and turned to face him.

"A putting green at the campsite, and get this," he paused for emphasis, "a nine-hole golf course and a leisure centre outside the village of Acharacle! But I'll give him this much: any normal entrepreneur would have stopped or folded by now. Not Percy Somerville. For him, there's always one more thing to do, one more idea to earn money, and it all piles more work on me."

Rebecca gave a faint smile. "Talk to him, David. I'm sure he'll listen. And you must admit, in the long term, all of this will benefit the estate and the surrounding area. I think you'll find the boss will slow down after the castle renovation. He hasn't come this far, this quickly, to abandon his plans for Dubh Artach. I know that's why he bought the boat."

David muttered something under his breath and stormed out of the office.

***

Friday came in the blink of an eye. Percy prepared carefully for his visit to the castle. After the tradesmen evacuated the ongoing work around the courtyard, he overheard some say they would work through the weekend while the weather held.

He made his way to the boathouse and manoeuvred the pleasure craft from its berth. The tide was high when he set course for the castle. There was no need for a zigzag route; he had learned how to use the drift of the tides to ease gently against the landing steps.

He threw his rucksacks onto the concrete platform, glancing once more at the central window, pretending he was merely admiring the stonework of the east curtain wall. Passing through the cobbled tunnel, he went straight to the kitchens and struck a match to the prepared range fire. He knew now that the heat would rise to the first-floor dining room, newly arranged into a dormitory.

Everything was ready for his so-called ghost hunt. All that remained was to wait for the semi-darkness to fall.

*** 

Percy spent the early evening moving coal, logs, and peat blocks into the storage cupboard near the kitchens before concealing himself in the second-floor toilet. Time dragged. He checked his watch by candlelight at regular intervals. It was well past midnight.

He smirked faintly at the thought of a ghost keeping a strict timetable. Yet, as the minutes stretched, impatience gnawed at him. Finally, he abandoned his hiding place and went to the dormitory, lying on one of the beds and staring at the ceiling.

"Maybe the ghost's waiting for the right moment," he thought. "Or perhaps I've picked the wrong corridor." He had, after all, made it very clear to MacDonald that the Grey Lady haunted the north and west wing corridors—a deliberate ploy to set a trap.

That night, nothing came of it. Percy slept soundly and indulged in a long lie-in before breakfast. The next day passed slowly. He walked the corridors, checking that every item on his carefully noted inventory remained untouched.

***

By nightfall, he was back on the second floor, stationed in near-darkness, waiting. Time seemed to slow, each passing minute thick with anticipation. At last, sometime after midnight, he considered giving up when he heard the small door on the northwest wing slam shut; just as it had before.

"Whooo… whooo… whooo…"

At first, Percy thought it was an owl hooting in the distance. But as he snuffed out the candle and stepped quietly into the north corridor, he realised he was wrong.

There, at the far end, stood an apparition: a woman in a grey Victorian dress, her long, straggled hair hanging around her shoulders, holding a lamp that cast an eerie, trembling glow.

"Stop!" Percy shouted, his voice echoing off the stone walls.

The figure turned and hurried down the western corridor. Heart pounding, Percy gave chase, quickening his pace to a trot. He rounded the corner, but she was gone.

He checked the south corridor below the battlements, then raced along the north corridor, down the stone steps, and into the courtyard. Nothing. Retracing his steps, he tested every locked door on every floor.

Doubt crept in for the first time. How could a spectre in a long dress, carrying a lantern, disappear so quickly? He should have heard footsteps, or at least seen a flicker of movement, but there was nothing.

He climbed to the southern battlements, scanning the sea for a departing boat. The Sound of Mull lay still and silent. No vessel approached or left the rocks below.

It was impossible. There was nowhere to hide. Every bedroom was locked, along with the library and the guardhouse. No one would risk hiding in the kitchens or dining room, either, now converted into a dormitory.

The thinking gave him a pounding headache. Finally, drained, he made his way back down through the semi-darkness, collapsed onto his bed fully clothed, and fell into a deep, dreamless sleep within seconds.

It was a troubled sleep. Percy tossed and turned beneath the heavy wool blanket, his mind replaying the strange events of the previous night. At last, he sat up, exhaled sharply, and decided to undress. He slipped into his jam-jams, the cold fabric clinging to his skin, and slid back beneath the covers. The castle was silent—eerily so—the kind of silence that makes one wonder if even time itself has paused. Eventually, exhaustion claimed him, and he drifted into another uneasy sleep.

When he woke, a thin shaft of sunlight filtered through the high stone windows, cutting across the dusty air of the chamber. Percy rose, lit the range in the kitchen, and cooked himself a modest Sunday breakfast. As he sat down, the aroma of frying bacon and fresh toast almost soothed him. He poured a pot of tea and ate slowly, going over in his mind the peculiar events of the night before.

Despite the strange sighting, Percy was calmer now, in a better frame of mind. Yet he was not the kind of man to accept the supernatural without reason. Something about it all nagged at him.

If a ghost truly wished to frighten him, why had it run off the moment he approached? And the lantern—too convenient by half. His thoughts wandered to stories he had read, of Florence Nightingale—the famous "Lady with the Lamp"—who was said to appear in the wards and corridors of certain hospitals. Could this, too, be an act of deliberate misdirection?

He leaned back in his chair, sipping his second cup of tea, and sat for a while contemplating his next move. Eventually, he scraped his plate clean, stacked his cutlery into his rucksack, and resolved to investigate the mystery further.

The castle looked different in the morning light. Gone were the oppressive shadows of last night; the sun streamed brightly through the tall corridor windows, illuminating motes of dust as they drifted lazily in the air. There was no need for paraffin lamps or storm lanterns now. The castle, bathed in daylight, almost seemed to breathe again.

But Percy's unease remained, and his first task was clear. The western second-floor corridor—where the entity had vanished—would be his starting point. The so-called spectre couldn't simply have disappeared into thin air. So how had she managed it?

He climbed to the battlements once more, scanning the layout in silence. There was no way anyone could have climbed or descended the narrow circular staircases so quickly, especially wearing such cumbersome Victorian attire. That left only one explanation: there had to be another route, something hidden.

Percy thought of the old tales he'd heard: of priest holes and secret chambers, built during the reign of King Henry VIII to conceal Catholic clergy from the king's purges. It was not uncommon for castles of this age to hide entire passageways behind walls. Could Dubh Artach Castle, too, hold such secrets?

There was only one way to find out.

Starting at the far end of the corridor where the windows admitted the brightest light, Percy methodically examined each wall panel from floor to ceiling, working between the narrow recesses one by one. His fingertips brushed across cold wood and uneven stone, seeking any sign of movement. Finally, he reached the southern door without success.

Undeterred, he crossed to the west wall and continued, crawling on hands and knees to test the lower panels and stretching up toward the ceiling where the carved mouldings cast long shadows. A heavy tapestry obscured some panels, its once-rich colours now dulled by centuries of dust. He carefully lifted it down and placed it on the floor, revealing hidden sections of the wall.

Then, at last, it happened.

A faint, distinct *click*.

One of the panels sprang open beneath his hand.

Just as he'd suspected, a narrow stone staircase descended into darkness. These were not part of the main stairwell—they were broader, purpose-built for easier passage—and from the depths below came a breath of damp, cold air. Percy shivered. Fetching his torch and storm lantern was the next step. He closed the panel, hung the tapestry carefully back in place to conceal his find, and descended swiftly to the kitchens.

As he gathered his lighting equipment, his heart pounded with the thrill of discovery. At last, he had proof: the so-called Ghost of

Dubh Artach Castle was no spirit at all, but someone flesh and blood using the castle's hidden architecture for mischief, and perhaps much more.

Back upstairs, he lifted the tapestry once again and pressed the panel. It swung open silently, revealing the spiralling descent. Lantern in one hand and torch in the other, Percy stepped cautiously into the stairwell. Each step echoed faintly, swallowed by the oppressive silence below. The descent seemed endless - a twisting coil of cold, ancient stone.

Then, faintly, he heard it. The muffled rush of waves.

He emerged into a low overhang carved from black volcanic rock, the walls slick with condensation. He raised his torch, and the beam fell upon an inscription chiselled deep into the stone:

*Charles Edward Stuart, 3rd of May, 1745.*

Percy lingered only a moment—perhaps some old dignitary marking a visit—before pushing on. The passage curved sharply and then opened into a cavern of astonishing size, its ceiling lost in shadow. Natural forces had sculpted this hollow over centuries, and a damp breeze whispered through it, carrying with it the briny tang of the sea.

Then Percy realised the truth: there was a hidden entrance somewhere below the west wall, an opening to the sea itself. From there, small craft could slip in and out unseen. That explained the cold breeze… and the gentle sound of waves breaking against what looked like a natural landing stage.

The mystery was beginning to unravel. This was how furniture and valuables had been ferried from the castle without a trace. And this, too, was how his "ghost" had made her escape.

But as Percy turned his torch, something else caught his eye; something bright and unexpected against the cavern's black stone.

Four canoes, propped neatly against the wall.

And then, just beyond them, he saw what made his breath catch in his throat.

Three small skeletons lay huddled together, still clad in faded scout uniforms. Their tiny bones, half-hidden beneath tattered cloth, spoke of final moments spent in terror and confusion. Beside them sprawled a fourth figure—taller, broader—the scoutmaster, still wearing what was left of his own uniform.

Percy's stomach turned. He forced himself to look away from the empty sockets of the skulls, as though they were staring straight back into him.

But there was more.

A fifth skeleton, larger still, slumped against the cavern wall. Its clothes were little more than rotting threads, its clogged boots cracked with age, a floppy hat lying askew upon the skull. Percy didn't need to guess who it was. This had to be Jan van Ecklon, the disgraced Laird of Acharacle, who had vanished years earlier under a cloud of scandal and debt.

The air in the cavern felt thicker now, charged with secrets long buried. Percy's grip tightened on the lantern handle. He turned sharply, retraced his steps to the spiral staircase, and climbed quickly back up into the safety of the corridor above. Once there, he closed the panel and replaced the tapestry carefully, his hands trembling slightly.

He had to tell the police, but not yet.

If he acted too soon, cancelling the replacement of the steps and landing stage, the thieves would know their secret had been uncovered. And if they were desperate enough to kill once, they might kill again.

The skeletons had lain there for over a decade. A few more days would make no difference. Better to let the culprits believe their secret is safe, draw them out, and catch them in the act.

Percy had a plan forming in his mind.

This coming week, he would spread whispers through the village: tales of ghostly sightings, strange noises, and missing valuables. Let the thieves believe their plan remained undiscovered. Let them grow greedy enough to come back for more.

Once the Aqua engineers completed their work, he would contact the police in Fort William directly - no small-town sergeants, no local gossip. This needed to stay quiet until the trap was ready.

And so, with his plan taking shape, Percy headed for the post office, the beating heart of the village rumour mill.

Inside, the usual gossip-mongers clustered around the counter, Catriona MacDonald among them, leaning in as she served a customer but clearly listening to every word. Percy let his voice carry just enough for all to hear.

"I know the time of night and the exact floor where this ghost walks," he said gravely. "Never thought I'd believe in ghosts… until now. Come next Saturday, I'll know the truth about the Grey Lady of Dubh Artach Castle."

The little group fell silent, wide-eyed, before parting to let him pass. Percy collected his stamps, paid without fuss, and stepped back into the sunlight.

"And when does the work start on the new steps and landing platform?" Catriona MacDonald asked from behind the post-office counter, her hands folded neatly on the polished wood as she watched Percy carefully.

"Today," Percy replied, adjusting the strap of his satchel. "In fact, I hope they're waiting for me already so I can ferry them out to begin work. The reconstruction should be finished by Friday."

He remembered that Aqua Marine had promised the job would take no more than two or three days, but he kept that to himself. The fewer people who knew details, the better. Percy didn't want anyone snooping around the castle before his plan was ready to unfold.

He was in high spirits as he left the post office. The idea of trapping the so-called ghost filled him with a quiet satisfaction. Now it was time to drive up to the lighthouse slipway.

The Aqua Marine team arrived shortly afterwards, their van loaded with equipment. Percy strode down to meet them, nodding to one of the divers as they began unloading their gear.

"Would it be possible," he asked casually, "to survey the seabed between here and the castle?"

The diver wiped a hand across his damp forehead and smiled. "Yes, we can do that for you. In fact, we can survey the entire seabed surrounding the castle if you wish. It wouldn't take us long, provided you supply the boat."

"I'll supply the boat," Percy assured him. "And there'll be a bonus waiting for you once the job's completed."

Soon, the drills, tools, and prefabricated steps were loaded onto the boat. Percy made three trips ferrying material across the short stretch of water to the castle, each crossing marked by the gentle slap of waves against the hull and the cries of seabirds wheeling overhead. The physical work, though tiring, did wonders for clearing his mind.

He showed the men the dormitory and the kitchens where they would eat and sleep. "I'll visit every morning, at noon, and again at 6:00 p.m.," he told them. "Just in case you need anything."

Leaving them to their task, Percy turned his attention to the foundations for the static caravans. By the time he arrived, work was already underway: turf stripped, rock exposed, and two labourers mixing concrete, their boots coated in grey dust.

The week passed quickly. By Friday, the work on the new landing stage was complete. The divers had also finished their underwater survey, charting the seabed around the black volcanic rock on which the castle stood.

The findings were conclusive. Somerled MacLeod had lied to him. On their very first crossing, Somerled had taken an elaborate zigzag course, insisting on the presence of hidden rocks and jagged pinnacles. But the survey proved otherwise. The seabed was perfectly safe: sandy, stable, and teeming with marine life—lobsters, crabs, scallops, prawns, shrimp—but no treacherous formations except for Lady Rock, far to the south of the castle's outcrop.

Percy's suspicions hardened into certainty. Somerled MacLeod had been involved in the thefts. And soon, the proof would come.

***

By Friday afternoon, Percy drove to Fort William to meet with Detective Chief Inspector James Macnab. It took considerable effort to convince the seasoned officer that his delay in reporting the hidden cavern and skeletons was justified.

Percy explained everything: the thefts, the ghostly ruse, and the murders hidden deep beneath the castle. He laid out his plan to catch the culprits red-handed, emphasising how much work it would save the police if they captured the thieves in the act rather than chasing them afterwards.

He added, with studied nonchalance, "And I daresay there might be some recognition for you in all this, Inspector. Perhaps even a promotion."

That sealed the deal.

An agreement was struck. The police would cancel leave, recall officers if necessary, and dispatch a contingent to the estate office on Saturday afternoon. From there, they would prepare for the boat trip to Dubh Artach Castle and the arrest later that night.

"This better work, Somerville," D.C.I. Macnab said sternly, leaning forward across the desk. "Or you'll be charged with wasting police time."

Percy opened his mouth to respond, thought better of it, and simply nodded. Arguing would be pointless. Instead, he glanced up at the ceiling, smirking faintly to himself where the inspector couldn't see.

Saturday brought a flurry of activity. Before meeting the officers, Percy sailed out to the castle to collect laundry, used plates, and cutlery.

He paused at the new landing stage, admiring the sturdy steel steps and wide platform, complete with double handrails and rope securing rings. The improvements made the climb far easier and safer. He secured the boat, strode up to the castle door, and set about tidying the dormitory and kitchens. He decided to leave the beds and mattresses in place; they might prove useful when renovations began in earnest.

Back at the estate office, he was greeted with good news. Work on Sanna Lodge had been completed. Apart from a minor snagging list, it was now fully habitable.

Percy was over the moon. Walking through the lodge, he marvelled at how far it had come: transformed from a disaster zone into something warm, livable, and welcoming.

But there was no time to dwell. He locked the lodge door and returned to the office, laying out several chairs for the arriving police contingent.

***

By late afternoon, the officers had assembled, and Percy went over the plan repeatedly until he was sure every detail was clear.

"I think I can explain it better out at the castle," he said at last. "We'll take the Land Rover down to the lighthouse slipway, where the boat's moored. Five minutes across—even for those who don't like the water." He grinned, but few smiled back.

The crossing was smooth. When they reached the castle, Percy showed D.C.I. Macnab opened the secret panel and led him and two officers down into the hidden passage.

"As you can see, Inspector," Percy said quietly, gesturing with his torch, "the crime scene is intact. Likely just as it was when those poor souls were left here." He then outlined the trap:

"There'll be two men and a woman arriving through that tunnel." He swept his torch beam toward the opening before shifting it to the platform above. "The woman will disembark and make her way to the second-floor wall panel, readying her ghostly act. Once the two men step off the boat, you move in from the shadows and arrest them. When they're cuffed, one of you runs up and jams the panel latch so the woman can't escape. I'll show you how it's done."

It was a simple process, and once everyone understood, Percy moved to the central corridor, where two constables were waiting on a wooden bench.

"It shouldn't be long now, lads," he said softly, lighting a candle. "I just hope the thieves—and our ghost—take the bait. If not…" He managed a wry smile. "…then I'm in serious trouble."

Minutes crawled by. Percy glanced at his watch; it was well past the witching hour, and still, nothing. He prayed silently that nothing had gone wrong below.

Then it came: a faint, haunting sound at the far end of the corridor.

The ghost had begun her moaning.

Percy and the constables moved calmly toward the north corridor. As they turned the corner, they saw her—the Grey Lady—

hammering frantically on the panel. She rattled the stair door, then the south corridor door, both locked. Spinning back, she pounded the secret panel again and again, her wails rising.

By now, Percy and the constables were almost upon her. There was no rush; she wasn't going anywhere.

"Faither, where are ye?" she cried, panic cracking her voice. "The panel's jammed; they're getting closer!"

"It's no good, Catriona," Percy said firmly. "It's over. Your father and your lover have been arrested in the cavern."

Her face blanched, and she offered no resistance as the constables handcuffed her and read her rights. At that moment, the secret panel opened and D.C.I. Macnab stepped through.

"Well, Mr. Somerville," he said, his tone grudging but respectful, "that went far smoother than I'd imagined." Turning to Catriona, he added sharply, "All right, young lady, time to go."

He gripped her arm and escorted her down to the waiting boat. Percy started up the pleasure craft, carefully guiding it out of the cavern beneath the west wall and toward the lighthouse slipway.

Back on shore, Percy rode with a constable to fetch the police van. When they returned, D.C.I. Macnab personally oversaw the loading of stolen booty recovered from the cottages.

Percy watched closely as Duncan MacDonald glared defiantly, his jaw tight with anger. Beside him, Catriona's face was pale with fear, while Somerled MacLeod's expression was a mixture of guilt, shame, and resignation.

One by one, they were secured in separate compartments of the police transporter bound for Fort William station and the cold silence of the holding cells.

The plan had worked.

# Chapter 5 - Boom Years, Film Crews, and a Fracture

Before he knew it, Mhairi and Archie had arrived for Christmas and the New Year.

She had agreed to move to the estate in the hope that a teaching post would become available at either of the village schools. This was much to the delight of her son, Archie Lawson, who was enrolled at Kilchoan Primary School.

Time had flown by. The 1970 summer bookings had proved a success; with planning permission granted, all ten static caravans were fully booked. The six holiday cottages were also reserved—some right through to Christmas 1971 and into the New Year.

Percy's choice of construction firm had been the right one. Once the stolen items had been taken back to the castle and stored in the two eastern rooms, work began on the two lighthouse keepers' cottages. These would be ready for use by spring 1970. Percy was so overcome with emotion that he vowed Alistair Dean and his company would get the Dubh Artach Castle contract when the time came for full renovation.

The caravan park and campsite had been slow to fill at first, but once it became known as a Blue Flag beach, it turned into the perfect destination for family caravan holidays. The Acharacle Estate was now generating so much profit that it was decided to press ahead with the other thirty static caravans. It was not too much of an upheaval, since twenty of the concrete foundations on the other two tiers had already been installed. All that remained was to purchase the caravans and put them in place. The fourth-tier foundations, beside the caravan park, could be laid in the winter of 1971 in preparation for the following spring, summer and even autumn, judging by the current bookings.

It was not just weeks or months that had slipped casually by. Archie had proved a great help during his time at Kilchoan Primary, but now he was in his fourth year at Oban High School, where he lived in the boys' hostel. He had consistently scored no less than 98% on his report cards from the day he started at the prestigious secondary school. His teachers spoke of him as a model pupil.

He had been given the honour of being dux of the school and captain of the Legendary Giant Fingal group, helping to maintain discipline among pupils from different academic years. Though Archie had tried football, shinty, and athletics, he was more drawn to books than the playing field. He went on to Glasgow University to study business management and mathematics. Gaelic remained his preferred language, which he had taken at school and continued at university. In addition, he enrolled in evening classes at the Glasgow School of Art, where he met the first love of his life, Jennifer—Jenny, as she liked to be called. She shared with him her talent for painting, and would later play a significant role in his life when they graduated together.

That was what Percy felt he had missed with his stepson, whom he had legally adopted. There had been no family holidays as such: no lazy days on the beach, no swimming together like other families. Percy often wondered whether it was his own disinterest or Archie's academic focus that had prevented such pleasures. Mhairi occasionally managed to persuade Archie to accompany her, but she usually pursued her own escapes to warmer climates during the holidays.

Percy could not dwell on such thoughts for long. The Dubh Artach Castle planning permission had been granted, but estate business was delaying renovation. Staffing was the main problem. Most men and women in the surrounding area were already employed by the estate, and those who were not were largely unemployable.

At one point, in the middle of the season, Percy had to sack the caravan park manager for pilfering from the shop—mostly cigarettes, though Percy suspected she had also been dipping into the till. When she was dismissed, her husband, who usually worked nights, left with her. Percy suddenly found himself "up the creek without a paddle" until a teenager, Alison McLoy, and her partner, who had just moved to the village, stepped in and filled the vacancies perfectly.

The serious work began: transporting men and materials to the castle. Then the surveyor arrived with another problem. Percy, not for the first time, wondered what his estate manager was doing; surely it was his job to sort out such issues before they reached Percy's desk.

The surveyor stood on the slipway, scratching his head as he studied the castle. He introduced his companion.

"This is Ron, a stonemason. He's agreed to work with me on this conundrum. Please don't ask me to explain just yet, because I don't have the answer. We need to go out to the castle immediately, before the planning Clerk of Works halts the renovation."

"They can't do that, Conan—we have planning permission," Percy protested.

"Oh yes, they can, Mr Somerville. They have the authority until we can give them a reasonable explanation."

Percy started the boat and sailed them out to the castle. Together they made their way to the first-floor east wing corridor.

"Okay, Ron, take the measuring tape to the north wall. Mr Somerville, if you could hold the reel to the south wall."

When they had carried out the instructions, the surveyor noted the distance and divided it into three, placing markers every fifteen feet.

"This is as much my mistake as anyone's," he admitted. "But it's not too late to put right at this stage." He measured again and marked a spot with chalk on the floor, to Percy's bewilderment.

"If you look at the markings every fifteen feet, we have three. The end room towards the south wall. The other room, located towards the north wall, is in the centre position of the…" He stopped briefly, then continued. "Two end rooms with doors and windows on the outside east wall. Then three windows on the east wall outside—but no door entrance here. We're missing a room, Mr Somerville. Fifteen feet of space, in fact—and that's what the planning authority wants answers about. It's as much their fault as mine; the plans should never have been passed without investigating this gap earlier."

"How could we have missed this, Conan? I've walked up and down this corridor countless times, with you and with every other foreman." A dark chill passed over Percy as he recalled the central window on the first floor, where he once thought he had seen a shadowy figure with a green, shell-like face.

"Right," Conan said firmly. "I need your permission to knock down part of this wall. I think we'll find a door to the missing room."

Percy could only nod. For once, he was speechless, and fear filled the silence as the stonemason began to hammer at the wall. Percy dreaded what they might uncover.

His relief was palpable when they found nothing sinister, only an oak door that matched the others in the east wing corridor. The stonemason cleared enough brick and plaster to allow entry, revealing that the large key was still in the lock.

Percy struggled with it. The lock was stiff, unused for decades, but eventually it clicked open. The handle squeaked as he turned it. He stepped into what could only be described as a large walk-in freezer.

The nursery was strewn with broken toys. Cobwebs hung thickly from ceiling to floor. Some toys that remained intact began to stir: the boxing monkey sparred with the boxing hare, while a small quartet of cymbals clashed into eerie music.

Percy pushed through the dense cobwebs, unprepared for the horror awaiting him. In the corner, on a single bed, were three skeletons—an adult and two children—huddled together. He gasped, frozen in shock at the grim sight.

He seemed transfixed to the spot until the rocking chair, facing the lighthouse through barred windows, began to move. It rocked slowly at first, disturbing the dangling cobwebs. Pushing them aside, Percy edged towards the filthy, barred window. He felt and heard a sickening crunch beneath his feet. He had stepped on skeletal remains—bones that had crumbled and fallen from the rocking chair. A few brittle pieces still clung to the chair's arms, grotesquely positioned as though the occupant were still at rest, gazing out at the sea.

Percy longed to escape this frozen hell. Yet as the rocking chair quickened its pace, he found he could not move. Trapped in the corner by the window, panic clawed at his chest. He flailed his arms desperately.

"Stay away from me! I've done you no harm. Please… oh please…"

The next thing he knew, the surveyor was shaking him by the shoulders in the corridor, his clothes and hair covered in cobwebs.

"Mr Somerville, get a grip on yourself. Everything is all right."

Percy slumped against the wall beneath the window that looked out onto the courtyard. Trembling violently, he accepted a bottle of water and gulped it down before forcing himself unsteadily to his feet.

"What in heaven's name is wrong with you, man? Pull yourself together. You need to see a doctor as soon as we leave this damned rock."

"So you saw it!" Percy's voice cracked. "You know this castle is cursed. You must have felt the freezing air, seen the toys moving of their own accord."

"There's no ice-cold room, Mr Somerville. Skeletons, yes—but I saw nothing else."

"And the toys—you admitted you saw them!"

"There's a logical explanation," the surveyor replied. "Those Victorian toys are finely balanced. The slightest vibration sets them off. Watch." He stepped into the room and stamped on the dusty floorboards. At once, the half-wound toys jerked into life; cymbals clashed, and the monkey resumed its eerie sparring.

The surveyor stepped out and locked the door behind him. Brushing cobwebs from himself and Percy, he said firmly:

"I want this room sealed, Conan. Do what you must—just seal it."

"You're not thinking clearly, Mr Somerville. This is a crime scene. The police must be informed. They'll close this wing until a pathologist has examined the remains and arranged proper burial—just like the cavern skeletons."

He paused. "I'll notify the planning department about this discovery. You must contact the Fort William police as soon as you reach Sanna Lodge. And one more thing: no more work today. Call your doctor."

Percy found even berthing the pleasure craft in the boathouse exhausting. Breathless, he trudged up to the riverbank, climbed the veranda steps, and dragged himself to the phone. He called Fort William police station.

"Can I speak to Chief Inspector McNab, please?"

"What is it regarding, sir?"

"Another four skeletons, I'm afraid. Found at Dubh Artach Castle."

"The Chief Inspector is on holiday. I'll connect you with another senior officer."

A pause. Then: "Inspector Murray speaking. I understand you've found another four skeletons?"

"That's correct. Two adults and two children."

"Right. Make sure nobody tampers with the scene. I'll send a pathologist and two constables."

Percy gave a wan smile. "The room is locked and secure, Inspector. They're not going anywhere." The line went dead.

He longed to lie down. Too weary to climb the stairs, he collapsed onto the settee and fell asleep.

It was Mhairi who woke him with a gentle nudge.

"It's the Fort William police, Percy. They're waiting to be ferried out to the castle. What on earth is going on?"

"I'll explain later, Mhairi. For now, I must hurry."

He drove quickly to the lighthouse, where the inspector, two constables, and the pathologist were waiting.

"Sorry about the delay," Percy said with forced cheer.

One constable grinned. "Any more finds like this, and you'll be keeping the match ball."

The inspector silenced him with a sharp look. Percy barely noticed—his gaze was fixed on the first-floor central window of the castle.

They climbed swiftly to the east corridor, where Percy unlocked the door and stepped back.

"Well, Mr Somerville," the pathologist remarked, brushing past the cobwebs, "you certainly have found a collection of bones." Toys gave their last jerks as the wound-down springs faltered. "Yes… most interesting."

After examining the scene, the inspector rejoined Percy.

"We'll await the pathologist's report. For now, let's go down, have a cup of tea, and you can tell me how you stumbled upon this carnage."

Percy boiled the kettle, laid out cups and a tin of biscuits, and poured tea. When they finished, the inspector instructed the constables to return upstairs and assist.

"One of you will stay to guard the room until the mortuary van arrives. That may not be until tomorrow. Mackay—you're on guard."

The young constable paled. The inspector smirked, then quickly hid it.

"Remember your training: it's not the dead you need to fear, but the living. Still, keep your truncheon handy—just in case."

Once the constables had gone, the inspector poured another cup of tea and leaned back.

"This is a curious place, Mr Somerville. I was just a constable during the cavern arrests, but that case fast-tracked my career. And now here I am again, back at your haunted castle." He smiled wryly. "Don't mistake my tone. I do believe there's something here—a curse, perhaps."

He lit a cigarette. "I've long been fascinated by the paranormal. Call them what you like—spectres, spooks, apparitions. The question is: do they exist? I believe they do. Not as we know human form, but as a force trying desperately to communicate. Sometimes, through a medium, they succeed. I once attended an Ouija board session at university—not participating, just observing. Four students placed their fingers on the planchette. It moved, spelling out the name of a girl, Lena Dixon. The light dimmed, the fire in the grate died to embers, then roared back to life. Weeks later, Lena was pulled from the River Clyde, terror frozen on her face."

He exhaled smoke. "That's why I believe there are both good and evil forces at work. I've seen objects move, doors slam, glasses smash in supposedly haunted pubs. Friends say I carry a light that wards off evil. All I can say is: I've witnessed enough to know the supernatural cannot be dismissed."

He reached into his case and pulled out a sheaf of papers.

"Here's a record of Dubh Artach Castle's inhabitants. It goes back to 1747, when the first laird was appointed after Culloden. Many rebel estates were confiscated. This castle went to Clan McCrimmon. The estate passed through generations until John McCrimmon took over in 1864. He was respected, but tragedy struck. His wife, Anna, gave him three sons—two of whom, I believe, lie upstairs. The eldest, Shamus, had no interest in the estate. He served in Queen Victoria's army and was killed in India. Eventually, a distant relation, Colin McNicol, inherited, but he too neglected the land. He sold it to a Dutchman, Jan van Ecklon."

The inspector took another drag, his eyes narrowing as he changed the subject.

"At first glance, I believe the woman whose bones lie scattered on the floor is Anna McCrimmon, John's wife, dating back to 1876. I also suspect the other adult skeleton on the bed is the nanny, Morag Dempsy. At the time, it was reported that they had run off to start a new life in America. However, I have the passenger list from the ship that sailed from Tobermory Bay in May 1876, and Anna, her lover, and the children never boarded."

"That's right, Mr Somerville. Anna had relationships with women. When the laird discovered it, he could not risk the scandal. He shot the lover and the children. He did not kill Anna outright, but he beat her before walling her into her chamber and leaving her to die slowly. It doesn't take a great deal of imagination to see that Anna suffered a terrible, drawn-out death." He gathered his papers. "Come, let's go up and try to make contact with Anna. Perhaps the pathologist has something new to report."

Percy shuddered. He had no appetite for contacting spirits—he had already seen far more than he wished.

The inspector placed a firm but friendly hand on his chest. "Before we go upstairs, I want to give you a piece of advice you'd do well to heed." He flicked his cigarette into the fire.

"By all accounts, Anna McCrimmon is a vengeful spirit. She cursed this castle, and her wrath is directed at the Lairds of Acharacle. Look at the facts. The laird who entombed her later died of mushroom poisoning—not mysterious in itself, as the cook had gathered the fungi herself. He had three sons. The eldest, Shamus, inherited the estate but died in India. Very little is recorded of the fourth laird, Colin McNicol, though we know he eventually sold the estate and emigrated to Australia. Jan Van Ecklon, the Dutchman who purchased it, was stabbed to death, leaving no laird on whom Anna could exact her revenge—until you came along." He gave a thin smile.

"To linger in this world, Anna has bound herself as one of the undead. I believe she made a pact with darker forces—demons who granted her time here, but at the cost of a debt that will one day be claimed. That price will not come due until a laird dies. Until then, she stalks these corridors." He withdrew his hand.

"That is why you must never be alone in this castle. Never give Anna the chance to punish you for her husband's cruelty more than a century ago."

"Come now, Inspector. I've wandered these corridors countless times alone. The only place I've not yet explored is the dungeons—but the contractor will need me there soon enough when the generator and septic tanks are installed."

"You may think so, Mr Somerville, but consider this: Anna was sealed into that room and had no escape until the wall was demolished and the door unlocked. Now she roams Dubh Artach Castle freely. She could be in the kitchens listening to us right now. But, as before, she cannot leave these grounds until her vengeance is fulfilled and the demons claim her soul."

Percy shook his head. "I don't wish to call you a liar, Inspector Murray, but the idea of a ghost wandering these corridors stretches belief."

"Think what you like, Mr Somerville. But how do you explain your extraordinary actions in that room? The surveyor and the stonemason both saw you."

Percy muttered excuses of fatigue, overwork, and imagination.

"Very well," said the inspector, "but mark my words. Anna McCrimmon will wait for the right moment. It may not be tonight, next week, or even next year—but she will be watching you. If you want my advice, sell this cursed place and never set foot in Dubh Artach Castle again. Lecture over. Now, let's go upstairs."

The constables were waiting at the door. The storm lantern still flickered in the corridor when the pathologist appeared, brushing himself down.

"There's not much more I can tell you, Inspector. Two adult females, around twenty-five years of age. Two infant males, one about five, the other three. The children and the woman on the bed were shot at close range with a twin-barrelled shotgun. I'll know more once I've examined them at the mortuary."

Pathologists rarely betrayed emotion, but Harry Stewart's grimace spoke volumes. "It's difficult to say how long the other woman took to die. If starvation and dehydration were the cause, I'd estimate a week, perhaps two. There are deep scratch marks on the door and gouges on the plaster by the window, where she tried to dig her way out. In the end, she must have given up and lain down to die. A dreadful end."

The inspector stepped into the room.

"Anna, we now know how you and the others died. I cannot harm you, and I ask you not to harm me. Let us be friends."

The rocking chair creaked into motion.

"Ah, so you are still here. I promise you this: before the mortuary attendants arrive, your remains and those of the children will be given a Christian burial. But grant me one favour in return—leave Percy Somerville, the Laird of Acharacle, in peace. He has done you no wrong."

The heavy door slammed shut.

"Are you still with me, Anna? If so, show yourself—or at least rock the chair once more."

There was no reply. The inspector opened the door and stepped back into the corridor.

"She has gone, but she is still bound to this cursed castle." He turned to the bewildered pathologist. "Let's go down for another cup of tea while we wait for transport."

The years passed almost unnoticed. The lighthouse keepers' cottages, restored and returned to rightful use, were now popular holiday lets. Yet for Percy, there was always one last task.

He had Sanna Lodge sprinkled with holy water and blessed by both a priest and the local Presbyterian minister. The site was consecrated as holy ground where future Lairds of Acharacle and their families would be laid to rest. A twenty-foot-high obelisk of red polished granite was erected on a deep foundation strong enough to withstand the Atlantic gales that battered the coast.

The castle itself had been transformed. Renovated and modernised, it now welcomed visitors from around the world, who came as much for the ghostly tales as for its grandeur. Double glazing, crafted to preserve the old look, kept the warmth in, while central heating ensured comfort in winter.

Meals were prepared by a capable kitchen staff, the rooms maintained by housekeepers, and service overseen by a modern-day butler. Electricity, telephones, and water mains—long since installed—kept the castle connected to the mainland. Luxurious en-suite bedrooms offered home comforts for those willing to pay the steep fees.

So frequent were the comings and goings that Percy hired a boatman, John MacKinnon from Barra, to ease his burden. But Percy, ever unwilling to step back, continued to help ferry tourists in the pleasure launch he had purchased from Rebecca MacLeod, whose husband was serving time for theft. At the slipway, disembarking visitors thanked him and pressed coins into his hand.

Yet one afternoon, as Percy watched them depart, he felt a tightness in his chest. Turning to John, he forced a smile. "I'll go to the chemist for some Rennies. Just a touch of indigestion."

But the chemist took one look at him and knew the truth—Percy Somerville was in the grip of a heart attack.

He was rushed to the Belford Hospital in Fort William. Wired to heart monitors, he felt utterly confused. "This isn't me, Sister," he said in anguish as she tidied his bed and propped his pillows.

"I'm afraid it is, Mr Somerville. You're lucky—this was a warning. Some people don't get one. Please lie back and relax. The doctor will see you on his rounds tomorrow morning." The officious nursing sister left him to ponder.

Rebecca visited that evening, bringing the usual necessities—pyjamas, dressing gown and slippers. She set grapes and juice on the bedside locker.

"I thought Mhairi would have come with you, Rebecca, but thank you for coming."

"Mhairi's in Glasgow on business. She won't have heard about you yet," she replied, a trace of anger in her tone.

"I don't know what business Mhairi has in Glasgow; she's never mentioned anything to me. Any idea what she's up to?"

"You stop worrying. The estate is running smoothly—before you ask. And David will visit tomorrow night. If you think of anything you need—and I don't mean estate business—tell me now or ring tomorrow and David will bring it."

Visiting hour ended too soon. Rebecca kissed his cheek. "You're here to rest, Percy Somerville. No estate business until you're home and well." She left the recovery room.

How could he relax, with the tourist trade in full swing and arrangements to be made for upcoming events? He picked up a local magazine and flicked through it. The first thing that caught his eye was an advert for a local fast-food chain. His heart monitor quickened alarmingly, bringing staff hurrying to his bedside.

The ward sister whisked the magazine away. "Right, Mr Somerville, time for your tea and tablets—then sleep." She drew the curtains.

It was already too late to stop the idea taking root. He had always felt something was missing at the castle and now saw it clearly in that advert: a tearoom on the ground floor, in the north-western corner. It would mean trimming the kitchen space but without interrupting daily operations. Guided tours could finish at the foot of the north-western stone stairs—an ideal point to entice visitors to refreshments after a long circuit.

Percy smiled faintly as a nurse brought tea and a plain digestive. The night passed quietly. In the morning, after breakfast, the doctor arrived with his cold stethoscope and examined him, then addressed the matron.

"Good. His heart has responded to the medication—keep him on it for now." He turned to Percy. "You've had a warning, Mr Somerville. Habits and diet must change, or the next attack could be fatal. Walk when you're discharged—build up gradually—and reduce stress. Personally, I'd leave the running of your business to your employees. I'll examine you again before discharge."

"When will I be allowed home, doctor?"

"We're awaiting the blood tests taken on admission. Let's not speculate." He left before Percy could ask more. The nursing sister straightened his bedcovers and pillows.

That evening, Percy spoke quietly with his estate manager about the tearoom. He held a finger to his lips for discretion. "I'm not supposed to get stressed, David, but there's something I want done while I'm stuck here." He glanced at the door. "Call the surveyor. I want a tearoom at the north-west corner of the kitchens. There's room to reduce the kitchen size. Conan will know how. We've missed years of income—my fault."

He changed the subject. "Has Mhairi returned from Glasgow? And what's Rory McGilvery up to?"

"No, Mhairi's still in Glasgow—hasn't disclosed her business. The gamekeeper's busy with shooting parties, chasing the deer."

Percy nodded with relief. David continued, "Alison McLoy and her partner, George, are doing a great job with the caravan park and the forty statics. Small issue with Billy Semple grumbling about mowing and tidying, but Alison threatened the sack if he didn't improve—problem solved."

Percy smiled. "Billy's always been a moaner—ever since the estate let the Hornbys go."

The visitors' bell sounded, ending their talk. "Just make sure my idea goes ahead, David."

There were no visitors on Wednesday—the day the wires were removed. On Thursday evening, Mhairi finally appeared.

"Where have you been, Mhairi? I've been worried," Percy said softly.

"Let's leave that until you're home and recovering, Percy. How are you feeling?"

"Home tomorrow, thank goodness. Rebecca's picking me up." He sat in the chair. "Who brought you tonight, Mhairi?" he asked, suspicious.

"Rory had shotgun cartridges to collect and other bits and pieces. It was too good a chance to miss a lift."

"So—it's Rory now. You know his reputation. You'll be the talk of the village tomorrow. Why use him of all people?"

"Sod the village—and anyone on the estate with twisted minds."

"Does that include me? I'm trying to protect your reputation."

"If the boot fits, wear it, Percy Somerville. I'm sick of gossip-mongers. I'm a big girl; I can look after myself. And if it eases your mind, Rory MacGilvray isn't the first and won't be the last to try to get my knickers off—without success, I might add."

Seeing him agitated, she changed the subject. "Archie and Jenny send love and best wishes. They'll visit when you're home. My word—so many cards and flowers. You're well liked—perhaps for what you've done for the area, lifting it from poverty with hard work and investment, which nearly cost you your life."

"That's what life is, Mhairi—vision and improvisation. Investment for long-term outcomes and income. That's why I bought the Acharacle Estate: I needed to escape the drudgery of my so-called life in the city stockbroker belt."

"I understand, Percy. Let's save it for later." She checked her watch. "I must dash. Rory will be waiting." She was gone before the bell sounded. Percy leaned back, suspicious and unsettled. He reached for his Nitrolingual spray to slow his pounding heart and ease the tightness in his chest.

Next morning, he felt better and was cleared by the doctor. "Remember the warning, Mr Somerville. Short walks at first, increasing daily—don't overdo it. Your GP will prescribe a heart tablet to take once a day, every day, for life."

"Thank you, doctor—and thanks to all the staff who looked after me."

Rebecca lifted his small case and walked him to the car. "Right, boss—ferry or Loch Eil?"

"Let's enjoy the scenery—and your company—a little longer, Rebecca. The Road to the Isles and Loch Eil, please." They smiled as she started the engine.

The local doctor advised Percy to take it easy for a month. He tried to heed the advice: short walks, lengthening each day; fishing on Loch Mundle every other day; climbing the stairs at Sanna Lodge without getting breathless. The two-mile walk to the village and back helped enormously. Yet he struggled to pass the junction to the lighthouse slipway. It felt like an angel on one shoulder urging him back to the lodge, and a devil on the other whispering, "Go on— what harm can it do? A short visit to the castle is what you need."

Percy took the road to Sanna Lodge. The brilliant sunshine tempted him to climb the mountain path of Meall Nan Con—something he had never done in all his years as laird. Reaching the summit, he challenged himself further with Beinn Na Serg and then Beinn Na Breac, the last conquered with ease. A picnic at each summit gave him time to relax and take in the breathtaking views.

After two months of rest, it was time to return to work. It felt as though he had never been away. The castle booking chart revealed that the BBC was interested in filming a documentary. One of the big American studios had also shown interest: the location was perfect for their historical film, and the resident ghost was an added attraction. As always in business, once one company took an interest, others followed, afraid of missing out. A film location manager and her entourage were scheduled for a flying visit in early spring 1978.

Letters from various American studios continued to arrive. Percy was particularly intrigued when a syndicate of film studios proposed buying the castle outright. As a businessman, he would have preferred them to compete individually, driving the price up. Still, the syndicate was clearly serious, and he would have to consider their offer carefully, particularly with his son Archie, the future Laird of Acharacle.

He had no firm price in mind but could already calculate roughly what each studio might be willing to pay. The syndicate was prepared to wait until 1981, since Universal had secured a lease for filming a historical epic starting in December 1979, hoping for snow. Production was expected to last five months, with a hefty penalty clause if it overran. Meanwhile, the BBC completed its documentary in stages, without requiring the castle to close—only certain areas were restricted from tourists.

This arrangement gave Percy and Archie time to deliberate. Meanwhile, Percy pressed ahead with alterations, turning part of the kitchen into a tearoom—a venture that quickly proved profitable.

The film location manager arrived by helicopter with her secretary and a boom-camera operator. They took notes, measured, and were guided around the castle by a tour guide well-versed in the ghost stories. After two nights in the castle, Percy was summoned to sign the film contract. The agreed price delighted him—secured during the quieter winter season when tourist numbers were low.

The manager was effusive. "The perfect location, Mr Somerville. We'll be in touch."

Percy watched the helicopter lift from the helipad. Another bumper season lay ahead; the estate was thriving once more.

By mid-November the film crew and chefs began arriving with their equipment. As the month progressed, the director, actors, and actresses came and went. Filming went smoothly—helped by a fall of snow exactly as they had hoped—and was finished by April 4, 1980.

Discussions with Archie settled on a sale price of $3,000,000 per studio, totalling $15,000,000. If any syndicate member dropped out, the others would cover the shortfall. Yet negotiations faltered when the syndicate deemed the price excessive. Archie urged patience: "Hold out for the price. Negotiate only if absolutely necessary."

Percy was less confident. "We don't want to lose this chance, Archie. If they walk away, it's gone forever."

"Alright, Dad. I can see you're nervous. Let's put our cards on the table—$500,000 off each member. Final offer: $12.5 million. I'll go to the States to sign if they accept."

Percy agreed, albeit reluctantly.

For a while, it seemed the deal had died. Then, one summer's day, an American solicitor telephoned the estate office.

"My bosses want this castle sale tied up quickly. The $12.5 million has been accepted. Payment will be made in November, with ownership transferred once funds clear. All I need is a signature at our London office."

"Excellent, Mr Dorsey. I can no longer travel far, but my son Archie will sign, and my solicitor will act on my behalf." Percy noted the date, time, and address carefully. "I think your clients have got a very good deal."

"That's what everyone says, Mr Somerville. Let's get this sewn up." The line went dead.

Percy phoned Archie with the news.

"Yes, clever of you to push the price up, Dad, knowing they'd try to chip it down. We still got what we wanted—with a little extra." Archie's laughter rang down the line.

Percy reflected with quiet pride. He had turned a £230,000 investment into assets worth £2.3 million, a bank balance of £1.8 million, and now the castle would bring in $12.5 million—all within eleven years. Hard work and sacrifice had given his family a comfortable life, and the Acharacle Estate would continue to provide income even after the sale.

Standing at the bay window, he savoured a Havana cigar and a glass of Rémy Martin brandy. Two luxuries he rarely indulged in, but the occasion warranted it. Beyond the glass lay the Inner and Outer Hebrides. Yet for all the triumph, he had no one to share the moment with. Archie and Jenny were finishing their university studies. As for Mhairi—she was spending far too much time in Glasgow, and not with their children. Suspicion gnawed at him. He considered hiring a private detective but decided instead to confront her directly. Gossip spread quickly enough on the estate; if something were amiss, it would come out.

He did not wait long. That night Mhairi returned to Sanna Lodge.

"Great news, Mhairi. Dubh Artach Castle has been sold—at a very healthy profit. Just what you always wanted: to be rid of it."

"Congratulations, Percy." Her tone lacked warmth.

"I think you should sit down. I have something important to tell you." She paced the lounge before finally lowering herself into a chair opposite.

"I'm leaving you, Percy. I've found my vocation at last."

"This comes as a shock. Is it someone I know? Rory MacGillivray, the gamekeeper? I've suspected him for some time."

"Now you're being ridiculous, Percy Somerville. There's nobody else. I've been faithful to you all these years, despite your lack of compassion in the bedroom. I'll admit, there were times I considered taking a lover, but I refrained. Recently, though, I drove to Glasgow Airport, desperate to escape this dull existence. It was just my luck—I had no passport, no holiday."

"After dinner at the hotel, I sat with my coffee in the lounge. A flight captain joined me, and I was utterly transfixed by my imagination. I wanted to give myself to him completely, without reservation. I lost count of how many times I whispered my room number, hoping he would take the bait—but my luck was out. He was waiting for his second flight officer and told me he was flying to Tenerife. If I'd had my passport and there'd been a spare seat, I would have followed him to the ends of the earth had he asked." She paused. "I was mesmerised when he stood to leave. My underwear was so wet I had to hurry to the lift and shower. Not that it helped—I lay awake all night dreaming of his body on mine, giving me what you never could."

"I had no idea you felt that way, Mhairi. Why didn't you tell me sooner?"

"That's the trouble, Percy. I did—on several occasions—but your head was always buried in business, especially that damned castle renovation."

"That's behind us now, Mhairi. The castle is sold, the estate is running smoothly. We can have a new beginning. What do you think?"

"It's too late for that, Percy. I've bought a semi-detached house on Archerhill Road in Knightswood, Glasgow. It's close to Knightswood Primary, where I'll be teaching after the summer holidays. That's why I've been in the city—not to take a lover, as you suspected, but to return to the vocation I've always longed for, ever since I graduated from Jordanhill College of Education. When I came here, I hoped for a post at Kilchoan or Acharacle Primaries, but nothing came up. I'm starting a new life before it's too late. Besides, the estate will always need something. When you talk about planting forestry on the mountain slopes—they say the Forestry Commission plants up to fifteen hundred feet. That's a lot of trees."

Percy reached for his briefcase, took out a notepad and pencil. "I'll take a note of that, Mhairi." He began scribbling calculations of how many trees might be planted, and the income it could bring to the estate.

He didn't hear Mhairi whisper softly, "I rest my case."

# Chapter 6 - Halloween, Fall, and the Legacy

When Percy finished his quick calculations, he looked up to find Mhairi gone. Rushing to the veranda, he caught only the glow of her taillights disappearing down the winding lodge road. Breathless, he reached for his heart pump spray.

The Forestry Commission was delighted with his decision to plant trees, and there was still time before winter set in. October winds swept through, and green leaves turned to brown before falling.

It was also time to erect the marquee on the helipad for another local celebration. Yet Percy felt a tinge of sadness. Archie and the estate solicitor had signed the castle sale contracts, meaning this Halloween would be the last event held there—though not the last on the estate.

Percy had already earmarked the campsite for future gatherings. For years he had organised annual events at Dubh Artach Castle: the Easter Bonnet Parade, the Chestnut Conker contest, the Halloween fancy dress for adults and children, bonfire night on the village green with fireworks provided by the laird himself, and, of course, Christmas and New Year celebrations. Time had carried them all along.

One tradition he loved most was the Argyllshire Gathering at Mossfield Park in Oban, where lairds and clan chiefs marched together. There were piping competitions, athletics, wrestling and tossing the caber. He remembered the sad incident of Jock McColl, a famed wrestler and caber-tosser. On one attempt the caber, instead of falling away, toppled back on him, breaking his shoulder and ending his career. Jock never competed again but became a respected judge.

Even so, the Highland Games always lifted spirits. The pipe band led the crowds back to the town centre, and the day ended with the grand ball in the Argyllshire Halls. For the first time in years, Percy had not attended the spectacle.

He rarely admitted mistakes, but losing Mhairi was one. Still, he believed she would come back eventually—perhaps once she realised what she had given up.

For now, his focus turned to the Halloween party. He relished judging the competitions, watching children beam as they won their prizes. No child went without; there were always apples, nuts and oranges for all. There was dooking for apples, treacle scones strung from a line, and for adults, a free bar, a buffet, and a jazz band in the marquee.

October passed swiftly. John MacKinnon, the boatman, ferried children and their parents back and forth. Once the children's competitions ended, they were returned to the mainland buses for the journey to their villages and crofts, before the adults came back later for the castle dance.

Percy breathed a sigh of relief as the night went smoothly. Under a star-filled sky, with the moon peeking over Ben More on Mull, he climbed to the battlements—his favourite place. Often he had stood there to gaze at the distant light of Dubh Artach Lighthouse, the warning buoys, and the Hebridean isles of Mull, Coll and Tiree.

But tonight, as he turned to step down, a green, shell-like face and a figure in a grey Victorian dress rushed from the western corridor door. "Woo… woo…" came the ghostly cry as she drew closer.

Percy stumbled back onto the cannon platform, flailing. Alison stopped immediately and called up to him.

"It's me, Mr Somerville—Alison, the caravan park manageress. Please don't be afraid, come down."

"For God's sake, Alison, you're only meant to scare him," her partner hissed.

But Percy was beyond reason. He flailed his arms in wild self-defence, shouting uncontrollably. "Get back! Horrible creature—get back, I say! Please—no—!"

As Alison pleaded with him to calm down, terror consumed him. Percy Somerville toppled backwards over the battlements of Dubh Artach Castle.

It was later assumed he struck the black rock below before his broken body was carried into the dark waters, snagging on Lady Rock. The wind shrieked like a banshee as the rock clutched him.

The boatman was summoned at once in case the body drifted towards the raging Corrievrechan Whirlpool. Percy Somerville was recovered and taken to the Fort William mortuary, where the pathologist soon required additional expertise from Glasgow.

Percy Somerville was dead before he fell over the battlements. Heart failure was the cause, according to the coroner's verdict. He had long been known to suffer from a weak heart, worsened by smoking, drinking, and relentless overwork. Yet there was one thing the pathologists and coroners could not explain: the look of sheer terror frozen on the laird's face.

Inspector Murray pulled back the mortuary sheet, glanced once, and replaced it without a word before walking out. He had already questioned the young couple, who swore on oath that Percy Somerville had been shouting before letting out a piercing scream as he plunged between the battlements to his death.

Murray knew in his heart what had happened that Halloween night, but his superiors warned him not to voice his suspicions at the inquest. To speak of it would invite ridicule and jeopardise his career. Promotion would never come his way if he stepped out of line.

The church was overflowing. Loudspeakers had to be hastily erected in the churchyard to relay the service to the crowd of mourners, who came from every walk of life. Clan chiefs and lairds, resplendent in their tartan kilts and plaids, lined the road to the church before joining family and friends at Sanna Lodge, where Percy Somerville, Laird of Acharacle, was laid to rest.

The piper played Flowers of the Forest and Amazing Grace before the minister gave a short sermon, thanking everyone for their presence. Afterwards, a buffet of soup, sandwiches, and refreshments filled the crowded dining room at Sanna Lodge.

It was after midnight before the last guest had gone. Archie, Jenny, and Mhairi walked together to the lodge. The sky was clear, stars twinkling brightly, and the moon bathed the obelisk in pale silver light.

Mhairi placed a wreath against the gravestone and raised her eyes to the heavens. "I was coming back, Perse. I just needed time—and a little courage." A tear welled as she bowed her head.

Archie laid his fingers on the cold black iron fence. "Well, Dad, you finally achieved your dream. The castle is sold, and the syndicate's money has been paid, just as promised." He smiled faintly. "I don't think we should tell him about Anna's disappearance. It would spoil it for him." Folding his hands together as if in prayer, he added, "Jenny is expecting our first child—a boy, they say. That gives us an heir to the estate."

Jenny raised her eyebrows, startled, as she realised Archie was speaking to his dead stepfather. She moved forward to take his hand, but Mhairi gently held her back.

"We'll explain everything, Jenny," she said softly. "Over cocoa and a peat fire at the lodge."

Archie kept his hands on the fence. "Before I go, Dad, there are a couple of things I want to tell you. While walking the heather-clad slopes, we came up with some ideas. A cable car from Loch Mundle to the summit of Meall nan Con, with a restaurant at the top so visitors can enjoy the view. A small return fare could include tea and a sandwich.

"And here's the icing on the cake: a ski centre on Beinn na Breac, with a lift up to the nursery slopes above the tree line, and another extending to the higher slopes for the experienced skiers. Perhaps even a little tearoom at the summit.

"We'll talk more about this later, when you've had your rest."

The two women linked their arms through the new laird's. Together they walked slowly back to Sanna Lodge, the beating heart of the thriving Acharacle Estate.

## The End

# The Affairs of Deborah Rupert

# Chapter 7 - Innocence and Awakening

Deborah Rupert was born in the early spring of 1915 and brought up in the country village of Welwyn in Hertfordshire. A quiet, reserved but intelligent girl, she found it hard being raised by her father and older sister, Chloe, after her mother died of pneumonia when she was ten years old. Her father eventually married again. Marjory had a kind way about her and would often sit with Deborah, helping her with school homework.

Deborah reached puberty early and harboured fantasies, just like any other young teenager wondering what the birds and bees were all about. She was an avid reader and soon discovered the meaning of sexual involvement with the opposite sex. Not that she was about to lie down with any Tom, Dick or Harry, or sneak behind the bicycle shed at school, where most of her friends indulged in innocent kissing and touching. She wanted something much more—a relationship where there was no going back.

At the age of sixteen, she would lie in her bedroom imagining all kinds of encounters, when the blacksmith gave her all the encouragement she needed. Her older sister, who had given her so much grief as a child, married the handsome, muscular blacksmith of the village. Barney Woodthorpe was considered a prize catch. Many of Deborah's school friends fantasised about him, and they would giggle as they shared their wild imaginings.

For Deborah, that chance came when the family spent two weeks of the summer holidays in Bournemouth, at Aunt Ada's apartment. Much of their time was spent on the golden spit of sand, a short bus ride from the town. Aunt Ada had her weekly hairdressing appointment. Then, much to Deborah's disappointment, her sister—who disliked being out in the sun—was undecided. Would she go, or would she walk around the shops? Finally, she said, "Okay, I'll cover myself and bring a parasol." Deborah remembered how disappointed she had felt at her sister's decision.

So, the trio caught the bus to Beachy Head. It was a typical hot English summer's day. Chloe lay on her beach towel, face down, reading a book, with her large parasol providing plenty of shade. Deborah and Barney frolicked in the water, splashing each other, until Barney, the muscular blacksmith, lifted her and threw her in. He pulled her to the surface and hugged her. In that moment, a spark flashed between them. When Barney held her close and asked if she was all right, Deborah wrapped her arms around his neck and smiled into his eyes. She could feel his hardness as he drew her nearer. She didn't pull away, glancing at her sister, who seemed engrossed in her book. Deborah gave him a long, salty kiss, sending him a clear message when their tongues collided that she was his for the taking.

She was unsure of his reaction; perhaps he would come to her later, when the timing was right. He pushed her away into the surf. "I think it's time to go home now," he roared, making sure his wife heard. "The tide is ebbing, and it can be dangerous if we stay in the water."

As a sixteen-year-old virgin, that was the end of her dream encounter. Chloe and Barney moved to Kingston upon Thames, a suburb in south-west London. They bought a cruiser, which Barney was forever tinkering with.

It was during a weekend break from teacher training college that Deborah was invited down to help with the decorating. Barney was on the cruiser, while Chloe said they had run out of paint. It would mean a trek to the shop. Deborah finished decorating and then took a shower. She put on her swimsuit and wandered down the path to the landing stage before climbing aboard.

She lay back on the deck beneath the boat's awning, eyes closed, when she felt a gentle touch on her arm. It made her senses stir. Barney was standing above her. "Lunch, Deborah. Chloe should be back soon with the tomatoes." He helped her up and led her down to the galley below deck.

Barney released her hand and gave her a knowing smile. "We must stop torturing ourselves like this, Debs. I'm not the one you want or need." She was about to embrace him when the dreaded voice of her sister rang out from the bungalow: "Coo-ee, I'm back."

Barney raced up to the deck, shouting, "We're about to have lunch. Did you bring the tomatoes?" Chloe handed him the fruit and veg. "I'll just put this paint and shopping away first, then I'll join you," she called. Barney began setting out the utensils and crockery, then put the kettle on the gas ring.

Deborah went back on deck and lay beneath the awning, another dream in tatters as her sister clambered aboard. "I hope you've been behaving yourself, Deborah, and not causing Barney any trouble." The chance would be a fine thing, Deborah thought with a wry smile.

It was back to Hatfield training college after another disappointing weekend.

She awoke fully from her dream, and for a few moments wondered where she was. She reached for her wristwatch and was about to get up when she remembered it was Saturday. No tutorials. She lay back, pulling the blankets up to her chin. She knew all too well where she was: stuck in a loveless marriage, unable to find a place of her own that suited her needs and her job at the new secondary school in Welwyn Garden City. Her husband had threatened to throw her out of the villa at 5 Oakland Avenue, but granted her a stay of execution until the end of the month. How things had changed.

She knew her estranged husband would be off on the train to watch Watford FC. She stretched her arms and put her hands behind her head. There wasn't much on her agenda today; perhaps a jog around the avenue would relieve her boredom, as it usually did on Saturdays.

She began to reminisce again. She had never been a lazy or careless student. She studied hard to achieve her aim of becoming a primary school teacher, often preferring her books to nights out with other students, especially the males who made it clear they were keen to show her a good time in more ways than one.

She had befriended an art student named Veronica Courtney, a bit of a tearaway who was too fond of marijuana cigarettes. Veronica went to drug parties that usually ended in orgies. Deborah, however, made it clear she was not interested in smoking dope. If she accompanied her friend, she left the party early, before the room filled with the sweet-smelling haze and passions began to run high.

Deborah would often lecture Veronica on the dangers of drugs and her reckless sexual exploits.

There was a twist of fate when Deborah and Veronica took a two-week holiday in Bournemouth, again staying at Aunt Ada's apartment. The fortnight had nearly passed with no available males in sight. One evening they were enjoying a drink in the Cliff Top bar, overlooking the bay and the entertainment pier, when a teenager pulled his chair towards their table. "Colin Freeman," the bold one said. "This is my friend Amadeus Rupert. Let us buy you a drink, then we can chat." Deborah remembered Colin signalling to his disinterested friend.

The taller of the two was calmer and more reserved, even as Veronica began to ridicule him, comparing his outfit to that of a bear in yellow-checked trousers, red polo-neck and yellow scarf. After a few glasses of wine, Deborah excused herself, saying she was tired and ready to return to her lodgings.

Veronica and Colin ignored her excuse. They were heading to a party, after a stop on the shingled beach below the pier. Deborah smiled as she remembered her past. A past that would become the beginning of her serious relationship with Amadeus Rupert.

She had allowed Amadeus to walk her home. She trusted him because he was a policeman who had just graduated from Hendon Police College in London, along with his friend Colin Freeman. "A celebratory weekend," he had said.

She recalled with a smile how, on that first night, it was only a peck on the cheek, as Amadeus had attempted to embrace and kiss her. She had no intention of seeing this boring character again. This was where fate played its part. Veronica, who had gone to the party but had been left on her own when Colin travelled to Cornwall on business, returned to Aunt Ada's in a drunken state—bra-less, her dress torn—and was then sick all over her bed.

Aunt Ada was furious, which made Deborah decide that they would both leave on the London-bound train on Monday morning, once the washing and ironing of the soiled bedding had been done.

Fed up with her Saturday morning, Deborah strode off into town. She had decided to relax by the swimming pool. However, things did not work out that way. She spotted Amadeus reading his newspaper at a café on the promenade. She hesitated, then took the bull by the horns and joined the lonely policeman, who was sitting in his shorts and T-shirt.

Deborah fondly remembered the beach cove and the spit of sand, how the pair had decided to join forces and spend the day there. They went to the supermarket for sandwiches and juice, and Amadeus bought two beach towels. They caught the bus, which dropped them near the sandy beach. It was a quiet spot—one she had visited with her family two years before, when she had frolicked with her brother-in-law. She reached for Amadeus when he applied sun cream to her back. That was where and when she lost her virginity.

She remembered that Amadeus was not a passionate lover. He was inexperienced and awkward, though they made love time and again. After frolicking and washing in the tidal surf, she had no regrets. A mistake—huge, in fact. She was fertile and unprotected, but like a bitch in heat, she reached for him again and again.

She had always imagined her first lover would be confident and commanding, but instead found herself guiding Amadeus, almost teaching him what tenderness ought to mean. It left her conflicted: unsatisfied yet strangely reassured that he belonged entirely to her.

She knew this tall, slim character was not the 'Charles Atlas' of her dreams. Yet it became inevitable when she missed her period and went to the doctor, hoping for confirmation that her sickness was only a virus. She soon discovered the truth when the doctor presented her with the hard facts.

This was not a good time to fall pregnant. She still had over a year to finish at teacher training college. How could she have been so foolish?

Deborah and Amadeus were married in a London registry office—Colin as best man and Veronica as maid of honour. There was no wedding reception or speeches, no honeymoon. All they had on that windswept London afternoon was a meal in a small restaurant and a drink in a pub before returning to a basement flat.

Deborah had never dreamt her wedding day would be so stark and loveless. No flowers, no music, not even a toast—it felt more like an obligation signed and sealed than the beginning of a romance.

Deborah thought her dream of becoming a primary school teacher in Welwyn had ended when her belly began to swell. She finally decided she would return to Hatfield College after the baby was born. This would need careful planning.

Life in London wasn't all bad. They moved into a larger flat. Amadeus was promoted to sergeant within two years and soon fast-tracked to inspector. But she remained determined to follow her dream. They discussed moving to Welwyn in Hertfordshire, and eventually, that was what happened.

With the help of her father and stepmother—who looked after the baby while she travelled to Hatfield—Deborah Rupert finally passed her exams and was registered as a bona fide teacher. It had been an arduous journey, but worth every minute.

Better days lay ahead. She was offered a position at Welwyn Village Primary, the very school where she herself had learned so much. She discussed it with her husband, now a well-known Detective Inspector at Scotland Yard.

It came as a surprise to the Commissioner when D.I. Rupert applied for a transfer to the Hertfordshire Constabulary. He would be a floating inspector, travelling around the county to help solve complex cases.
"It's in the sticks, Rupert. Nothing happens up there," a senior officer remarked, trying to persuade him to change his mind. But Amadeus was adamant it would be for the best.

The couple bought a bungalow at the edge of Welwyn village. With two jobs and a doting stepmother, life began to improve. Amadeus was given his transfer—reluctantly—from London, and the couple settled into wedded bliss until Deborah fell pregnant again after a birthday bash at the local pub.

This time the birth did not cause problems. She worked until her eighth month of pregnancy. By chance, her delivery was perfectly timed. Their daughter, April, was born four weeks premature in the first week of the school summer holidays. This gave Deborah time to recover before resuming her teaching duties when classes began. With her stepmother on hand to care for both children, everything worked out.

Deborah often marvelled at her stepmother's devotion. Without her steady hands rocking the cradle and keeping the household afloat, Deborah knew her career would have collapsed before it had even begun.

After their marriage in 1934, the couple enjoyed five wonderful years together. Then came the Second World War. Amadeus, who could fly, applied to the RAF to become a Spitfire pilot. Colin, his dear friend, was accepted. Amadeus was rejected due to colour blindness. Instead, he was drafted into essential Home Front Services—exactly the work he was already doing.

The sad news arrived that Squadron Leader Colin Freeman had been killed in action. The letter from Mr and Mrs Freeman did not say that his Spitfire had exploded over the English Channel after overheating. It simply said that his body had not been recovered.

Amadeus seldom expressed sorrow, but Deborah knew it affected him deeply. He had mood swings she had never witnessed before. Was it really Colin's death—or the frustration of his own dull workload?

Not that Amadeus took it out on her. It was more to do with the bureaucratic red tape that had kept him from the war. She knew her husband wanted to strike back at the Germans who had killed his friend.

Life began to spiral downwards. Amadeus was still not a tender or loving man. With the phoney war over, his duties increased. He became a warden in his spare time. Deborah saw little of him, and when she did, he was often asleep before she got undressed.

She had her own problems. The primary school was closed, and the children—including her own—were evacuated to the countryside. This left a void in her life.

It was Veronica who came to the rescue. "The American Air Force has taken over the secondary school. They want typists for administration. I'd get up there today and put your name forward. Don't dilly-dally, Deborah, there won't be much work around here in the future."

The two friends went to the evacuated school and entered their names and occupations in the register.

Deborah smiled, remembering how her husband had joined Coastal Command as a flying officer in Oban, a small town in Scotland. The memories of those early war years came flooding back. How she missed his company. The nights were long and lonely.

She tried to pass the time by joining the village quiz team, and by playing darts and dominoes most nights of the week.

She sat in front of the fire, debating whether to venture out or practise her typing. She chose the latter, hoping to hear from the American typing pool soon.

Then she recalled the prominent knock at the door. She glanced at the clock, wondering who could be calling at that hour. When she opened it, she had to look twice at the smartly dressed officer in his naval uniform.
"Barney," she gasped, uncertain of herself. "What are you doing here? Come in, come in," she said in astonishment.

"I'm catching a train north tomorrow to join my ship. Rather than book into a hotel, I knew you and Amadeus lived nearby, so here I am."

She took his overcoat and jacket and hung them on a peg. "Can I get you something to eat? I'm afraid I can't offer much, not even a drink. War shortages and all that." She smiled.

"Never mind, Debs. I've brought some of my own we can share."

She raised her eyebrows as he produced a bottle of French brandy and two bottles of French wine from his kit bag. Deborah remembered clearly how, when she had gone to fetch the glasses, Barney followed her into the kitchen and, as she stretched up to the cupboard, he cupped her breasts. She recalled his words: "I thought that might turn you on, Debs. Let's have a drink first." The brandy and wine flowed with much hilarity.

They sat reminiscing about old times, when the family visited Aunt Ada, the old battle-axe. She remembered most of the conversation that was to follow. Barney placed an arm around her shoulder.
"Where is Amadeus? Do you expect him home shortly?"
"My husband is a flying officer with Coastal Command. I'm afraid I can't say where." She remembered how he had tried to placate her.
"Never mind, Debs. I understand. But it must get lonely when he's away from home. I know how to remedy that—with my company."
"I keep myself busy, Barney. Pub teams take up most of my time. I also keep myself in shape by running."
"Yes, you still have a fine body after having two children."
"Please, Barney. The feelings I had were those of a frustrated teenager. They were just a young girl's fantasy. I'm now a responsible married woman who loves her husband."

Deborah was surprised as the memories of the past came flooding back. But so much had changed since those days. She felt a dampness in her pyjama bottoms. As much as she now wanted to begin her day, she couldn't escape those memories. She slid back beneath the sheets again and recalled her time at the American Air Force typing pool in 1942, when she was accepted into the general staff, often tasked with informing American families of their loss. Sometimes it brought back memories of her own.

She recalled the night she attended a quiz competition, which she won. Her overindulgence in gin and tonics was to celebrate her 27th birthday. Drinks kept arriving at her table from the bar. The smartly dressed American was her boss at the typing pool. His uniform displayed his rank as he lifted his glass to toast her. She had tried to stay aloof from this Major, about whom she had heard much gossip. Was he the one who found it all too easy to get into the married and unmarried women's knickers?

She remembered how she had made it clear to this American upstart that she was not available. Nylons and perfumes would not turn her head. Yet she sighed when she recalled what happened next.

The Major had escorted her back to the bungalow and her bed, where a night of passion ensued before he left her worn out and sleeping, just as the dawn chorus began. It would be some time before she would again have the pleasure of Major Pressley's company.

How could she forget such a traumatic moment? Her husband had joined Bomber Command, flying the new Avro Lancaster heavy bombers over Germany. She remembered receiving the telegram in 1943 that would have a profound effect on her life: Wing Commander Rupert's plane had been witnessed dropping in flames during a bombing raid. He was reported missing in action, presumed dead.

Deborah winced and pulled the covers up over her head. She was utterly devastated, so much so that she had begun to give up on her life. There was nothing more to live for. It was her friend Veronica and her stepmother who pulled her through that sad time, reminding her she still had children who relied on her.

Major Pressley visited her, assuring her that her job was safe and still available once she recovered from her trauma. That became another chapter in her life. She was offered the job as his personal secretary—with no strings attached.

Of course, it could not last. While accompanying him to the War Office in London, they stayed in a country hotel, where intimacy became inevitable. Nights of passion followed. It was not merely lust, or so she thought, but the beginning of a bond. Or so she believed—until the truth came out.

Major Pressley was bedding many women in the typing pool and beyond, their husbands absent or lost to the war. Deborah had not been alone in her deception. By the time he flew back to the United States, she was pregnant. Worse, Amadeus returned from a prisoner-of-war camp at the war's end to find his wife expecting.

It was to be a testing time for their marriage. She knew there would always be confrontation whenever the subject was raised. She was relieved when he was reinstated as Inspector, a job he had once loved, just like in the early days of their marriage—dedicated to her and to the children.

But things changed. Inspector Amadeus Rupert became moody; there were long spells of frustration, and when they did have sex it ended with his brusque, "Wham-bam, thank you, ma'am." She knew he was parroting an American phrase, before rolling over and turning his back to sleep. Many a night she lay there, breaking her heart, frustrated and lonely.

There was little or no love between them now. His work seemed more important than ever, especially with the children at boarding school.

Deborah was glad when she graduated with a degree in secondary education. Yet there were no congratulations, no card, not even a word from her husband.

For Deborah, life became the same old routine: rising from a lonely bed, showering, breakfast, driving to the secondary school, retrieving the books from the cupboard, teaching her classes, then locking everything away again. Clean the blackboard, drive home to a silent house, cook dinner, correct papers, pour herself a glass of wine, then go to bed. When Amadeus arrived home, there were no long conversations as there once had been.

She longed for the school holidays. Somewhere—anywhere—she needed a break.

There was one pupil who showed her an unusual kindness in English class. He always hurried to the front row, despite his good grades, and took his place at the top. Norman Brackley was tall, broad and handsome, a popular boy among the girls. A keen all-round athlete, he played rugby for the school. Unlike the others, he often helped her with textbooks and stayed behind to clean the blackboard.

She began to tease him, arranging a stool in front of his desk and reading Shakespeare aloud, slowly crossing her legs to reveal a glimpse of silk stocking tops and suspender fastenings. Perhaps even her cream thighs and white pants fell into his line of vision. It was unfair of her to tempt him this way, but she got a secret thrill when class ended and his trouser bulge was obvious.

Norman would hurry to the blackboard, pick up the duster and sweep the chalk away. He would gather the textbooks into a pile, return them to the cupboard, then leave with a broad smile.

This became a natural rhythm as the weeks moved from spring to summer.

One day, Norman paused, staring at her twin set. "What a beautiful outfit, Miss Rupert. You certainly are a woman of fashion."
She pulled the cardigan across her breasts. "You should not be saying such things to your teacher, Norman. Now, get a move on and take the books to the cupboard." He smiled as he began to stack the books.

"The bottom one is you, Miss, and the top one is me. Or, if you like, we can change that position."

He watched her blush as she dropped her pen. "Now look what you've made me do, Norman Brackley. I've a good mind to report you for sexual harassment." She hurried to the cupboard, cheeks burning.

Norman switched off the classroom lights as usual before the lunch break, but this time he locked the door from the inside and walked towards the cupboard. Deborah tried to squeeze past the tall, muscular pupil in the dimly lit book store. She was slightly confused and was about to ask what he was doing.

Norman touched the fabric of her blouse. Deborah gasped loudly. The touch felt good on her most vulnerable spot. Norman began to massage her breasts through the material of her blouse and brassiere. She was soon breathing heavily at his touch.

She remembered how much she enjoyed his massage and how she could feel his hardness pressed against her. She reached for his trouser belt and unfastened it. Norman led her further into the book room, unbuttoning her blouse and unclipping her bra with surprising ease. She knew then she was his for the taking. Sliding the garments from her shoulders, she unclipped her skirt as well.

After a moment of hesitation, panic flickered across her mind. *What if the janitor or someone else came in?* "I've locked the door so that we can relax," Norman whispered. "I want you again, Miss Rupert."

They made love quickly before the dinner bell sounded, which meant the pupils would be assembling outside for their return to class. They dressed in a hurry. Norman kissed her gently. "Until the next time, Miss Rupert." He unlocked the door and darted down the corridor.

Deborah hurried to the ladies' washroom to tidy herself before taking another class. Her concentration was broken. *How stupid I've been to get involved with a senior pupil,* she thought. It could have destroyed everything she had worked so hard to achieve. Her career would not have survived had she been found out. She recalled telling him, "It must never happen again."

But it did happen again, and again. Their trysts became so frequent that they sometimes drove to the countryside to lay a blanket in Bluebell Wood, making love naked beneath the trees.

There were occasions when her husband was away at a football game or attending a police seminar, or when Norman's parents were out of town. They spent the night together at his parents' house, where Deborah had taught him the art of oral sex and different positions to spice up their relationship. Yet she knew they were playing a dangerous game.

She felt both dismayed and relieved when their affair ended. Norman and his parents were emigrating. He was to enrol at the University of Western Australia in Perth.

It was another let-down, another betrayal. She had wanted to end it on her own terms at the summer break. Unlike with the American Major, this time she had taken precautions—using her contraceptive coil at the beginning and later ensuring Norman always used a condom. Arguments arose when he wanted to take her unprotected, but she held firm.

In the end, it was Norman who brought things to a close. Deborah wondered what would have happened had she been the one to end it—would there have been gossip, or repercussions? She suspected there would. All she could do was wish him well as they said their last goodbyes, leaning against the bonnet of her car.

When the summer holidays came, there had been no tittle-tattle among Norman's friends. She felt relieved, even satisfied, that he had not boasted about their affair. It was something she had always feared would come out.

Her husband, meanwhile, was occupied with a probation officer from Stevenage. In a way, Deborah felt glad. It kept him distracted and cleared the way for her own independence, leaving her free to explore the villa.

Mrs MacGinty, the housekeeper, worked Monday through Friday. That left Deborah with her Saturdays free, especially when her husband travelled to distant football grounds.

On good days she would jog down Oakland Avenue, cut through Oakland Lane, and turn up Oakland Drive to Oakland Terrace. It was a long route that made her sweat. The uphill stretch to the terrace always left her breathless. She would stop at the hedge fence to catch her breath, jogging lightly in place before resuming along the terrace and back down to 5 Oakland Villa. There she would take a tepid shower before dressing in summer clothes and tending to the garden.

Sometimes it was peaceful. At other times, boring, especially with no secret tryst on the horizon.

# Chapter 8 – College Days and Amadeus

There was always a cheerful wave from Geoffrey Bunter, an aircraft engineer with Boeing International at their factory in Hatfield. Sometimes he would stop and hold a polite conversation with her. Other times, he would run past with a quick good morning or afternoon. Her Saturdays were always full of promise.

It usually started with the milk cart delivery, six days a week without fail. Cecil Williams made the deliveries. He was a right forward, cheeky scamp who made it clear he could provide a "special delivery" when her husband had gone to the football.

"You just concentrate on your milk round, Cecil," was her response while standing on the doorstep in her dressing gown.

"You better cover them up, Mrs Rupert; you could catch cold." Deborah hadn't noticed that her dressing gown had opened, and her breasts were exposed in clear view.

"Say the word and I'll tuck them in for you after a bit of fun, Mrs Rupert." He laughed and walked down the path to the milk cart.

Deborah always made sure she was up and dressed in her jogging outfit, or that her dressing gown was securely fastened. It still didn't stop Cecil from making some comment about her figure.

She thought it was no more than harmless fun until Friday, the dairy's milk money collection night. She had just showered after working in the garden, enjoying the warm evening air drifting through the windows.

Cecil arrived with his money bag, book and pencil. It was the usual procedure.

He was taken into the lounge and told to take a seat while Deborah counted out the payment. She stood in her short baby-doll pink nightdress before sitting beside him on the couch. She handed him the money due before attempting to get up.

Her nightdress crept up her thighs. Cecil, emboldened, chanced his luck like he had done with many married women on the estate.

"My God, Mrs Rupert, what a beautiful pair of tits." He got no response from the customer.

He sat for a while, staring at her erect nipples through the lace, before finally making a move.

"I best be getting on with my collection, Mrs Rupert. There have been complaints about my timekeeping. But we could hold a conversation, or something more adventurous, some other time."

"Perhaps, Cecil. But stop calling me Mrs Rupert; it becomes tedious after a while. Call me Deborah. And another thing, it's not every Friday night my husband is out of the house, so be careful the next time you open that big mouth of yours."

Cecil nodded, then took the money, placed it in his bag and scribbled quickly into his notebook, 'Paid,' before handing her the receipt and making his way swiftly to the door.

Deborah smiled at his embarrassment while showing him out.

There were no more opportunities for the milkman. Deborah was either out or her husband, Chief Inspector Rupert, was at home. Cecil would just have to content himself with Mrs Dunaway further down Oakland Avenue, before his bosses found out about the reasons behind his delays and sacked him.

The longer her husband was at home, the more frustrated Deborah became.

There were times he brought that shameless hussy from Stevenage up to stay for the weekend. They would pass on the stairs without a word. Deborah knew it was becoming untenable, and she would sometimes go to London just to stay out of their way, take in a show or simply relax in their luxury apartment in Mayfair.

Barbara Sedgeway was a condescending cow. It was usually just a sneer in passing, until one morning, looking the worse for wear, she stopped on the landing and smiled.

"Amadeus and I talked about you last night after a roll in the sack. You've become a problem in this house. Why he's let you stay so long is beyond me."

Deborah was about to shove past her and go down to the kitchen when Barbara grabbed her arm.

"He wants you out, Mrs Rupert. There is no room for two women in this house or in his life. I'm moving in permanently. He'll talk to you about it. I thought I'd give you a warning about your future." Barbara Sedgeway laughed and went downstairs.

This was a setback. Deborah had never expected it to come so soon. To hear it from his lover came as a shock and a deep disappointment.

She watched from behind the lounge curtain as they drove away to a football match. This was something they shared each Saturday. If it were an away game, they would book into a hotel for the night, return to the villa on Sunday, and Barbara would drive down to Stevenage on Monday for work.

Deborah confronted Amadeus after Barbara had left, and before Mrs McGinty arrived to do the house cleaning and change the beds. Not that Deborah's bed needed changing – she had already made it to save the housekeeper extra work.

"I need to speak to you about my eviction, Amadeus. I don't mean to sound harsh, but if you do throw me out before I find alternate accommodation, I'll take you for half of everything you own. You know as well as anybody the way the courts handle divorce cases where there are children."

Amadeus stood up. "I'm glad you mentioned divorce, Deborah. I was going to give you a chance to get settled, but I think it's time we seek a new beginning. I would like you and your belongings to be out by the end of the summer, before you begin teaching again after the break. I'm prepared to allow you that time before Barbara moves in permanently."

"Oh, Amadeus, how has it come to this?" Deborah said with tears in her eyes.

"I don't have time for this. We'll discuss it further tonight." He turned to face her and pointed angrily. "Come the end of August and you're out." He walked out of the villa and strolled down the Avenue to work.

That was the way it ended, although when they spoke that night, the conversation was much more civilised. They made a pact with each other that the children would not be drawn into any divorce settlement, and there would be an amicable agreement about who got what. But that would change when the wolves of the courts sank their fangs into such a juicy divorce case.

Detective Inspector Rupert would get the best out of the settlement: the luxury apartment in Mayfair, the villa at 5 Oakland Avenue, all his business income and department stores. This was deemed part of a gift from his dear, dead friend and the Freeman family fortune. Deborah's barrister had argued and asked the question, Why? Because Colin Freeman was her friend, too.

Detective Inspector Rupert was given custody of the children on the grounds of Deborah's affair with the American Major. A lot of water would flow under the bridge before this divorce settlement was finalised.

She couldn't believe how cruel Amadeus could be. Forced to take drastic action, Deborah visited the estate agents in town in the hope they would have something for rent on their books, while she considered buying her own small property.

There was nothing suitable on the estate agents' books. She extended her search throughout the county. The property was still highly sought after, even a few years after the war, when the country was still struggling with its rebuilding programme. She often felt that the shortage of homes mirrored her own sense of displacement, as though society itself had little space left for her.

She still owned the bungalow in Welwyn village, but that was rented out on a five-year lease contract that still had eighteen months to run.

Deborah knew she was in a sticky wicket. Time was running out as the eviction notice had been served on her by her husband's solicitor.

It was by sheer chance and good luck that her friendly neighbour, Geoffrey Bunter, was rushing down the rain-and-wind swept Oakland Avenue. She was reversing out of the driveway and offered him a lift into town. He shook his oilskin coat before taking the passenger seat beside her.

"Thanks, Mrs Rupert, I'm in a bit of a hurry this morning. A bit of business to attend to before I catch the London train."

Deborah asked where he would like to be dropped off.

"The estate agents would be handy, Mrs Rupert. I need to get my house on the market before I fly out to the United States."

Deborah was all ears. "You're selling up then, Geoffrey? What has brought this about?"

"Not selling, Mrs Rupert, renting – but with a stipulation that my room must always be available for me when I return to the UK. It's not a significant issue, which occurs only once or twice a year. The reason for my move is that I have been given a job with Boeing International in Florida, part of the NASA space programme. I'm excited."

Deborah stopped the car at the railway station.

"I have a proposition for you, Geoffrey. I'm moving out of 5 Oakland Avenue at the end of the week. I would be only too happy to rent the villa on Oakland Terrace from you. Your room would be available anytime you returned from the States. We can agree on a rental price now, if you'd like, and have our solicitors handle the legal aspects. It'll certainly save you an estate agent's fee. You know how much they charge."

"Gosh, Mrs Rupert, this is a stroke of good luck. The house is ready to move into at your convenience."

At that moment, Deborah felt the faintest glimmer of relief, as if fate had intervened with an escape hatch just when the walls of her world were closing in.

Her time had come. There would be no more reminiscing, recalling the sad and dangerous times of her life. A rental figure was agreed, and Geoffrey Bunter handed her the villa keys.

For the first time in a while, Deborah felt as if the gods were smiling on her. She saw Geoffrey off on the London-bound train before driving up Oakland Drive and along to number 17 Oakland Terrace. She parked the car in the drive, hurried to unlock the door, and stepped into the villa out of the rain. The place was clean and tidy. All she needed to do was make up a bed and set the coal fire ready to light when she moved in.

There was also food to consider, so she began to plan her move come Saturday when the slut and her husband were gallivanting. No hint would be given that she had found the ideal accommodation, albeit just a short distance from 5 Oakland Avenue. Why should she bother about that?

In fact, it was an ideal place to keep an eye on the pair of scallywags. She smiled at the description she had given them before inspecting the rest of the house.

She found one bedroom door locked and had no intention of prying, so she made her way out to the car and drove down the Avenue. She pulled two large suitcases from the hall cupboard. She intended to fill them with her clothes until she heard Mrs McGinty climb the stairs.

"Are you looking for something, dear?"

"My tennis racket and shoes are in here somewhere; I need to find them for the court singles on Saturday." It was as good an excuse as she could think of on the spur of the moment, as Mrs McGinty walked away.

Her timing would need to be better. Saturday would be D-day – that's when she would pack and make the move.

The days seemed to drag by slowly. Deborah contented herself with the fact that it wouldn't be long until she escaped from this awkward, bitter, and resentful situation she had found herself in when Barbara Sedgeway appeared on the scene.

She often wondered if there could have been a compromise with her husband, had it not been for Barbara's expertly trapping him. Like a lobster creel: an easy way in to take the bait, but after feasting on the delights, it would find it impossible to get out.

Deborah was sad that Amadeus had not seen through this woman. She knew the affair with the probation officer could never last. How long was the big question? Deborah gave them five to six months before the honeymoon period evaporated and reality set in.

She could almost picture herself months later, quietly laughing when the cracks began to show, knowing deep down that Barbara's allure would fade as quickly as it had flared.

She gave a wry smile as she pulled on her sweatshirt, nylon running shorts and shoes. Sometimes she would change the route of her run. It made no difference whether she ran up to Oakland Terrace and down Oakland Drive to the narrow Oakland Lane that linked the Drive with Oakland Avenue.

It mattered not. The summer sun was shining when she chose the steeper route, along the lane and up the steep drive to the Terrace.

She always had to run lightly on the spot and take five at the corner of the Terrace.

A head looked over the hedge. "Oh, it's you, Mrs Rupert." Lawrence Tinsley was a teacher at the secondary school. Deborah had noticed that he ogled her in the staff room during their lunch breaks. And now it was no different, as he watched her braless breasts move up and down while she caught her breath.

"You should treat those breasts of yours with care, Deborah. You never know when someone like me might come along and give them a little massage."

She smiled. "The chance would be a fine thing, Mr Tinsley." She began to trot along the Terrace and back for a well-earned shower.

She selected a different route each day, again stopping to catch her breath at the corner of the Terrace. The face appeared from behind the hedge. He was ogling her heaving chest.

He switched off the spraying hose and opened the gate. "I've got some lemonade chilling in the fridge, a slice of lemon and ice to complete the drink."

Deborah felt the need for some fluid. She followed her colleague, who held her by the hand, into the bungalow.

"Where's your wife, Lawrence? Has she gone to the shops?"

"She and the kids have gone to Cornwall for a couple of weeks to visit her mother." He smiled. "That leaves you and me alone to enjoy our drinks." He put ice cubes into the glasses and poured the lemonade.

They sat at the breakfast bar on their stools.

"How is that separation of yours coming along? That husband of yours must be off his head to let you go. Now if it was me…"

The sentence ended when he pursed his lips and blew her a kiss.

He laid his hands on her bare thighs and moved them up towards her running shorts. She held his wrists firmly.

"Kindly don't do that, Lawrence. You have a wife and family to consider."

"I've seen the way you've looked at me, Deborah. Especially in the staff room. There were times I would have laid you down there and then and let you see what I could give you."

"Don't be ridiculous, Lawrence. Now let me clear and wash the glasses, then I'll be off."

She slid down from the stool and took the glasses to the sink. Lawrence came up behind her and slid his hands into her sweatshirt, gently massaging her breasts until her nipples stood hard and erect. Deborah gasped and began to breathe heavily as he massaged her vulnerable spot, making her want more of his touch.

It was so good to feel a man take her nipples between his thumbs and forefingers, then gently rub them. Lawrence heard her panting.

"They're just what I imagined, Mrs Rupert. Please remove your sweatshirt and face me. I want to see them in the flesh. I'm going to fuck you and give you something that I've always dreamed of."

Deborah lifted her sweatshirt over her head, then turned to face her colleague. She gasped and responded to his kisses. Then she guided his head back to her throbbing nipples that needed his attention.

Lawrence answered her demands.

God hadn't stinted when he handed Lawrence Tinsley a snake-eyed weapon.

He lifted her into his arms and walked to the small ground-floor bedroom. Lawrence pushed her down gently on the bed, where they made love for the rest of the afternoon.

Of all the penises she had encountered over the years, none compared with Lawrence Tinsley's. He touched her like no other. There were times she thought he would come out of her mouth. She lost count of how many times she had orgasmed. After several encounters, she knew she had never ejaculated like this before.

Lawrence was a compassionate and considerate lover. They would caress each other and talk before answering each other's needs, becoming as one.

Deborah left him exhausted and sleeping when she put on her shorts and sweatshirt from the kitchen. She walked back to Oakland Avenue. Every step of the way was irritating her.

There were to be plenty more trysts with Lawrence. They even took lunch breaks in the country; having sex in the open air in Bluebell Wood excited her just as it had with Norman Brackley, her loving, attentive pupil.

Saturday had come along quickly after her sexual experience with her colleague.

With an empty villa, she packed the two large suitcases from the hall cupboard. There were a lot of her items, such as perfumes and jewellery, to be loaded into the car.

But Deborah worked tirelessly, removing what was hers. It took her three runs with the car to finally get her belongings shifted. She left a short note for her estranged husband.

'Hi Amadeus, out of your hair and out of your life at last. Good luck for the future with the probation officer.' This was written with a stern face.

'You'll be hearing shortly from my solicitor, who is applying for a quickie divorce. That will come at a cost. We'll leave the legal buzzards to get on with it.'

Debs. x

***

The stage was now set for the future. After putting her clothes away in the wardrobes and drawers of 17 Oakland Terrace, she arranged her perfumes and jewellery on the dressing table and then drove down to the grocery store to stock up on food and wine. She put a match to the fire on her return.

After a light meal, she sat in the lounge, content and relaxed with a bottle of red by her side. She browsed through the evening local paper that had been delivered, and arranged with the newsagent to include the delivery of the Sunday broadsheets.

She sighed as she got up to open another bottle of red.

But after a good night's sleep – the best she had enjoyed for some considerable time – she was up early on the Sunday. After a cooked breakfast, she went to church to pray for redemption.

Sunday being the day of rest, that is exactly what she did. After cleaning out and setting the fire, she sat back on the couch with the Sunday papers.

For the first time in months, she allowed herself to exhale deeply, letting the tension slip away, telling herself that perhaps she could still rebuild something of her old life.

She had prepared the Sunday dinner the way Mrs McGinty had taught her.

How relaxing it was to heat the soup and put the roast beef, vegetables and potatoes into the oven. With nobody else to cook for, it became a simple chore. She savoured the quiet clink of crockery and the gentle tick of the oven, a homely rhythm that steadied her nerves.

The days and weeks passed. The summer school holidays were over in a flash.

There was no sign of Lawrence in the teachers' staff room.

She was informed that Mr Lawrence Tinsley was on compassionate leave due to a car accident.

All Deborah could do was raise her eyebrows in disbelief and speak, "Poor Lawrence."

However, she knew the truth about Lawrence, and now was not the time to be asking questions. She knew, as the estranged wife of a police inspector, not to get involved in conversations that could open a can of worms.

It was back to teaching. The months rolled by as usual. Geoffrey Bunter arrived home for Christmas, but that was not the reason for his surprise visit. He shocked her by announcing that he was putting the house up for sale.

"And what about my lease agreement, Geoffrey? Surely that must mean something?"

"I instructed my lawyer to delay any formal undertakings until I was sure of my position in the United States. He has told me that no agreement has been signed. However, I'm not going to throw you out on the street," he said, smiling.

"I wanted to discuss your position before I make any move to sell."

Deborah listened to his achievements with the aircraft conglomerate in the States: how he had been promoted to an engine test foreman for Boeing's new aircraft engine; how the company had helped him buy a beautiful house in Pine Grove Springs, just north of Miami; that he was supplied with a Chevrolet convertible and free travel around the world; and how he would work with a captured German scientist called Wernher von Braun on thrust and rocket propulsion.

Geoffrey went on to say that, with the Germans' knowledge, it just might be possible to put a man on the moon sometime in the future. "All hush-hush, Deborah, so let's get back to the basics." He scratched his head.

"If you wish, I can give you the first chance to buy. But that comes after you consider my proposal." Geoffrey stood up and paced the room. He was hesitant before he spoke.

"I knew of your untenable position at number 5 Oakland Avenue concerning your husband and his lover. I felt sorry for you…"

"Let's get this straight, Geoffrey Bunter, I don't need your sympathy," Deborah said, frustrated.

"I'm not getting this across in the right manner, Deborah. What I would like to offer you is a position in the United States as my housekeeper and secretary. You would be based at home in Pine Grove Springs, with a room of your own, free to come and go as you please. Who knows, in time we might form a more permanent relationship.”

“Is that some kind of marriage proposal, Geoffrey?” Deborah asked, laughing.

“I suppose it is. I was never much good at getting my point across.”

“We can soon rectify that with a little tutoring, but I’ll need time to consider this monumental proposition. It’s a big step to take. It would mean me giving up my teaching job, giving up my way of life, Geoffrey.”

“Forget it, Mrs Rupert. It was silly of me to suggest such a thing.” He looked disappointed.

“No, I won’t forget it. In fact, I think it’s a very admirable proposition for you to make.”

This brought a smile back to Geoffrey’s face.

Deborah spoke with aplomb and authority, like a teacher.

“While I give your proposal some thought, here’s one for you. Why do I not buy half of 17 Oakland Terrace? This would give both of us a place to land if things went pear-shaped in America. Please remember I know what those villa prices are; when your lawyer draws up the contract, this time there will be two signatures on the document.” She smiled.

Geoffrey gave her an unexpected hug.

"Yes, what a marvellous idea. I'll attend to that this very morning."

Deborah had slight misgivings about becoming a secretary. Her mind went back to the days of Major Presley, when they romped their way through the latter part of the war; how she had fallen pregnant and was left in the lurch when he returned to the United States.

But this could be a new beginning. It would enable her to leave behind all those sex trysts – dangerous sex trysts, should they ever be discovered.

It would be a cheap move on her part, using Geoffrey Bunter as a get-out clause, an ideal way to bury her past. She concluded it must be done.

When Geoffrey returned from his solicitor's, she gave him the answer he wanted.

"I've made up my mind to join you in the United States, Geoffrey, and who knows, in time we might enhance our relationship."

They didn't waste any time. After a celebratory drink, they went to bed together.

Deborah went through the motions, accompanied by the sounds of "Oohs" and "Ahs," but Geoffrey did nothing for her. There was only one large manhood that Deborah craved, and he was bettering himself and his family in Cornwall. She tried to ignore the hollow feeling that followed, telling herself this was a practical decision, not a romantic one.

It was deception at the lowest level when Geoffrey kissed her and said he would organise her US visa and residency with Boeing, who, in turn, would contact the United States Embassy in London. They would organise the necessary documents for her to sign and arrange for a medical. "It might take a few months, but we'll get it done as quickly as possible."

He rolled over and went to sleep.

There seemed to be a lot happening after Geoffrey left for the United States.

The house-share purchase had gone through smoothly. She signed the documents.

Her quickie divorce had come through. She received more than she expected, and after agreeing with her ex-husband's solicitors, she sold her share of the Waterloo Mansion apartment in Mayfair to her ex-husband, with a clause allowing her to use the apartment when she visited London in the future. It fetched a tidy sum. The same deal applied to 5 Oakland Avenue, except there were no clauses; she was no longer welcome at that address. It also fetched her a tidy sum. Now she could move on. She signed the papers.

Several visits to the United States Embassy helped speed the process. Her character and medical results proved unblemished. She signed the necessary documents.

All she had to do was wait and let things unfold as they would. She marked the likely departure week on a small calendar by the hearth, counting the days with equal parts dread and anticipation.

Her colleagues expressed their sadness at her leaving.

Geoffrey phoned and wrote to her regularly with information on her arrival.

There was something in a letter that intrigued her.

"Should I not be at the airport to meet you because of the hush-hush work, I'll instruct a colleague of Boeing International staff to meet you. Love and best wishes, G."

Like the others, Deborah filed the letter in her file box and forgot about it.

As the winter months turned to spring, Deborah noticed a distinct atmosphere in the teachers' staff room. She had to ask the reason and wished she hadn't.

Lawrence Tinsley was not involved in any car accident. He had upped sticks and moved to a teacher's post in Cornwall. There was disbelief in the staff room.

Deborah put her hand to her mouth, then said, "How can this be? He was perfectly happy here, according to his wife."

"So, you had assignations with Lawrence, too?" the French teacher said with suspicion.

Deborah couldn't answer her. She hurried from the staff room to the female toilets, where she vomited into the W.C. bowl. After rinsing her mouth, but still in shock, she went to her classroom to prepare for the next class.

After the revelation by the French mistress, a registered letter from the American Embassy arrived, with her departure date to Miami airport enclosed. It had all the usual jargon:

"If unable to keep this date, please inform us immediately."

She knew that any delay could prove catastrophic if her true character were to become known.

She folded it neatly. She was not in the mood to read any more, but persevered with the multiple papers that she had to sign at the US Embassy.

To alleviate the attention required to understand the requirements, she began to pack her belongings, slowly and carefully selecting what she would keep and discard. The car would need to be sold. Different suppliers would need to be cancelled. That included the newspapers and milk.

The education department would need to be informed, but that would be the last to be attended to.

While sitting in the villa lounge, her thoughts were interrupted by a knock at the door.

Two young people, who turned out to be trainee teachers at Welwyn Village Primary, asked about renting a room.

Deborah explained that it was a joint ownership, and she could not make that decision on her own. However, she would ask her partner's advice.

Deborah had already made up her mind. It would be better to have sitting tenants to look after the place. It would also provide an income to her bank account, something else that would need to be attended to.

She was sure Geoffrey would go along with her decision, and after a discussion, he agreed wholeheartedly.

There was one stipulation Deborah laid down firmly with the young teachers.

"You will each rent a room. No wild parties. I know what you young teachers are like. I was one myself, don't forget."

She paused. "An agency will report monthly to me directly and, if there is any damage or such activities as smoking dope, you'll be out on your ear. Is that understood?"

The young couple nodded.

Everything was now arranged.

Her rail fare to London had been paid. All her taxi receipts would be kept for reimbursement. Her hotel bill would be settled by Boeing International.

Deborah made her way to the Ritz Hotel, where she was met by a representative from Boeing, who checked her passport. After conferring with reception, she was escorted to the penthouse suite, where the representative ensured she was comfortable and satisfied with her room. She was informed that a limousine would pick her up at 9:00 a.m. the next morning and take her to Heathrow Airport, where she would be met by another Boeing representative and shown to their executive lounge before her departure to the UK by T.W.A. (Trans World Airlines).

Deborah couldn't have been more surprised at how organised everything was, including her luggage trunk, with all her belongings, that had been collected from the villa and forwarded to her new home in Pine Grove Springs, Florida, in the U.S.A. She was so excited that she hardly got any sleep that night.

It didn't deter her from rising early to shower and put on her freshly laundered attire, which had been expertly dry-cleaned and pressed by the hotel's laundry. After a healthy breakfast, she was ready to begin the second part of her journey.

The chauffeur-driven limousine arrived at 8:55 a.m. and took her out to the airport, where a representative was waiting for the car to pull up. The chauffeur swiftly got out of his seat and opened the back door.

The representative introduced herself as Eleanor and shook her hand.

"Please follow me, Mrs Bunter. I'll take you up to our executive lounge for refreshment before your flight."

Deborah looked around until she realised it was herself the representative was addressing. She was now registered in her maiden name, and even her passport had been changed. Deborah smiled and followed the Boeing representative to the escalator.

Her dad and stepmother greeted her. It had been a while since they had been in communication, and seeing them gave Deborah a lump in her throat. After many hugs and kisses, they sat together, discussing her decision to accept Geoffrey Bunter's offer and emigrate to the United States.

"If it doesn't work out, I can always come back, Dad," she said in defiance at his objection to her leaving her country, her job, and her children.

# Chapter 9 – War and Longing

"I've met with the children during the festive season and explained that they can come over anytime to stay during their school holidays. It was part of my divorce settlement." She sipped the champagne to ease the lump in her throat.

The young black waiter replenished their glasses.

There was still plenty of time before her flight was called. The representative had said she would return to lead her to the aircraft, allowing her to bypass the check-in queue. Deborah sat making promises to write often.

She was totally unprepared for the next surprise in her life. A tall figure, dressed in a worn brown coat and a trilby hat, approached the gathering. He simply nodded to her parents before taking Deborah's hand.

She suddenly realised who it was and sprang to her feet, tense and uncertain.

"Amadeus, what on earth are you doing here? Is there something wrong?"

"The only wrong thing is me, Debs. What a fool I've been. Letting you go so easily was a big mistake. I only hope you can forgive me." He hugged her tightly.

"I'm not here to ask that you change your mind – that's the way I am. But I want you to know that I wish you every happiness in the future, and should you need a place to lay your head, then 5 Oakland Avenue's door will always be open to you, despite what the legal beagles said in court."

He watched her parents rise and give her a final hug. Her dad opened with a salvo of disgust.

"You must excuse us, Deborah. The air in here has a pungent smell that lingers and leaves a sour taste in my mouth. We'll watch you take off from the observation lounge."

The last of her parents' hugs brought tears to her eyes. Inspector Amadeus Rupert felt like a fish out of water as her parents left without glancing in his direction.

Deborah offered him a glass of champagne.

"Better not, I'm on duty."

"A coffee then," she said hoarsely. Amadeus just shook his head.

"I must ask you, Amadeus, how are you and the probation officer getting on?"

He smiled. "That was over months ago. You were right. Barbara was a gold digger."

Deborah gave a wry smile.

"Mmm," was her only response. There wasn't much more to say, and she was glad when the Boeing representative appeared to take her down for departure.

She gave Amadeus a final hug before she was led from the executive departure lounge. Amadeus gave her a final wave but couldn't see that her heart was breaking. She finally broke down in sobs of despair on the escalator, knowing that Inspector Amadeus Rupert would now only be a love remembered from a distant past.

*****

The Boeing representative was kind and thoughtful as they made their way to the aircraft.

"Have a good flight, Miss Fox."

Deborah climbed the aircraft steps and was greeted by a T.W.A. hostess. She stood on the platform but had to turn and look back at what she was leaving behind. She quickly took her window seat before she started to bubble again.

As the aeroplane lifted into the clear blue sky above London, she couldn't help thinking of her ex-husband, Amadeus Rupert, a Wing Commander with Bomber Command during the war. A war that had brought her and him many problems. Her mind flickered with images of sirens, shelters, and hurried goodbyes—memories that seemed impossibly close, even now.

Her thoughts were interrupted by a stewardess who offered her refreshments before lunch. Deborah was thankful for the gin and tonic that helped ease the dryness in her throat.

She settled down and watched the green pastures of England disappear and the tip of southern Ireland's coastline loom ever closer. Then it was boring, as the waters of the Atlantic Ocean seemed never-ending.

After a superb lunch, she soon fell asleep.

She was awakened by the airline captain, who advised passengers to return to their seats. The steward gave her comfort.

"Just a bit of turbulence, ma'am, nothing to be concerned about."

Apart from that small incident, it was a perfect flight: a selection of dinners followed by teas or coffees, then a final refreshment before the crew prepared for landing.

Deborah watched the lights of Miami as the aeroplane circled and came in to land at 2:25 a.m. local time. They landed early due to a good tailwind.

***

Deborah was glad to stand on the American tarmac and stretch.

The Boeing International chauffeur and representative were waiting patiently by the silver limousine. The representative took her passport and handed it to the immigration official at the drive-through.

There was no sign of Geoffrey.

Deborah asked the obvious question.

"My partner was supposed to be here to meet me, although he did say work commitments might intervene."

"Unfortunately, Mr Bunter is delayed." It was short and to the point.

"Did he give any indication when he would come to Pine Grove Springs?" she asked quickly.

The rep ignored the question.

"It's a two-hour drive along the Interstate freeway, so catch up on your jet lag and have a sleep." This was said as an order.

Deborah didn't sleep but watched the traffic move along the freeway slowly.

The chauffeur spoke into the intercom.

"It looks like an accident up ahead, Miss Fox, so I'll be making a diversion."

"Damn," the rep said with irritation.

"Problems?" Deborah asked candidly.

This was met with stony silence, so Deborah settled down for a sleep.

The diversion must have taken a while. She looked out into the early morning light.

The representative spoke calmly.

"Not long now, Miss Fox."

Deborah was glad when the limousine pulled up outside a large bungalow. She was led up the garden path by the irate rep. But what path was she being led up, she asked herself, as the rep unlocked the door and handed her the keys, then quickly showed her around the beautiful bungalow.

"I have another person to meet at the airport this morning. Enjoy your stay in the United States, Miss Fox, and have a nice day."

Deborah was left standing as the representative hurried away. She watched her slam the limousine door and signal the chauffeur to drive.

"Condescending bitch," she said while climbing the stairs to the bedroom.

She stripped off and was asleep in minutes. It seemed strange waking up in a new bed, in a strange room, in another country. She didn't have much time to think about her circumstances after the long flight. But here she was, in the United States of America.

She stood in her nakedness, thinking how a huge burden had been lifted from her shoulders. She had briefly noticed on arrival that her trunk had been delivered, and her clothes hung up in the walk-in wardrobe. Her underwear and blouses had been ironed and put into the bedroom drawers. It only left her to set out her perfumes and jewellery on the large dressing table.

As she placed the bottles neatly in a row, she realised this was the first time in years she could arrange her life exactly as she pleased, without anyone watching over her shoulder.

She had no intention of doing much today. She gladly dressed in freshly laundered casual clothes before venturing downstairs to the kitchen. The cupboards and icebox were stacked with food and dairy products, so she began to lay out a cereal breakfast with toast and coffee. She sat pondering what to do next when the doorbell chimed.

The mail was lying on the floor, so she picked it up before opening the door and flyscreen. A tall blond man stood on the porch, clutching a bottle of wine and a bouquet of red roses.

"Good morning, Deborah. I'm Jordan Leigh, Geoffrey's lawyer. I live four blocks up the precinct, and I'm here to bid you welcome to the States. I hope I'm not intruding so soon after your flight, but I wanted to let you know that if you need any advice on the surrounding area, please don't hesitate to ask. I'm only too keen to keep a client of mine happy."

Deborah took the welcoming gifts and watched the neighbour descend the porch steps with a brief wave. She watched him get into his black sports car and drive away.

She wanted to get out for a walk in the fresh air and stretch her bones. While walking around the neighbourhood, she spotted a sign that read, "To the pond," so she took the path that was surrounded by trees until it opened out into what she could only describe as a wonderland of trees, flowering bushes, and wildflowers of every colour. These plants surrounded a large lake that had a path leading up either side. She began to explore the vista that lay before her. Birdsong threaded through the canopy, and the soft mulch underfoot released a clean, woody scent that made her shoulders loosen.

She walked about a mile up one side of what she described as a lake, with wildfowl and swans racing to pick off the floating titbits. There were benches to rest her weary legs by the water's edge. When she reached the point where she would walk down the other side of the lake, she marvelled at the two Canadian red pine trees that could grow to a height of sixty feet, with a circumference of twenty feet.

It suddenly struck her that this would be an ideal place for jogging. The thought of swimming entered her head, but she would need to check that out with Geoffrey or Jordan.

She strolled lazily down the other side of the lake, which had many of the same colourful trees, scented bushes and wildflowers. She realised she had discovered her paradise, where she would walk and run daily, regardless of the weather. She made her way home to a nice surprise. Geoffrey had returned and was cooking their steaks with eggs over easy and a mixed vegetable salad. He had uncorked the wine gift to let it breathe.

"Sorry, I wasn't able to meet you at the airport, honey bunch, but something came up at work." He changed the subject. "Are you ready for this, my precious?"

"Yes, I'm famished after my walk around the lake," she said, taking a seat at the table.

"Excellent, you've discovered the pond then. I was going to walk around it with you, but we can do that some other time. This is a flying visit, honey; I must be back at the factory by tomorrow night, duty calls."

"So, when am I going to see you on a regular basis, Geoffrey?"

He smiled and changed the subject.

"Let's eat, then I can show you what needs to be done regarding my files. It's important they're documented and stored in the correct order."

After dinner, they sat in the lounge with their wine before Geoffrey took her upstairs to his small office. He went through the filing system before venturing out to the Chevy. He brought in two large piles of paperwork and laid them on the desk.

"That should keep you busy for a month or two, honey. I'll bring the second part of the documentation the next time I visit."

"Whoa there, cowboy, does this mean it's going to be two months before I see you again?"

"Give or take, honey, but I'll be home for much longer after we've finished this work programme that is top secret."

Deborah shook her head. "That's not what I expected when I came out here, Geoffrey. As your secretary, yes, but not as your slave. And that reminds me, we need to talk about wages. I'm not prepared to be at your beck and call twenty-four hours a day, seven days a week, for nothing." She listened to his wage offer and felt pleasantly surprised.

"Just one more thing, Geoffrey, I don't want to be known as Miss Fox. In fact, 'Debs' or 'Mrs Rupert' sounds better, so get your blessed company to get my passport and my name changed back to what it was." She had to pause.

"And another thing, stop calling me 'honey' or 'honey bunch,' or you and I are going to fall out big time."

There was a quick romp in the bedroom. When she woke the next morning, Geoffrey had gone back to the Boeing International factory at NASA. He had never mentioned the abbreviation in their conversations. She had noticed it on the pile of documents with their headed notepaper. She began to wonder what she had let herself become involved in.

Right now, there was nothing else to be done but follow her partner's instructions. She began work on the files, which were all gobbledygook to her. Numbers and drawings meant nothing to her.

It was Saturday morning. The sun was up and shining. She wanted to get into a routine like she had in the United Kingdom. She pulled on her sweatshirt and nylon running shorts, then put on her running shoes and walked up to the entrance of the pond path. She heard an American voice cry out, "Hang tail there, Debbie, I take my pond run every Saturday morning at this time."

Jordan Leigh trotted up beside her. "We can do this together. I'll be glad of some female company after a frustrating week in court."

Deborah smiled. "Sure, Jordan. If you can keep up."

They set off together at a reasonable pace. After some distance, Deborah had to sit down on a bench seat. She was still looking good, fit and healthy, but age always takes its toll. Now, in her mid-thirties, there were things she could and couldn't do, and she couldn't run a circuit of the lake without a rest.

Jordan sat beside her and teased. "You're asking if I can keep up. Now, who has collapsed in fatigue?" He laughed loudly.

Deborah tweaked his nose.

"Come on then, I'll race you to the red pines." She was up and off like a greyhound, leaving Jordan to rub his nose.

"You little vixen," he shouted after her, not knowing that her maiden name was Fox.

He began to sprint after the slowing jogger. He caught her around the waist and lifted her off the ground, much to her indignation but delighted squeals. His hands momentarily slid below Deborah's breasts, and she gasped. He let her down slowly, but moved his hands to feel her beautifully shaped hips as she stood firm. She was breathing deeply, and not because of the run. Jordan rubbed them tenderly while kissing her neck.

He turned her body to face him. They kissed with passion before Jordan led her up the embankment behind the bushes and trees, among the wildflowers. After an extensive time of sexual favours, they lay in the warmth of the morning sun with only their running shoes to hide their nakedness. A dragonfly skimmed the water, and somewhere a dog barked in the distance, ordinary sounds that made their secrecy feel even sharper.

"I think we had better move, Deborah. The pond gets busy come lunchtime when people bring their picnics and walk their dogs and children."

They put their garments back on and stealthily walked back down to the path. Jordan pulled her behind a red pine tree and kissed her. He fondled her naked breasts below her sweatshirt.

"I believe you enjoy what I'm doing. Can we do it again sometime?"

"Yes, Jordan, I enjoyed you very much," she croaked, before kissing him hard.

"My girlfriend is a nurse at the local hospital. She starts night shifts on Friday. It would be an ideal time for us to go to bed together and make real, passionate love." He kissed her.

"You could always come to the bungalow any time of the day or night. Geoffrey leaves his car in the driveway because mine is in the garage. So, if you see it there, please don't come near."

"Don't worry. There is always some business to discuss with Geoff, so don't be surprised if I come knocking on the door."

They jogged slowly down the other side of the pond. Deborah stood waiting for a kiss that didn't come.

"I need some advice, Jordan. What about swimming in the lake? Sorry, I meant the pond. Is it safe to do so?"

"Of course it is, I do it regularly, but bear in mind that it is spring water, very cold, and no one knows its origin. Usually, around early evening, the water is warm enough to go swimming. But I urge caution if you're not a good swimmer, and I'll be pleased to accompany you. Just let me know."

With the underhand sex trysts arranged, they went their separate ways. But it was only until Friday night when Jordan appeared at the back door. They made love often before the dawn chorus advised them that his girlfriend would be coming off her shift at 6:00 a.m.

This was not the first or last time they would gorge themselves on sexual pleasure. Sometimes his erection and lovemaking were so good that she removed her contraceptive coil. This was much better for both lovers. After many sexual encounters without protection, Deborah – still in her prime – fell pregnant. It came as no surprise to her, but her lover was furious at her recklessness.

"You could have worn a condom, Jordan," she said in self-defence.

He shook his head in anger. "You told me you were protected by some device. I need time to think this out, Deborah, so I think it best if we call a halt to our deceptive trysts."

"No, you don't, Jordan Ley. You're not going to wriggle your scrawny legal arse out of this unfortunate situation."

He touched her breasts and watched her gasp before giving her a warm kiss, then placed her down on the carpet with a cushion behind her head. He had her knickers off before she could recover her composure. Once inside her, she moaned with pleasure.

There would be many more quickies before it became awkward and dangerous to continue penetration. They would then content themselves with oral sex.

Geoffrey was informed of her pregnancy. The difficult part was telling him. It was the deception she disliked most, having taken Jordan's advice to blame her partner.

"I wasn't the only one who was humping you. It could be Geoff's baby. Who is to know any different?" he said callously.

"We'll know, Jordan. Have you no shame?" The question was futile.

She sat down with Geoffrey on one of his rare visits home.

"I have good news for you, darling." She had never used that word when addressing him.

"I'm going to have a baby." She didn't know what kind of reaction she would receive.

Geoffrey lifted himself lethargically from the couch and hugged her.

"That's wonderful news, Debs. I'm going to be a father at last." He smiled. "The company will be so pleased to hear the news. They like their workforce to be settled into marriage with children. This deserves a celebratory drink." He poured two large glasses of red wine.

"A toast to little Geoffrey." He clinked their glasses and swallowed a large amount.

Deborah sat trying to hold back the tears.

"Don't be upset, Debs. I'm delighted, and I have another surprise for you." His tone had changed. Deborah expected the worst.

Geoff took a real estate magazine from his briefcase.

"Feast your eyes on that, dear heart. I wanted to talk it over before going ahead with the purchase, but we can't wait too long.

According to my friend in the property business, this will be snapped up." He handed a relieved Deborah the magazine.

"It's a shack, Geoffrey." She looked at the rundown building, which resembled a ghost house.

"Idaho? Where in hell's name is Idaho?"

"Ah, now we have a misconception. Why? Well, it's like this. Idaho is located in the Pacific West and Mountain West regions. It's a landlocked state, which includes Montana, Nevada, Utah and Wyoming. It's sometimes called the 'Northern Rockies.' A little bit of Canada encroaches on the border, but who is arguing? A staunchly Republican state, most Idahoans believe they live in the Midwest, where the summers are hot and the winters are cold, but not severe. Temperatures can vary significantly in winter, with heavy snowfall. A friendly, welcoming state whose claim to fame is its potato crop, which has a 25% yield that supplies all of the United States. Idaho is a never-ending state of nothingness. Its vastness makes it seem empty. They still regard themselves as cowboys from a bygone era. The state has three beautiful cities: Boise, Meridian and Nampa. This property is situated in the mountains, twenty-five kilometres from Meridian City." Geoffrey sat down on the couch.

"You've certainly done your homework, Geoffrey. It sounds like an ideal place to bring up children. Perhaps another two or three before I reach the dangerous age."

Deborah meant what she said. She would have more children – but with Geoffrey Bunter, nobody else.

"So, Geoffrey, how much is this fresh air going to cost us?"

"Seventy-two thousand dollars. And with over an acre of ground at the back, enough to install a swimming pool, a solarium and a vegetable garden. There is also plenty of ground at the front to install a terraced garden. That will take a bit of work, but think, Debs – an eco-pond that could be used as a skating rink in winter. Surrounded by a forest of evergreen trees to protect the cabin from the winter blasts." He went into his briefcase and took out some detailed drawings.

"It clearly shows there is enough room at the gable end to erect an extension. Three, perhaps four extra rooms for family and guests. But we can undertake that once we're settled in. There will be the extra cost of the renovation work, but I could carry out most of it with the help of a few local cowboys."

Deborah nodded. "It certainly could be an investment for the future, so yes, let's go with it."

Geoffrey was delighted. "I'll make a phone call right now."

"You're surely not going to phone Jordan Ley at this time of night, Geoffrey?"

"No, the chief of Boeing's legal team will handle this. Besides, Jordan Ley is a small fish in a big pond. There is something going on with him and Boeing International's legal team. I don't know much about it, but there's no smoke without fire."

Deborah was trying to disguise her discomfort. Geoffrey gave her a stern look.

"It was he who brought the wine and flowers from me when you arrived in the United States. Has he ever been inside the bungalow, on the pretence of a business acquisition?"

Deborah solemnly shook her head as she listened to Geoffrey expand.

"Apparently, he was screwing the previous foreman's wife, who left all kinds of important documents lying about. That's where Jordan Ley made his big mistake. He couldn't keep his pants zipped up, and when the Boeing legal team found out about his sex trysts and his interest in some of the documents, the factory foreman was sacked. I believe he divorced his wife at a later time. That's why I urge you, Debs, to keep the top-secret documents locked securely in the filing cabinet, or it could be our neck in the noose."

Geoffrey went to make the phone call. Deborah was flabbergasted at the news. There were times when she was filing that she had left important papers on the desk. Even before and after sex with Jordan, there were times she had left him alone while she went to the corner shop for milk or some other commodity. Should she tell Geoffrey or keep stum? The latter was her decision.

Geoffrey returned in a jovial mood.

"By tomorrow, we'll be the proud owners of a log cabin in the mountains of Idaho."

They went to bed and made boring love. The next morning, Geoffrey was gone.

Deborah kept herself busy. She was interested in an advert in the local paper about a paedophile ring operating in the area. She had enough experience with such unsavoury characters from what her ex had mentioned. A lot of people misconstrued them, thinking they were unshaven men in dirty raincoats, but nothing could be further from the truth. They were highly respected, well-dressed individuals from all walks of life.

She also took an interest in abused women and men. There were men out there under constant abuse from domineering spouses. She felt a stirring of purpose, the old instinct to dig deeper and uncover hidden truths, the same drive that once helped her husband solve difficult cases.

Deborah hadn't lived with a highly intelligent police inspector from Scotland Yard for twenty years without gaining some insight into the low-life operators who had a vast network of influence in the corridors of power. That was why so few paedophile rings were ever caught. That was the case in the UK. She wondered if they had the same protection that created a problem in the United States of America.

The more she read of the newspaper article, the more interested she became. It would certainly fill up her day if she opened a small agency for investigating abused children and adults in the town of Pine Grove Springs. She knew the questions to ask and the people to visit.

Now was not a good time, with her baby due at any moment – and the secret sex-tryst visitor who always came to the back door from the fields.

She said nothing about Geoffrey's idea to buy a log cabin and made sure all the aircraft engine documents, when placed in their proper order, were securely locked away in the filing cabinets.

While resting between sex sessions, she asked Jordan a question about the paedophile situation in the States. With him being a lawyer in the Boeing syndicate, he would surely know what was going on further afield as well as what was happening in the local court.

"Massive," was his reply. "The trouble is they can see you from a mile off. I've personally tried to take them to court, but it never got that far. There was always somebody in the justice system who could bury it for decades to come. Why the sudden interest?"

"Just a small article in the local newspaper, and something that might occupy my time when the baby is born."

Their sex trysts went on until she could not take him any longer. She had taken advice from her doctor that she was pushing the boat out by having a child, especially at her age.

To her astonishment, she gave birth to triplets – two twin girls and a boy.

Geoffrey was over the moon. The company kindly granted him extra compassionate leave, accompanied by many handshakes and congratulatory cards.

It took Deborah weeks to get over the trauma of childbirth. The last time she had felt so tired was when she aborted the American Major's baby in front of her ex-husband. He had unexpectedly been found alive and returned home from a prisoner-of-war camp. That was when their marriage began to fall apart.

She had to scold Geoffrey, who was strutting about the private recovery room like a mother hen about to lay a free-range clutch of eggs.

"I must insist you and the children have a nanny. There's enough room in the bungalow. We can convert the office into a nursery and sleeping quarters. Now you get some rest. I'll come by tonight."

It was for the first time that Deborah realised she had no friends. Nobody apart from Geoffrey came to visit her. Not a card or flowers from Jordan Ley, who had apparently moved to Miami to be closer to the Boeing International central offices and legal team.

Slowly but surely, Deborah began to feel stronger. She felt as if she was living in a florist's shop. Every visit, Geoffrey brought fruit and flowers. There were also flowers from Geoffrey's workforce, accompanied by a well-wisher's card from the company, but no visitors.

She had plenty of time to think while lying in the recovery room. Her mind was made up. When she got home, she would search for an office. Nothing too big – enough to share with a receptionist. It would be called The Deborah Rupert Agency.

She imagined her name in bold letters above the door, a small but defiant claim of independence in a new country.

What she didn't realise was how fast her name would rise, not just in Pine Grove Springs but across the state of Florida and beyond.

Before all that happened, her prime instinct would be that of motherhood. She needed to hire a nanny for the children to ensure they would be cared for during her time at the office.

When she was released from the hospital, she was pleasantly surprised. Geoffrey had organised everything. Even the bungalow office had been converted into a nursery with the nanny's room attached. A nanny was already employed.

She was now experiencing something she thought would never happen again. She was beginning to love and appreciate her partner, Geoffrey Bunter, more than ever, despite his failings in the bedroom department. This, she told herself, could be resolved with time.

***

The Deborah Rupert Agency office had been decorated and was ready for occupancy. A bright young receptionist called Mary-Jo Hemmings was employed. Geoffrey attended the opening day, along with business associates from the town.

It took a month before business began to pick up, but she need not have worried. By the second month, the agency was overwhelmed with telephone calls and clients who wished to remain anonymous until Deborah assured them that their meetings would be held in the strictest confidence. She even put a notice in the window highlighting the need for privacy.

She now realised that the agency would need bigger premises. There was a vacant furniture store that had closed on Vermont Street, just off the bustling, busy 3rd Avenue. After inspecting the building, it was exactly what she was looking for.

However, she needed to employ counsellors – people who knew how to handle domestic abuse and child abuse. She knew those cases were entirely separate from the paedophile rings, so she decided to keep the small office to investigate that part and move the other business to Vermont Street, along with the receptionist.

It took some time to put her dream into place. Two counsellors were employed, along with a solicitor who would handle the legal aspects.

Deborah could scarcely believe how quickly her idea had grown; what began as a way to fill her time was becoming a beacon of hope for the vulnerable.

That now left Deborah the time to investigate what she was determined to stamp out.

She paid a visit to the primary school and explained that she, too, had taught at the primary level. This helped to win over the headmistress. They discussed the problem facing the United States at length.

"The trouble is, Mrs Rupert, even the F.B.I. can't catch those responsible. It's almost as if the paedophile rings are protected in some way or another." She stood up, indicating the meeting was over.

Deborah could only thank her for her time. She had learned nothing from the headmistress that she couldn't learn from any newspaper office. She would take that route when all other avenues closed.

Deborah always remembered what her ex-husband, Detective Inspector Amadeus Rupert, had told her: "Patience, stealth, softly, and a softer approach to catch the monkey."

That gave her the inspiration to hang about incognito for a while. The school bell rang at 3:00 p.m. precisely. As always, children ran from the school to the arms of their waiting parents. Deborah noticed a green Ford camper van parked close to the school.

The driver got out of his seat and waved enthusiastically. A young girl ran up and gave him a hug. There was nothing wrong with that – a father and daughter exchanging fondness for each other. But then she noticed the girl had trouble getting into the passenger seat. It wasn't until the camper van pulled away that she saw the young girl sitting on an adult's lap in the front passenger seat.

Now that did strike Deborah as strange, considering there were seats in the rear of the camper. She quickly jotted down the registration state number.

Had she gotten lucky on her first assignment? The trouble was that her car was facing in the wrong direction. Much as she wanted to tail the camper, it took her time to turn the car around. She gave chase, but the camper had disappeared.

# Chapter 10 – Betrayals and Recklessness

There was always tomorrow. By tomorrow, she would be prepared.

Deborah stood at the school gate in the early morning sunshine. Children with their parents began to arrive. She lingered, hoping to glimpse the driver of the camper van.

That didn't happen. The girl she had spotted yesterday arrived with the woman Deborah assumed was her mother. When the young girl had gone into the school carrying her bag and lunch box, Deborah struck up a conversation.

"It's a job getting them to and from school, in between holding down a job or looking after a younger family," Deborah said, fishing for information.

"Exactly. I've tried to tell my husband that since Emmylou was born. Does he pay the slightest heed? No, he doesn't. Although I'm very lucky. I have an understanding boss who lets me work from nine-thirty until five-thirty."

Deborah had the mother talking. "That is the hard part for me. I must take a job that corresponds with my daughter's schooling."

"Again, I'm most fortunate. I have good neighbours who take turns collecting Emmylou from school. I don't know what I'd do without them."

The woman stood back. "You're not one of the parents, are you? I've not seen you around before."

Deborah had to think quickly. "As I'm sure you can tell by the accent, I'm new to the area. In fact, new to the United States. I'm from England and have settled here with my partner, who is an aircraft engineer. Today I got my daughter enrolled before classes started."

This seemed to please the woman, who said, "Good luck in this dreary, no-good town. Now I must dash, or the boss will be spanking me again."

Deborah raised her eyebrows in disbelief. She tried to continue the conversation, but the woman was gone.

She was determined to know who was picking Emmylou up from school. After spending time in the office, she drove back to the school in the afternoon.

The camper van arrived on time as the bell sounded, and the children poured into the playground to be collected by either parent or, in this case, a neighbour.

The young girl, as yesterday, ran towards the waiting driver and his passenger. The driver lifted her into the air in a seemingly friendly gesture. But was it friendly? Deborah noticed where his hands were—below her skirt, on her bottom. This was not how a neighbour should welcome a child or anyone else. Her stomach tightened as she watched the girl scramble onto the knees of the passenger, who handed her a candy bar as the camper drove away.

She followed until it parked in the driveway of a bungalow. The driver got out quickly and helped the youngster to her feet. She grabbed her bag and lunch box, then followed both men indoors. A single question pulsed in Deborah's mind: *What were they up to?*

It could have been innocent enough, but it was the girl sitting on the passenger's knees that troubled her. She must talk to the young girl urgently.

That chance came three days later when Emmylou was walking home alone.

Deborah stopped the car beside her. "Can you help me? I'm looking for 22 Elm Grove Crescent." She had noted the address the day she tailed the camper.

"I live next door to twenty-two," the young girl said with a smile.

"Excellent, then you can show me the way."

"I'm not to accept lifts from strangers," she said, backing away from the open car door.

"I'm not a stranger, Emmylou; I'm a friend of the two men who pick you up from school."

The young girl smiled and walked towards the open door. "Then that's all right. They're so good to me."

Deborah couldn't believe how easy it was to pick a child up off the street. Her fingers tightened on the steering wheel.

"Do you sit on the man's lap every time the two men collect you?"

"Yes, and I get a bar of candy."

"What age are you, Emmylou?"

"I'll be nine in August. Mr Sawridge says I'm a big girl for my age."

Deborah pressed on, her tone sombre. "Do those men interfere with you, Emmylou?"

"I don't know what you mean. Now let me out of the car."

Deborah slipped up when she said, "I bet you're relieved now we've reached number 22."

She pulled up at the door.

"I thought you needed directions to the address," the sharp young girl said.

"That's strange, because here we are outside my neighbour's front door without any direction from me." Emmylou grabbed her bag. "I don't trust you, whoever you are."

She got out in a temper. "I've a good mind to tell my dad." She slammed the car door.

Deborah was stuck for words. She hastily drove away.

This was going to be a long-drawn-out process. Trying to get photos of the two men who, she believed, were responsible for the degradation of Emmylou would be difficult without giving herself away or endangering the young girl.

Deborah spent weeks sitting in her car observing the bungalow at 22 Elm Grove Crescent. She managed to get several photographs of people entering and leaving. There seemed to be many comings and goings.

Could it be a gathering of church members? Or perhaps a birthday party, given the number of children present? Deborah had her doubts.

The camper van was always there. Emmylou was never allowed to walk home. She was always collected from school by different people and in different vehicles. Sometimes a man, sometimes a woman, sometimes both stood at the school gates.

Why were they so keen to treat this young girl with kid gloves? It became impossible to talk to Emmylou on her own.

Deborah felt she was at a dead end. She had no proof of what was taking place inside the bungalow.

There was, however, one sign that whoever was involved with Emmylou Carson was running scared. Deborah's small office had been targeted with hate mail, and the large window was smashed.

This led to a police investigation.

The local sheriff's office made inquiries. They asked why she should suddenly start receiving hate mail.

She explained her suspicions in depth, supplying photographs and timings of meetings. She recounted her talk with Emmylou, who had told her what took place with her neighbour and another man. She gave the sheriff a typed list of names she had tracked. Some of the visitors to 22 Elm Grove Crescent were prominent citizens of Pine Grove Springs and the surrounding areas.

His response was a criticism. "You should not be interfering in police work, Miss Fox. We've checked you out. You want to change your name back to Deborah Rupert. I don't think that will be done, but hear this: you have absolutely no proof of paedophile activity in this town. Your battered wives and husbands club has certainly expanded, but once again, you're interfering in police investigations and that must stop."

Deborah looked at the overweight sheriff chewing his tobacco.

"And what about the evidence of Emmylou Carson? Are you going to ignore that, sheriff?"

"The rantings of a young girl entering puberty. Often the case. Having wet dreams about the boy next door."

"The only difference is that it's not a boy next door but an adult. I also have photos of the so-called friendly passenger who takes Emmylou to 22 Elm Grove Crescent, with her on his lap."

The sheriff spat his chewed tobacco into a bin and struggled to stand up.

"Miss Fox, if I were to arrest every friendly person or relation for letting a young girl sit on his or her lap, our jails would be overflowing. Now, if you'll excuse me, I have a town to keep safe from real criminals."

Deborah knew she had been fobbed off. As she left the stale fug of the smokers' office, another thought crossed her mind. Was the sheriff, or his friends, involved? She still had no concrete proof that a paedophile ring was operating in the town, and with no help from the sheriff, she felt as if she had hit a brick wall.

But there was a dim light at the end of the tunnel. As she walked to her car, she was pulled into a lane by a deputy sheriff.

"I can't spend much time talking to you, but you're on the right track. Stay with it, ma'am. My own daughter was approached by those paedophiles until I threatened to shoot the man if he or any other paedophile even spoke to her again. You'll find most are involved in coaching staff in any sport where youngsters are involved. Also, youth organisations, like the Boy Scouts or Girl Guides. I can't talk anymore."

The deputy ran to the far end of the lane and disappeared.

Deborah stood looking out at the main street. It felt as if every pair of eyes was staring at her. Now she was becoming paranoid.

She walked quietly to her car only to find the back window smashed. If before she had only felt paranoid, now she was afraid. A cold draught moved through the vehicle, carrying the smell of broken glass and dust.

She felt relieved when Geoffrey came home for the week. She talked it over with him: the damage to the office and the car, her visit to the sheriff's office, her surprise meeting with the deputy and what he said.

Geoffrey sat listening to her suspicions.

"Let me think about this, Debs. I might have the solution to your problem. However, now might be a good time to visit our log cabin in Idaho. What do you think?"

"Yes, Geof. I could do with a break. The domestic abuse office is doing well; I think I can leave the counsellors and lawyer to get on with it."

"Talking of lawyers, Debs. Have you seen Jordan Ley recently?"

Deborah shook her head, wondering what was coming next.

"I haven't seen his sports car around. I often used to see him drive to work on the Monday run to Miami. But hasn't he moved there with his girlfriend? Why is there a problem?"

Geoffrey changed the subject.

"I've purchased two camp beds and sleeping bags. All we need now are pillows and food. We'll take some pots and utensils, just in case there's nothing there. The drive time is approximately thirty-eight hours, forty-six minutes, on Interstate-84 and I-184. That takes us from Miami, Florida, to downtown Meridian in Idaho—2,655 miles. This means an overnight stop at a motel. However, I have some good news. In the future, we can fly from Miami Airport to Meridian, Idaho, in five hours and fifteen minutes. That's something to think about when we see what's what at the cabin and get settled."

Deborah smiled. There was one thing about Geoffrey Bunter—he was always precise in his explanations. He had clearly done his homework long before bringing it to her attention.

"Sounds good, Geof. I'll pack a bag." She trotted off upstairs.

Geof picked up the telephone and dialled a number.

"Danny boy, it's Geof from Boeing International. I have a conundrum I hope you can deal with. It concerns a paedophile ring operating in Pine Grove Spring."

"That's not a conundrum, Geoffrey; that's a huge problem throughout the United States. Give me the details and I'll see what I can do, but let me remind you—there is no easy fix to this problem."

"I understand, Danny. I'm off to Idaho for a couple of weeks. Perhaps we could meet up, buddy, swap anthologies."

"Okay, my friend. Phone me when you get back." The line went dead.

Geoffrey rubbed his hands together and followed Deborah upstairs to pack.

After loading the car and checking with the nanny, they set off on the long drive to Idaho, each taking turns after three hours behind the wheel. One thousand miles behind them and sixteen hundred still to go.

They pulled into a roadside motel, tired but jubilant that they were nearing the journey's end.

They slipped off Interstate-84 towards the city of Meridian. After getting directions, they drove out into the countryside. The western snow-capped mountains looked spectacular in the distance.

They had to ask directions from a potato farmer who was busy in a field that stretched as far as the eye could see.

"You've missed the turn-off for Bear Creek by eight miles. Go back until you come to a crossroads, then a mile beyond is the track leading to the cabins."

"Did I hear you say cabins, Mr Farmer, sir? How many are there?" Geof asked quickly.

"A total of three, with seven miles between each of them. When you get off this highway, drive two miles to the T junction." He leaned on the tractor. "I take it you're the new incomers. That means your cabin is straight ahead for eight miles. Whatever happens, don't get out of your car. It's not called Bear Creek for nothing. We have a forest ranger who patrols this wood regularly."

The farmer jumped into his tractor and drove away.

Deborah couldn't help herself. "I don't like the sound of that, Geof. Maybe we should just turn around and head back home."

"I think he was just trying to scare us. I know that a local farmer wanted to buy the cabin with its land. Come on, let's see what we've purchased."

Deborah turned the car around and drove until they reached the crossroads. After a mile, they came to the T junction. As they progressed, the track narrowed, and the forest closed in around them. The eight miles was an uphill drive that seemed to go on forever until it opened out into a wide, clear area. The vista was spectacular, with the Bitterroots and Western Mountains in the distance and the forests surrounding the desolate, forlorn-looking log cabin.

A natural waterfall cascaded over a rock face at the side of the cabin.

Geof was delighted with the purchase even before they ventured inside.

Deborah was still unconvinced, her thoughts turning to bears roaming the forests. *The silence of the place was beautiful but unsettling, like a wilderness both inviting and menacing at once.*

After a quick assessment of the cabin, Geof raced out the back door and up the embankment. He stood with his arms outstretched in amazement.

"Come up here, Debs, and look at what we've bought."

Deborah followed him up onto the high embankment.

"A swimming pool here, close to the cabin. A solarium next to the pool. And just what you've always wanted…" He paused. "A large vegetable garden. I can't get over how much ground we have to work with."

"You have all this marked out, Geoffrey Bunter. How often have you been doodling and planning this when you were supposed to be working?" She smiled.

"I'm not finished yet, Debs. Follow me." He led her towards the gable end of the cabin. "Plenty of room for an extension. An underground water pipe from the tank or the stream on the embankment." He took her hand and led her down to where the Chevrolet was parked.

He pointed to a large, spacious circle of earth.

"Tell me, what do you see over there?"

Deborah shook her head, trying to figure out what Geoffrey meant.

"Okay, here it is." He led her to the circle of earth banking and stepped onto its ridge. "The underground pipework will fill this area with water, making it into an eco-pond in spring, summer and autumn. Then, come winter, when it freezes, it'll be a skating rink for the children when they're older. A water inlet at the far end will give oxygen to the water, and a mesh-covered underground overflow will let the excess water escape into the stream without overflowing the embankment. That keeps it at a safe depth for skating and gives pond life ample space to glide."

Deborah was impressed, especially when Geof pointed to the front of the cabin.

"A terraced garden for your plants. That will take a bit of work, but never say die, eh."

He gave her a hug.

"Let's get the bedding and food out of the car before a bear picks up our scent and has you for tea." He laughed loudly at her reaction.

"Don't joke about those things, Geoffrey." She glanced nervously towards the surrounding forest.

They were glad to have brought provisions. They lit candles and had the kitchen stove fired up. Supper beside a log fire in the lounge rounded off their long day.

Deborah was beginning to realise just how intelligent Geoffrey Bunter was. He had tremendous vision, not just for the here and now, but for the future. It proved true when he spoke about a skating rink for their children's future.

They spent most of the night on their camp beds by the log fire, talking about what could be done to the cabin and the surrounding land.

Deborah insisted that her share of the purchase would be signed and sealed when they returned to civilisation. She also insisted that any expenses for materials and machinery hire would be covered by her.

"Thanks, Debs. That's a load off. It means the work will be carried out quicker."

She fell asleep while Geof was still talking.

They woke to a misty morning. The sun rose to create a beautiful day, the morning dew disappearing as the haze burned off.

Deborah stood at the large window in her lace baby-doll nightdress, taking in the scene in front of the cabin. Now she could visualise, in her mind's eye, what Geof had spoken about on their arrival and what they had discussed the previous night.

Geof had breakfast cooking and brought her a mug of coffee.

"You should put some clothes on, dear. Or the bear will see what you've had for breakfast. Not that I'm not enjoying the view, but we must make the most of our time here. We have a busy day ahead. Cleaning this place is our priority, both inside and outside. There are a lot of dead branches lying about. We can burn most of it. So let's have breakfast before we start our chores."

"Slave driver," Deborah said with a smile, finishing her coffee.

The work began inside. Every room, nook and cranny was swept, dusted, and mopped with disinfectant. Everything not worth keeping was placed on the bonfire outside. The surrounding area was cleared of old wood and broken branches.

A Ford station wagon skidded to a halt. A blond man and a woman leapt from the truck.

"Can I ask who you are, and why you have this fire burning?" the stranger said abruptly.

"Ah, now I understand your concern. Thanks for the warning," Deborah said softly.

"No harm done, but be careful in the future. Come on, Sue-Ellen, let's be on our way." Stephen hesitated and turned to face the new owners. "You mentioned machinery. Are you planning to alter this area? If so, you'll need planning permission."

Geof smiled. "Nothing serious. Some internal alterations, perhaps an extension when the children grow up, a swimming pool, a vegetable garden, and an eco-pond over there."

Stephen nodded his approval. "That sounds interesting. Good luck with the project. I have a small construction firm in these parts;

I have some machinery and plant I hire out that might come in useful. I also have a small labour force, should you need any help."

Deborah interrupted. "I was wondering about that angle, so after my partner and I have talked it over, I can say we'll probably be in touch."

Geoffrey began to rake the leaves, indicating the neighbourly meeting was over. Deborah wasn't finished quite yet.

"Tell me, Mr Tuple, are there any wild bears roaming around these parts?"

"Yes, mostly found in isolated places like Hell's Canyon. The brown bear and the grizzly have different ranges and diets. The brown bear is smaller and found near coasts or waterfall creeks where they feed on wild salmon. Their diet is any kind of fish, but salmon in season is their staple, preparing them for hibernation. The grizzly is bigger, with a different geographical range, from Alaska through western Canada to isolated spots in Washington State, Idaho, Montana and Wyoming. It has a different diet. The grizzly eats berries, roots, grubs, moths and larger animals. They're normally found in the Cabinet and Selkirk mountains, and also the Bitterroots in northern Idaho. They are classed as an endangered species and cannot be owned or hunted."

"Thank you for that descriptive analysis, Mr Tuple, but the question remains. Do they eat you?"

"Only if they've had a bad summer and not built up enough fat to sustain them through a long, harsh winter in hibernation. But be sure of this: if they don't eat you, they'll make a hell of a mess of you. They'll tear you to ribbons, especially if they have cubs in tow." He paused. "Don't worry. Bears are tracked and captured quickly.

In all my years in Idaho, I've never heard of them mauling anyone, so you can rest easy at your swimming pool when it's finished."

Deborah gave the couple a friendly wave as their station wagon pulled away. As the engine note faded into the trees, the clearing felt suddenly larger, the silence pricked by the steady rush of the waterfall.

Geoff and Deborah talked about machinery and plant hire while they worked.

"A small digger would be advantageous when it comes to the swimming pool excavations. Perhaps it would help to bury the water pipe from the new tank down to the eco-pond."

Geoff paused. "Our next task is going to be hard. Moving the large stones from the ridge down to form the terrace. So we'll need machinery for that. We'll use the excavated earth from the swimming pool area as backfill on the terraces."

They worked on until the light began to fade. The surrounding area looked much better and cleaner after their efforts. They went to bed each night exhausted, with nothing in mind but sleep.

They drove into Meridian to purchase a pickup truck. They loaded it with heavy plastic sheeting to form the base of the eco-pond. They bought a trailer to transport gravel, sand and cement for mixing concrete. They decided to buy a small cement mixer rather than hire one, which would allow them to start on the eco-pond on their next visit.

Deborah drove the Chevrolet back to the log cabin, keeping a close eye on her partner in the mirror. She had every confidence in her newfound love.

The drive back to Pine Grove Springs was tedious. An overnight stop in a motel made it more tolerable, and they spent indulgent hours making love.

Deborah still had to go through the motions and noises. That was the only part of their love affair where Geoffrey Bunter failed: the bedroom department.

Back home at last, Deborah checked the children before going to the office. The window had been replaced, and the new pane was intact. She ventured across town to the marriage guidance clinic, as it was now called. Everything was running smoothly, just as she had left it two weeks before.

It was Geoffrey who spoke solemnly at the tea table. "If you cast your mind back to the time I made a phone call while you were packing the cases for our expedition to Idaho. I contacted a friend who works for the F.B.I., the Federal Bureau of Investigation. I gave him the information you'd given me regarding a paedophile ring operating in Pine Grove Springs." He hesitated.

"I'm afraid you've been misled by a young primary school girl who has made allegations about other men in the past. Emmylou Carson is living in a fantasy world. Her parents are considering having her committed to the state mental hospital. That will probably take place without their recommendation. The neighbour does look after her, and the other man whose knee she sits on is her uncle, a respected judge in the state of Florida."

Deborah was about to speak when Geoffrey held up his hand.

"It has been discovered that Miss Carson has been abused, not by a paedophile ring, but by older boys and men who took her to the woods to play. Emmylou Carson is a young sex predator, always game to play, especially with older men. That, Debs, throws a different light on paedophiles. I'm not saying those low-lives don't exist elsewhere, but not here, not in Pine Grove Springs, according to the F.B.I. investigation."

Deborah felt anger and revulsion creeping over her. "And how do they explain the deputy sheriff who grabbed me and told me I was on the right track?"

"Nothing more than a wind-up, Debs. Perhaps he had ulterior motives in mind."

"The broken office window, Geoffrey. How does your friend justify that?"

"The sheriff's department already has somebody locked up for that. An irate husband who wanted revenge because of the advice your marriage counsellor gave his wife: to leave him and seek a divorce."

"F.B.I. agent Danny Corrigan can explain it all in detail if you wish. The sheriff wants a word with you about this, so I would get over there and get it sorted sooner rather than later. I'll come with you for support."

Deborah put her head in her hands. "And the groups of people coming and going?"

"Members of the Mormon Church holding prayer meetings."

"All right, what about the so-called judge sitting with Emmylou on his lap in the passenger seat?"

"I think the sheriff has explained that, Debs. It was Emmylou who insisted she sit on his lap on the journey back to 22 Elm Grove Crescent. Now, enough of this; let's go to the sheriff's office."

"There's a cover-up somewhere, Geoffrey. An attempted whitewash. Well, I'm not giving up on this. There are paedophiles operating throughout the United States, and I'll make it a crusade to weed them out."

They drove to the sheriff's office, where Deborah was given a severe warning to stay away from 22 Elm Grove Crescent and any other addresses she had uncovered.

"Do you want to press charges against the window-breaker? If so, sign here," he said, continuing to chew his black tobacco square.

Deborah shook her head. "Let him go. The poor man has enough problems on his plate."

It was back to the same routine. The only difference was that time was going by so quickly. The older she got, the faster the days seemed to pass.

The children were now at primary school. Her marriage guidance agency had expanded throughout Florida.

The F.B.I. and the C.I.A. were now acutely aware of the real problem that was taking place. There were several arrests throughout the United States concerning paedophile rings. Deborah had been invited to speak at parental conventions. Some she attended, some she did not. She wanted to attend them all, but her marriage guidance business had taken off in a big way. The D.R.A. had expanded into several states, with outlets in towns and cities.

On top of that, she had her own children's education to consider. Then the log cabin project. There were many days and weeks spent travelling to and from Meridian, Idaho. The pickup truck was parked in the supplier's yard, loaded with materials and ready to go.

There was a problem when she reached the log cabin. If the digger operator or his labourer wasn't there, she had to unload the sand and cement herself. Sometimes it got so bad that her arm muscles were beginning to look like those of a heavyweight boxer. That was when she demanded to be shown how to operate the digger, much to the chagrin of the operator. The first time she gripped the levers, her hands shook, but the machine's steady grunt calmed her; for the first time that week, control felt tangible.

"All right, Mr Sidley, tell your boss that if you don't play ball, we'll buy our own digger and dispense with his services. I want you and the labourer here Monday to Friday when I get up, and here until I go indoors. That means 08:00 until 17:00, an eight-hour day with an hour for lunch. I'll permit a fifteen-minute tea break morning and afternoon."

She paused. "I'll reverse the pickup truck over to the eco-pond. Boris and I can start to lay the reinforcement rods onto the plastic sheets and begin mixing the concrete for the first base. Meanwhile, you can start excavating the swimming pool soil, which I want placed here, next to the proposed terraced gardens."

Geoffrey and Deborah had expressed their frustration at the slow progress to Steve Tuple, the contractor. Every time they visited, nothing seemed to have been done. Geoff noticed the machinery was in the same position as when they had left the site.

It was Deborah who gave Tuple an ultimatum. "Get things moving, or we'll bring in another contractor, Tuple."

It was obvious that backsides had been kicked. The operator reacted quickly. Climbing into his cab, he moved the machine up to the pegged-out area for the swimming pool and started excavating.

She and Boris unloaded the cement bags and reinforcement. They had the grids tied with wire and in place by lunchtime.

After lunch, the cement mixer was started, and Boris began mixing sand, cement and gravel. Three shovels of sand, one of cement and one of gravel had been recommended.

The mixer chugged when turning a heavy batch, which Boris tipped into the wheelbarrow and delivered to Deborah, who was standing in her shorts, Wellington boots and sweatshirt. She caught Boris ogling her chest with each barrowload, his gaze lingering despite her attempts to ignore it. [ADDED DETAIL for tension] The awareness unsettled her, but she forced herself to remain focused on the task.

She carried on, raking the concrete into the reinforcing squares, not being too fussy about the levels because Geoffrey had said there would be two more layers. The top layer would be screeded to a proper, flat finish, ensuring the base was strong and smooth for the work to follow.

# Chapter 11 – Divorce and Departure

They worked tirelessly on the first layer of the eco-pond foundation. By the end of the first week, she was exhausted. However, she had peace of mind knowing the first layer was completed and ready to begin again with the second on Monday morning.

She spent a quiet weekend reading and ironing curtains, grateful for a brief rest.

She was delighted when the second layer of concrete for the eco-pond was completed. The third and final layer would be made by those with finishing skills.

Time was not to be wasted; time was the enemy. They had taken delivery of rolled pre-grown grass, which was placed on the sloping embankment surrounding the pool. A gap was left for the wheelbarrow and the finishing layer of concrete. There was also the last section of the eco-pool to be completed.

According to Geoff's instructions, when the final layer of concrete was laid, levelled and hardened, another layer of thick plastic would be spread and covered with earth and small rocks. This was to give fish and other pond life places to dart behind. Deborah wanted the grass laid quickly so that the roots could take hold, giving the eco-pool a finished, natural look. All that would be needed then was the water supply, which Geoff could handle on his next visit. A lot of thought had gone into this part of the project.

In the ten working days she had spent on site, an impressive amount of manual work had been completed. She was glad to drive the twenty-five miles to Meridian. Going home gave her aching body respite, and as the aircraft took off for Miami, Florida, she felt her shoulders finally relax.

While in flight, she thought about all she had achieved and felt pride in her accomplishments—stories she looked forward to sharing with her partner when he came back from work at Cape Canaveral. That was all she truly knew about him: an aircraft engineer working with an ex-Nazi scientist captured when Germany was defeated.

She had once asked him his opinion on the subject when they were alone at home.

"If it wasn't the Americans who got them, it would have been the Russians. Now, for God's sake, Deborah, drop the subject once and for all."

She had never heard him speak so sharply. She changed the subject and told him about the progress at the log cabin, though his mind seemed elsewhere.

"Is there a problem you want to talk about, Geoff? A problem shared is a problem halved."

"No, nothing of importance, darling. I'm sorry. Go on with your stories about the cabin. I am interested."

Deborah explained everything in detail.

"I'm sorry, I won't make it with you this time. Duty calls. I'll be going back to the Cape early next Friday."

Deborah gave a slight moan. "Another six weeks without you. Never mind, I'll go back to Idaho once you've returned to work. There's no rush to finish the project, Geoff. Besides, we have a good labourer who knows the ropes."

They had an early night. There was something different about Geoff's bedside manner. He seemed to last longer before he ejaculated, and he was giving her the satisfaction she craved.

Perhaps it was her imagination playing tricks, but the false noises and endearments she had once made in the past were now genuine. For the first time, she found herself asleep before her partner, who was keen to excite her.

What had changed? She smiled at the thought. Perhaps it was her biceps and arm muscles that turned him on. Yet there was something else—something bothering him. Geoff didn't normally show emotions, and now she wondered if she was the one failing to satisfy him.

Their time together was short. Geoff left for the Cape on Friday. Deborah packed a small suitcase with underwear and clothes and caught a lift to Miami Airport.

She flew to Meridian, Idaho, arriving in mid-afternoon.

She collected the pickup truck as usual, finding it loaded with five-gallon drums of diesel oil and rolls of water pipe. Apparently, Geoff had placed the order by telephone, saying he would be flying to Idaho over the weekend. Those plans had clearly fallen through. She collected the ignition keys and paid the monthly account.

The drive out into the country excited her now that she knew the way. Turning off the highway, she spotted the change in the road surface: the first two miles had been widened and tarred to the T-junction. The eight miles to the log cabin remained the same—rough and narrow.

She was pleasantly surprised to see the two workmen still toiling, though it was close to 17:00. Boris came to meet her, explaining what had been done.

The third layer of concrete in the eco-pool had been finished. The final rolls of heavy plastic had been laid, and the sifted earth and rounded stones had been spread across the pool area. The rolls of grass had closed the gap on the sloping embankment.

The mesh-covered underground overflow pipe had been installed, channelled into the mountain stream that flowed down beside the road.

There was more. The swimming pool area had been dug out and prepared for the shuttering joiners.

"We still have the terraces and steps to the porch to consider, but we can begin that on Monday morning. Mr Tuple will bring the granite blocks and steps. He'll also bring the wood and ply for the pool shuttering. Once the terraces are in place, we can use the digger to lift the cement mixer up to the pool area, where it'll be needed for mixing the concrete."

"You've certainly been busy, Boris. I think a bonus is in order when the work at the cabin is completed."

This brought a huge grin from the dark-skinned labourer.

Deborah unloaded the pickup truck and watched the two men drive away. It had been a long day. She left everything by the pickup, cooked her meal, and afterwards settled down with a bottle of red wine. She spread her sleeping bag on the couch—anything was better than the uncomfortable camp bed, which had dumped her on the floor more than once during the night.

Saturday dawned bright and sunny. After a light breakfast, she set to work rolling the alcathene pipe up the steep embankment towards the water tank. From there, she uncoiled the pipe, rolling it along the top of the ridge and down by the gable end of the cabin. The second roll was less demanding; she rolled it from the parking place to the gable end to link with the first, which would eventually feed the eco-pool.

She topped up the digger with diesel before starting to bury the pipe. The hardest part was laying a bed of sand in the two-foot trench to protect it. Once the pipe was laid, it was covered by another layer of sand before backfilling commenced.

Deborah was delighted with her weekend's achievement. By the end of the week, the shuttering joiners had finished.

She decided not to interfere with the swimming pool project or the pipe couplings, leaving them for Geoff. She wasn't sure what he envisioned as the final result, though he had mentioned adding a separate tank to feed the eco-pool.

There were still the terraced gardens to install, which promised to be hard work. But she had an idea to save time and energy. She had spotted red and grey granite blocks at the merchants' yard. Instead of collecting large stones, the blocks could serve as the base—grey in the first layer and red on the second. She could reverse that if necessary.

She drove into Meridian with the pickup and trailer. She chose the grey granite blocks for the base. They were loaded onto the trailer and taken to the cabin, where the digger lifted them onto the prepared concrete base.

Now she could backfill and level the first terrace with a layer of cement, ready for the paving slabs.

By the second week, she was utterly exhausted. But an old saying kept her spirits up: "The devil makes work for idle hands." It drove her to work with gusto. With Boris's help, the last paving slab was put in place.

The first terraced tier looked good, with spaces left between the slabs for planting. Deborah changed her mind about the granite colour—the second tier would also be grey, matching the first.

However, she would need to let the groundwork settle. Work on the second tier was delayed. She felt she had done enough for the time being.

But there was no real limit on time. The project would take at least two years, especially if Geoff planned to add an extension.

She decided to stay for a third week. The boss of the construction company was keen to lend a hand at mixing and pouring the concrete at the shuttered pool. He worked tirelessly, spreading the base in preparation for the pool tilers.

He worked long after the workforce had gone home. As the light faded, his sweaty body stepped beneath the cascading waterfall. He rubbed himself down with soap before stepping from the cold mountain stream. He stood, letting the heat of the day dry him.

Deborah couldn't resist standing at the kitchen window in the candlelight, watching. She gasped when he brazenly grasped himself, his smile fixed on the glass as though he knew she was watching.

She stepped back, heart pounding, but it was too late; he had seen her. She forced herself to look away, yet curiosity drew her back for a second glance. [ADDED DETAIL for tension] The twilight outside seemed suddenly heavier, pressing against the cabin walls.

Opening the door, she stepped out into the cooling air, only to hear the contractor's station wagon start up and pull away.

She was left with mixed emotions. Did she truly want what she had just glimpsed, or was it nothing more than a fleeting, dangerous whim?

Whatever it was, she had an uncomfortable night on the sofa. She couldn't get Stevie Tuple out of her mind. This would prove to be a regular occurrence whenever he finished his work.

Deborah considered going out to hand him a towel, hoping he would take the hint, but she resisted. There was too much at stake. It would spoil her dream of having a place to relax, and there was Geoffrey to consider. She had grown fond of him. Now she was left in limbo.

There was still much to be done with the cabin project. She wanted to prove to Geoff she could carry out his wishes, both at the log cabin and in the bedroom. Much as she tried to erase the memory, it still plagued her: the vision of the contractor's muscular body stepping from the waterfall.

Deborah often fell asleep thinking of him.

By the end of the week, she was making plans to return to Pine Grove Springs; she still had her young family to consider.

On Saturday morning, she was up with the proverbial lark. Her heart leapt when the station wagon pulled into the parking lot, only to be disappointed. Sue-Ellen Tuple stepped out from the driver's seat. No one else appeared, which made Deborah wonder if there was trouble ahead. How could there be? Nothing had happened between her and Sue-Ellen's husband.

The contractor's wife gave her a wave. Deborah dried her hands and walked down to meet her.

"Hi, Debs. It's been a while since I was last here. I'm interested to know how the project is going. Stevie just says it's progressing, so I've come to see for myself."

Deborah showed her around the work that had been done and what still needed attention.

"My word, you have been busy. This should be finished by the autumn."

"Not quite, Sue-Ellen. My partner Geoff is going to build an extension onto the far gable end."

"Men… they always need to have something to occupy their time." Sue-Ellen laughed, then added inquisitively: "Ah, so you're not married then?"

"Not yet. Perhaps when the children are older, we will have a better relationship, the way we are. Why spoil a good thing?" Deborah smiled.

"Yes, I understand. Sometimes I wish Stevie and I had never married."

"Come on, Sue-Ellen. Nobody is forced into marriage. It's a commitment made by two people." Deborah could see the uncertainty in the woman's expression.

"Let's talk together over a glass of wine," Deborah suggested, trying to defuse the tension.

"Not for me, but I would kill for a cup of coffee."

The two women walked casually up to the back door. Deborah set the coffee pot on the gas ring, laying out mugs, sugar and milk. They sat on the sofa, talking small talk like long-lost friends.

Sue-Ellen spoke candidly. "I was forced into my marriage by my parents. I fell pregnant to Stevie while at college. My father said it brought shame on our family and our religion, which abhors the thought of sex before marriage. So, there it was—led down the aisle by a proud father. Then catastrophe struck. I had a miscarriage. We lost the baby. Dad and our doctor said we could have plenty more, but that was not to be. My ovaries were damaged to the extent I could not have any more children."

Deborah held her hand to her mouth. She had heard this kind of story before, though she herself had been fortunate to have children. She could only express her sympathy at Sue-Ellen's loss. This woman was still highly strung and suffering.

"There is one thing I should say, and that is my husband Stephen was warned there would be no divorce. Again, that is where our religion dictated our future. Stephen is what we American women call a fanny teaser. I know he struts about the swimming pools of Meridian and Boise—probably more besides—but that is as far as I allow him to go. He has been warned by my family: any extramarital affairs and his allowance will be cut off, and he'll end up at the bottom of our lake. A boating accident." She sipped her coffee.

"It is my money that keeps him in the style to which he has become accustomed. His casino debts are taken care of. His expensive clothes are bought for him. As for the rest of my wealth, I own everything. The log cabin with its lake and cruiser, the business, everything. I'm sure he's been parading around here in his shorts, flashing the only assets he has. But, as I've said, that is as far as he is prepared to go."

Deborah said nothing about Stevie flashing himself. In a way, she felt slightly sorry for him. Was he trapped in a loveless marriage, just as she had once been?

"You'll have to excuse me, Sue-Ellen. I catch a flight for Miami at 15:00."

"Of course. But we must do this again sometime. I enjoyed our little chat. Perhaps I'll find out more about your life and loves."

Deborah smiled, gave Sue-Ellen a hug, and watched the domineering, wealthy woman drive away.

On the flight back to Miami, Deborah thought about their conversation. Was Stephen Tuple a hen-pecked husband, forced to kowtow to the demands of a wife who held the purse strings? If so, it could only lead to disaster unless they separated.

Deborah had come across this situation many times in her marriage guidance work. The bottom line was always the same: unless common ground could be found and respected, separation was better for all concerned.

She had considered saying as much to Sue-Ellen but decided it wasn't her place to intrude. She would seek advice from one of the counsellors in Pine Grove Springs and pass on whatever friendly professional advice she could.

There was much to talk about when Geoffrey returned from the Cape. He seemed to be in a better frame of mind. So much so that an evening swim in the lake and a night of passionate lovemaking took up most of his two weeks' leave.

They made the most of their time together as a family before he went back to Cape Canaveral for six weeks. It was a time of sadness for Deborah, who longed for his next return. But Geoff, being Geoff, insisted on flying to Meridian to resume work at the log cabin.

Deborah smiled, and they agreed to meet in Idaho rather than her flying to Miami only to turn around again.

While organising granite blocks for the second tier with Boris, the station wagon skidded to a halt. Stevie Tuple jumped quickly from the driver's seat.

"Can I have a word with you in private, Miss Fox, if you don't mind?"

Deborah handed Boris the spirit level.

"Come up to the cabin. I'll put the kettle on. And please call me Deborah—or Miss Rupert."

"No cabin, Miss Fox. That is your true name. This is not a social or business call. We'll speak in the station wagon, where we have a witness working close by."

Deborah saw from his angry mood that something serious was on his mind. When they were settled, Stephen Tuple began.

"I understand you and my wife met recently and discussed my marriage. She told you about a baby she miscarried, about our faith preventing divorce, and about my so-called flashing."

"Where did you get this from, Stephen? I hardly think your wife would disclose our conversation. And you can't deny you were exposing yourself at the waterfall; I saw you with my own eyes."

"Do you have proof of that, Miss Fox? I don't recall anyone else around at the time. I was simply having a shower to wash off cement. I had no idea you were watching me, and should it ever come to court, it would be my word against yours. Then there is another scenario—if you did see me nude, why didn't you walk away? There are plenty of rooms in the cabin with no view of the waterfall." He paused.

"Let's talk about this so-called miscarriage. There was no baby, there was no miscarriage. Sue-Ellen was trying to gain your sympathy, to gain your support. If you can't understand why, then you're more naïve than I thought."

"That's unfair, Tuple, and this conversation ends now." Deborah reached for the door handle.

"Not until I give you the facts, Miss Fox." He lowered his voice. "My wife Sue-Ellen is a lesbian, preparing an assignation with you. Are you a lesbian? Did you give her encouragement? Personally, I don't think so; you've had a lucky escape. I know Sue-Ellen has drugged other women and taken advantage of them in the past.

"Now let's talk about me and my wife. She thinks she holds all the cards with her wealth, but I've played my own game. I let her cover my casino losses, but I never told her how much I won and stashed away. Shirts, ties, shoes, cars—they've all brought in a tidy sum. Then there are the business profits. This is what Sue-Ellen doesn't understand. One day, when I'm ready, I'll pull the plug on our marriage and sod the lot of them.

"One more thing before I go. Yes, I go to the swimming clubs—but with my girlfriend. That's right, Miss Fox, my girlfriend—the same one Sue-Ellen once tried to ensnare."

"I want you and your labourers off this site, Tuple, and I'll explain my actions to my husband when he arrives tomorrow."

"Don't be stupid all your life, Miss Fox. We have a contract signed and sealed by our solicitors. Any move like that would cost you dearly." He started up the vehicle.

He looked at her with contempt. "Be careful, Deborah. Those woods are full of wild animals. Accidents can happen. I'll be over this afternoon to remove the last of the shuttering, and there will be no cold shower."

He gave her a wry smile before driving away.

She was visibly shaken, wondering where he had got the information from. He had probably got it from his wife, threatening her as he had just now.

All she could do was go back to work on the granite blocks for the second tier. Slowly but surely, they were put into place, and the terraces were completed. She drove to Meridian airport to collect Geoffrey.

They talked about the log cabin and what had been done. Deborah said nothing about the altercation with Stephen Tuple.

All they needed now was the last of the shuttering to be removed and the tilers to complete the swimming pool with its large blue dolphin in the tiled depths.

Things always seemed to move faster when Geoffrey was around.

They pegged out the extension and dug out the foundations. The concrete was laid in preparation for the long timber logs that were coming from Wyoming.

"I think we can leave this job until next year, Debs. The foliage is starting to turn brown. That is why I want the oil-fired heating boiler and the generator installed before the end of the autumn and winter begins to bite. That gives us a chance to install the central heating. We can also work on a new bathroom and shower," he said, smiling.

"I've got to hand it to you, Debs. I'm impressed with the work that has been done. I always knew I had a winner when I met you."

Deborah went to give him a hug and lead him to the couch.

"None of that, precious. There is still some light left in the Idaho sky. I'll couple up the water pipe to the tank and the two ends at the gable. I might even have time to fit a stop valve at the eco-pond. Then we can let the pond fill slowly overnight."

Deborah noticed it was a stranger who dismantled the last of the shuttering and loaded the wood onto the station wagon.

She set about preparing the evening meal.

Geoff came in rubbing his hands. "It's all systems go, darling. The eco-pond is now filling up. We can bring some fish and pond grass on our next visit."

Deborah hugged him tightly before they sat down to dinner with wine. She tried to find the right moment to tell him about Sue-Ellen and the threat made by Stephen Tuple, but she could not bring herself to disclose what was said. It would only break their happy time together, which was few and far between. She poured another two glasses of wine.

***

It was a romantic setting in the lounge of the log cabin, candles flickering and a log fire softly burning. But they were both so tired that it was a race for the couch to see who would be asleep first.

Geoff suggested that, now the underfloor work had been completed, it might be time to start thinking about furniture and carpets. A bed would be their priority.

The first week had gone by so quickly. Geoff had laid all the underfloor central-heating and water-supply pipes. Drainage for the en-suite bedrooms was a massive undertaking. He also had the electric cables fixed to the joists, ready to connect to the lights, the switches and the wall plugs.

Deborah had hung a few radiators, and Geoff connected the tails to the flow and return valves. Outside, the housing for the generator was complete. The electric cables were connected to the generator. A large hot-water cylinder was installed in an airing cupboard.

There was still some work to be done in the interior.

Once again, time was the enemy when Geoff had to return to Cape Canaveral.

The eco-pond was looking fantastic and, overnight, had attracted dragonflies, while a bullfrog was hopping on the embankment. Birds hovered, hoping to catch a worm on the sloping grass or a fly from the pond.

Before he departed, he pointed to the fir trees close to the eco-pond. "Perhaps some coloured fairy lights on the trees will help illuminate the pond when it freezes and give the skaters some light. We can't rely on Diana, the Moon Goddess, to light the way all the time."

Deborah could only smile at his future vision.

After she had dropped Geoff at the airport, she went to an aquarium shop and purchased various species of fish, pond grass and fish food. She also bought some ornaments to finish the eco-pond surrounds.

She considered what Geoff had said about the fairy lights, but decided to leave that until the winter, which was approaching rapidly.

The children seemed to swallow up the years. Now at high school, they insisted on coming to Idaho for the holidays to witness for themselves the finished article of the log cabin, now that the extension had been completed and furnished. They had witnessed the marvellous achievement by their parents while construction work was still underway. They enjoyed the deep-snow winters and ice-skating on the eco-pond. The visits deep into the magic forest, where Geoffrey teased them about fairies and goblins, came with the rule that they must not venture far without an adult.

This always made Mary-Beth twitchy about going further. Isabella was more adventurous, as was their brother Timothy. The two would hide out of sight and then spring from behind a tree on their nervous sister. They were told to behave and threatened with no more visits because it was giving Mary-Beth nightmares.

In general, life at the log cabin was relaxing and educational, with many tasks still to perform. It was Timmy who suggested cutting down the forest that surrounded the cabin.

Deborah and Geoff remonstrated. "You'll do no such thing, Timothy, even after we've gone. This is a paradise of ecological importance, a place where your children and your children's children can enjoy the surroundings and the clean, unpolluted air."

Geoff added, "Besides, the forest protects the log cabin in the fiercest of winters. So no more talk of cutting down trees."

There were always the expressive talks on a winter's night around the log fire.

It came as a surprise to Deborah and Geoff to find that the last enemy, time, had played a cruel trick on them. Boy meets girl, girl meets boy. Marriage proposals made and accepted.

Each of the marriage ceremonies was held in Pine Grove Springs. Only Isabella and her husband honeymooned at the log cabin.

Then time proved a gift when each of the children announced their wives were pregnant and expecting a baby.

Deborah and Geoff were over the moon each time the patter of tiny feet ran across the lounge or the porch.

It was on a visit to Idaho that Timmy broke the sudden, unwanted news. "I've passed my medical and received my draft call-up papers for Vietnam."

Both parents were stunned into silence, then shocked.

Geoffrey broke the silence. "That's not possible, Timmy. You have an important job on the home front in the Boeing aircraft factory. I'll see to it that those papers are withdrawn."

"Please don't do that, Dad. As you know, I already have my pilot's licence, and I begin training on Angel Interceptors in two weeks. They're a lovely aeroplane—fast and deadly. We'll soon show Uncle Ho Chi Minh what he's up against."

There were wry smiles all round before Timmy and his wife, Marge, went to bed.

Geoffrey stood at their bedroom door. "Is there nothing we can say or do to make you change your mind, Timothy?"

Timmy just switched out the light and turned to face Marge.

The next morning, Timmy and Marge, with their two children, jumped into the station wagon and were driven to the airport, where there were lots of hugs and kisses with messages of "Write often and stay safe."

Deborah and Geoff watched as the aircraft lifted into the blue Idaho sky.

Geoff said nothing, but deep down, he had a bad sense of foreboding. He kept his hands in his coat pockets as if bracing against a wind that wasn't there, eyes fixed on the vanishing speck until it was lost to glare.

Deborah seized him by the arm. "Come, darling, let's buy some more tropical fish."

It was a sad moment they shared together. Timmy would serve a year in 'Nam, or fifty missions, whichever came first.

They both agreed that Marge and the children would not miss out; they would be flown to Idaho regularly.

There were other tasks to be carried out at the cabin. First was the road surface. It was widened and tarred, which made the drive through the forest to the main highway more pleasurable. An electricity cable was laid to the substations, then on to the cabin, where it was linked to the existing cabin cable. The generator was kept as a standby in case a bolt of lightning hit one of the substations. On stormy nights, Deborah still preferred the friendly thrum of the generator, a reassurance beneath the rain.

It was also agreed that a telephone line should be installed while they had a trench open. That brought the renovation work on the log cabin to an end.

There was a tearful goodbye to Timmy at Miami airport, where he boarded a flight to London before joining a United States aircraft carrier to complete the journey to Vietnam.

There were mixed emotions in the early years about the war taking place so far away. It would prove a futile effort for those who fell in that foreign land. The Ho Chi Minh Trail had been destroyed several times, in different areas and at great cost, only to be repaired quickly, allowing the transportation of supplies once more towards South Vietnam.

Deborah followed the war news in the papers each morning, circling articles with a trembling hand as if doing so might somehow keep Timmy safe.

# Chapter 12 – America and Uncertain Futures

Deborah was dusting and wiping down the window ledges in the lounge when she saw the black car with its Air Force flags fluttering on the wings approach the log cabin.

Her first thought was that Timmy had completed his fifty missions and that he and the family had driven out to the cabin to surprise her. She just wished Geoff could be there to share this wonderful moment.

She stepped out onto the porch veranda, wiping her hands on her apron.

That was when she saw two Air Force officers step out of the car. She was suddenly shaken as they walked up the steps, with one of them clutching a brown envelope.

"Good afternoon, ma'am. We called at Pine Grove Springs and, with nobody there, we phoned your husband, who will fly out to Idaho tonight."

Deborah realised it must be serious. She wiped her hands on her apron, then dropped to her knees and cried.

"Please tell me Timmy is safe. Please, I've got to know."

There was a heavy silence before one of the officers lifted her up and spoke gently.

"It's best if we talk inside over a strong cup of tea, ma'am."

They went inside, and Deborah insisted on making the tea. It helped her prepare for what was to come, though she could barely hold her cup and saucer.

The officer handed her the War Department letter. How many letters like this had she sent to the United States during the Second World War while working at the American Air Force offices in Welwyn, England? Airman missing, believed killed in action. Sad memories came flooding back like ghosts from another lifetime.

"Flight Lieutenant Timothy Bunter was shot down over the Vietnamese jungle close to the Demilitarised Zone, known as the DMZ line for short. It's confirmed that he ejected safely and his parachute opened. After that, nothing. Helicopters swept the area where he went down, but gave up when they came under heavy fire. The letter explains he's missing in action, believed dead."

Deborah sat up in hope. "So, it's possible he might be hiding somewhere in the jungle, perhaps taken prisoner by Viet Cong forces?"

The officer lifted his hand. "I wouldn't like to build up your hopes. We know what the North Vietnamese do to airmen who bomb their towns and cities. They play a game called Russian roulette. Sooner or later, the prisoner shoots himself in the temple."

Deborah took heart, though visibly shaken by the thought of Timmy being alive in some prisoner-of-war camp. It had happened to her first husband during the Second World War. Why could it not happen again? She felt sick, her heart twisting painfully in her chest.

The Air Force officers finished their tea.

"If we do hear anything, you'll be the first to know, Mrs Bunter." She watched them drive away, forgetting to thank them for their personal touch. Most families just received a telegram with a few cold lines.

The telephone rang loudly. It was a sympathy call from Geoffrey, explaining that Marge and the children had been picked up and were at Miami Airport, ready to catch their flight.

She washed her face before going to collect them. It was a long, lonely, and sorrowful drive that seemed to last forever.

It was a tearful reunion as the family walked out of the customs area into the Meridian Airport concourse. Hugs and kisses flowed freely. Deborah took the child from Marge, wondering how many other families were enduring the same sadness—the loss of a son, a brother, or a friend—as the Vietnam War took its toll on American boys.

There was one thing for sure: the American public would not stand for this Asian war. Already, there were signs of growing discontent among peace protesters determined to carry their message to the White House, the Pentagon, and missile plants.

On the solemn drive back to the log cabin, Geoffrey broke the silence, if only to speak. "I think the American military have a problem with the Vietnam War that isn't going to go away. The demonstrations we hear about are growing by the day." He hesitated. "Never mind—our great American nation has something in the bag to cheer everyone up."

"Please tell us, Geoff," Marge asked, tears in her eyes.

"Sorry, it's all hush-hush at the moment. But my family will be one of the first to know before the news breaks."

"That's typical of you, Geoffrey Bunter—building us up only to let us down. Don't forget, we have spare rooms at the cabin."

Deborah was only trying to lighten the mood. Mary-Beth was the only one who smiled and added, "I suppose there's always the station wagon."

The family gathering at the log cabin turned out to be a surprisingly positive occasion despite the news about Timmy. Geoffrey and Deborah knew they had to face facts and accept what had happened. But not Marge. She was seething—why had her husband been sent overseas to fight a war for a corrupt government?

It broke in The Washington Post and The New York Times that the South Vietnamese Government was riddled with corruption right up to the presidential level.

"Is it to stop Communism spreading, Geoff? Is that the real reason our boys are over there?" Marge paced the lounge. "When I get back to Miami, I'm going to join the peace movement."

Geoff smiled. "Sit down, Marge. You're wearing out the carpet."

The time at the cabin helped them through the initial shock of Timmy being shot down, although the mourning still lingered. Days blurred into nights, marked by silence and whispered prayers.

The compassionate leave granted by Boeing International was ending, and Geoff had to return to Cape Canaveral by Friday. The women and children stayed on for another two weeks, trying to recover from the devastating news.

Now it was time to face reality.

Deborah had a business to run. Isabella and Mary-Beth had husbands and families to care for. Marge had her two young children, now without a father.

On returning to Miami, Marge joined a "Bring Our Troops Home" group of hippies, who seemed to be the only ones brave enough to get the message across to the White House.

Marjory Bunter was arrested and charged with causing an obstruction on a public highway. Resisting arrest was added to the charge sheet.

The judge was sympathetic to her reasons but warned that if she appeared before the court again, she would be jailed and her children taken into care.

This brought an abrupt end to her radical activism. She would have to fight the cause legally, believing that the pen was always mightier than the sword.

She founded a group for women whose husbands had been killed, wounded, or gone missing in action. She always made sure that, when she stood on her soapbox objecting to the war, television and media coverage were recording the throng of protestors.

Marge Bunter became a well-known voice for the anti-war movement. She could see how much the warmongers and the U.S. Government loathed her actions, which were gaining momentum throughout the United States and abroad.

All the while, the American death toll escalated. She was sick to the back teeth of the lies and false reports given to the press, declaring how the war was being "won" by coalition forces. Deep down, she knew there would be more heartbreak before the war ended.

Once again, it was Geoff who came to her rescue when she had overstepped the line.

Then came great news for the family after such a grim winter—an invitation to witness the launch of Apollo 11 from the Cape Canaveral Space Centre viewing room. Geoffrey would be with the other technicians in mission control.

The Bunter family would be privileged guests, alongside the astronauts' wives and other engineers' families.

Geoffrey gave them a rundown of the programme once they were safely inside the Space Centre and all communication devices with the outside world had been removed.

"The rocket will be powered by a Saturn V booster, which Ernst von Braun and I have been working on for the past few years. The three astronauts are Commander Neil Armstrong, Lunar Module Pilot Edwin 'Buzz' Aldrin, and Command Module Pilot Michael Collins. It's hoped that Neil will be the first human to step onto the Moon's surface. Beyond that, I can't say much more. We have timings for each stage of the mission and hope everything goes according to plan.

"When the rocket fires and lift-off is complete, you'll be taken to a hotel where you can watch the mission unfold and see the capsule's return to Earth. I must leave you now, but you'll be well looked after."

Geoff didn't linger; he left the excited families chatting among themselves.

Now Deborah understood the reason for Geoff's long absences from home—something the other wives had also endured. She found it strange that Marge had refused to attend such an important event in American history.

The launch of Apollo 11 was spectacular. Everyone sat in awe as the rocket separated from the towers and lifted into a cloudless sky. The flames became a pinprick against the atmosphere before disappearing completely. A sense of pride and wonder filled the air.

The coach drive to the Ambassador Hotel was lively. They were handed flutes of champagne and strawberries, followed by a buffet. Then they were shown to a large room where a television had been set up with a direct link to mission control.

Deborah was immensely proud of her partner, Geoffrey Bunter—the man who had come from an aircraft factory in Hatfield, England, to become a leading propulsion engineer contributing to one of humanity's greatest achievements.

She made sure to reserve a prime seat for herself and the children. It was strange how she still thought of Mary-Beth and Isabella as children. She gave a wry smile as the conversation shifted from the space programme to the astronauts themselves.

The wives listened intently as the space module circled the Earth in an orbit of 114 to 116 miles above the planet. Communication was lost whenever it passed behind the dark side of the Earth, and later, the Moon.

The mission took three days, three hours, and fifty-six minutes to reach the lunar surface. They listened in awe to the message from Houston: "The Eagle has landed."

Then came the transmission that would go down in history— Commander Neil Armstrong's voice as he descended the ladder towards the Moon's surface.

"That's one small step for a man… one giant leap for mankind."

A thunderous cheer erupted from every room in the hotel. Even the staff stopped what they were doing to join in, many wiping away tears of pride.

There was still work to be done: samples of moon rock were collected, and the American Stars and Stripes was planted firmly into the lunar soil. The module then lifted off from the Moon's surface—that too went smoothly. The astronauts were soon back in orbit, setting a trajectory to re-enter the Earth's atmosphere.

Everyone knew this was the most dangerous part of the entire mission. Would the heat shields survive the inferno as the capsule hurtled back to Earth?

There was another collective gasp of suspense, followed by a roar of relief when, after seconds of silence, three vast parachutes opened and slowed the capsule's descent into the ocean. Divers and rescue boats were quickly on the scene, transferring the astronauts to a waiting ship.

A final cheer resounded when the capsule hatch opened and the first astronaut appeared, giving a weary wave to the world. It was a moment humanity would never forget.

Deborah gathered the family close and told them she had a few matters to attend to before returning to Pine Grove Springs. Once the business was checked, she said, they would head to Idaho and the log cabin—that peaceful haven which, she mused, shared its name with the landing site on the Moon: the Sea of Tranquillity. "What an apt name," she said with a soft smile to the children.

She was driven from Cape Kennedy back to Miami, where she asked the driver to drop her at an address in the city centre.

Taking the escalator to the fourth floor, she found apartment 407 and knocked softly. When there was no response, she knocked louder.

The door opened slightly, and a bedraggled-looking woman peered out. "Yes, what do you want?" she asked sharply, then gasped. "This isn't a good time, Deborah."

Deborah Rupert had not been an inspector's wife for years without picking up a few of his habits—and right now, she smelled a rat. She brushed her greasy-haired daughter-in-law, Marjory, aside and stepped into the muggy, stale-smelling living room. Overflowing ashtrays littered the table, and dirty dishes were piled high. Pizza boxes were strewn across the floor.

Deborah couldn't believe what she was seeing.

"I came to find out the real reason you didn't come to the Apollo launch. But now I can see it with my own eyes."

She stopped short when she heard a lazy male voice drawl from the bedroom, "Get rid of them, Margie, and come back to bed."

Deborah picked up a walking cane from the hall stand and stormed into the bedroom.

A long-haired, bearded hippie sat up abruptly. Deborah noticed a Jamaican cigarette smouldering in an ashtray, filling the room with the sweet, pungent scent of marijuana.

Without hesitation, she brought the cane down across his head several times before he leapt naked from the bed. "Hey! What gives, lady? You want a go with me, is that it?"

Deborah struck him again. "That's my son's bed you've been abusing, you filthy moron! Now get dressed—and if I ever see you here again, make sure your life insurance is up to date!"

The hippie scrambled into his jeans and shirt, hopping awkwardly towards the door without so much as a goodbye to Margie.

Deborah snapped the cane in two and threw it to the floor.

"Get yourself into the shower, Marjory. Then we'll talk."

She began by drawing the curtains and opening the windows to air out the stench. She cleared the lounge of dirty plates and fast-food boxes, her anger simmering under the surface. Then she walked back into the bedroom, extinguished the half-smoked joint, and opened the curtains wide to let in some light.

Marge appeared moments later, head bowed. Deborah grabbed her by the robe and shook her violently.

"Now you listen to me, Marjory Bunter—and you'd better listen well." She paused, her voice trembling with fury. "I will not allow you to drag my dead son's name through the gutter—not by you, or by anyone else. Now hear this, because it's the important part."

She held Marge tightly. "You'll clean this apartment until it's spotless and ready for sale. You'll put it on the market through an estate agent and buy a small bungalow in the suburbs. You'll stop living with that hippie commune and get off those drugs. No more soapbox protests or street demonstrations—I won't have my son's children put into care while you rot in a jail cell."

She gave her daughter-in-law another hard shake. "If you carry out what I've said, you'll always be welcome at the log cabin. But if you fail in any way, you'll find yourself in the belly of an alligator in the Everglades. Do I make myself clear, Marjory?"

Deborah released her grip, her breath shaking. "If you need help in any way, the Bunter family will always be by your side. The children are welcome in Idaho—that goes without saying."

She turned at the bedroom door and pointed at the distraught woman. "Make sure you follow my instructions, because I'll be watching you from now on."

Deborah was trembling as she descended the stairs. She couldn't wait to have Geoff by her side again at the log cabin.

After completing her business errands, she made her way to Idaho.

Summer was giving way to autumn—the green leaves turning golden brown and drifting lazily from the trees. Geoffrey had been held back at Cape Kennedy for debriefing and analysis of the Apollo mission.

When he finally arrived at Meridian Airport, he looked exhausted, dark shadows evident beneath his eyes. The drive from the airport was quiet, but the nearer they came to the cabin, the more Geoff began to speak.

"Do you know, darling, that the astronauts' return journey took two days, twenty-two hours, and fifty-six minutes? The overall mission—including their time on the lunar surface—lasted four days, six hours, and forty-five minutes."

She smiled knowingly. Geoff was blowing off steam.

"It was a marvellous achievement—true teamwork. It must have been intense, being locked in mission control for so long. But let's leave all that behind for now. A few days by the pool and a sauna will soon have you back to your old, grumpy self."

They both laughed heartily, their laughter echoing around the cabin and breaking weeks of heaviness.

Deborah decided to keep her discovery about Marjory to herself, at least until Geoff had fully recuperated.

He did recover and resumed his work at the Cape. The years drifted by, still with no word from the War Department regarding their son.

Meanwhile, political unrest grew on the home front.

A break-in at the government's Watergate offices inspired two investigative journalists from The Washington Post to look deeper into what was initially dismissed as a faulty alarm. They pursued the story with persistence and professionalism, uncovering layers of deceit and corruption.

Their determination finally paid off. On 11 January 1973, The Washington Post published a story about five men convicted of breaking into the Watergate offices to retrieve documents for shredding.

From there, the scandal snowballed through the corridors of power, leading to resignations, jail terms, and fines. By 1975, the illegal fundraising accusations were proven, and the stench of corruption began to fade into history.

During those three years, The Washington Post sold more newspapers than ever before—and probably ever would again.

On one of his visits home, Geoff and Debs sat in the lounge discussing the war that still raged in Vietnam. "Tricky Dickie"—President Richard Nixon—was the topic of the evening, and how he had tried to cover up the Watergate affair. There were now widespread calls for his resignation.

He refused to step down—that was on 6 August 1974. But not even his promise to bring American boys home from Vietnam could save him.

He was forced to resign on 9 August 1974.

At noon that same day, Gerald Ford was sworn in as the 38th President of the United States of America.

Geoff had taken to a pipe or his Havana cigars with a brandy and soda. The sweet, woody smoke seemed to soften the sharp edge of the news bulletins that never quite left their living room.

"We're losing this Vietnam War, Debs. It's been on the cards for some time now. These past six years, from the 1967 and 1968 offensives by the North Vietnamese Army onwards, there has been a steady decline in our ability to hold back the tide and the tactics of the Viet Cong, who are using guerrilla warfare, hit and run, then merge into the jungle. Tunnels below ground where they can eat and sleep, sheltering them from bombs. Their booby traps. But the most important reason we're losing this Asian war, though it goes without saying, is the media firing up political hatred against the war. Unemployed hippies protesting on our streets.

"War is a high debate in domestic and political life and plays a large part. I think the latter will bring the curtain down. How can our boys keep up morale when activists are burning the American flag in public? What those people don't understand is this." He paused.

"The South Vietnamese are determined to stop the spread of Communism. The French tried and failed. If we lose this war, it will make the Far East unstable." He paused again. "Talking of activists, what's happened to Marge? I noticed she wasn't at the launch. I don't see much of her on the TV these days, and when was she last at the cabin?"

Deborah knew the question would come and was ready to give Geoff an explanation.

"I meant to ask each Christmas when the children were here, but no Marge. Other things came to mind, and it was dismissed."

He looked puzzled, and Deborah explained the situation that had now been resolved.

"Well, she's the loser in all this, but I think we should give her a second chance, even if it's for the children's sake and the Christmas holidays at the log cabin. I'll see to it when I find the time."

He smiled. "Do you know what those doodlers in the Senate are doing? They're changing the name of Cape Kennedy back to Cape Canaveral. I wonder which one of those prats thought this up. Democrat or Republican?" He sipped his cognac.

"Do you know it was a Spanish explorer called Juan Ponce de León who landed on the peninsula in 1513 and named it Canaveral, which means barren, sandy scrubland? It wasn't until the start of the Second World War that it was turned into a military base."

"I think that Brandy is going to your head, Mr Bunter. Let's go to bed, where I can give you lessons on how to treat a sensual woman." Deborah giggled as Geoff downed the cognac and led her by the hand to their king-size bed.

There was not much happening in the lunar programme. Geoff had returned to the Boeing factory, in charge of redesigning aircraft engines, something he was very good at. It wasn't long before he was elevated from the shop floor to managerial status, in charge of production and sales.

The new year of 1975 brought hope for peace in that far-off, often forgotten land. President Ford had stood by his promise. The military were brought home, leaving behind war material of unimaginable cost, but the retreat left hundreds of thousands trapped in a country that had not wanted Communism. The Vietnam War ended on 30 April 1975 when North Vietnamese Army tanks rolled through the presidential palace gates in Saigon, South Vietnam.

A deal had been struck with the Viet Cong that American investigators would seek to find the remains of American servicemen. Of the sixty-three bodies recovered, Flight Lieutenant Timothy Bunter was among them.

There were still 1,244 servicemen unaccounted for. There were 470 bodies classed as non-recoverable.

The war's casualties had taken a brutal toll. A government survey showed the cost of the Vietnam War in human terms:

Killed in action: 42,240

Died of wounds: 5,451

Captured, declared dead: 151

Missing in action, declared dead: 1,085

The VC Spring Offensive of 1967 claimed the lives of 11,363 Americans.

The VC Spring Offensive of 1968 claimed the lives of 16,899 Americans, the biggest loss of life in a single campaign throughout the entire war.

There was no mention of the South Vietnamese losses. Deborah read the figures twice. Numbers on a page felt cold, yet every one of them belonged to a family that would set an extra place no more.

Deborah and Geoffrey were simply glad that they had the body of their son to bury at home in the United States. There would be many families still grieving, living in hope that their loved one would come back from Vietnam.

Timothy Bunter and his countrymen's remains were taken to the forensics department in Hawaii for identification. Their remains were then flown to the nearest airport to their homes.

The Bunter family, dressed in black, watched as Timmy's coffin, draped with the American flag, was unloaded from the military cargo aeroplane and placed in the hearse. The drive north to Pine Grove Springs was a sad but, in a way, relieved journey.

Flight Lieutenant Timothy "Timmy" Bunter was laid to rest in the town cemetery. Six Marines fired into the air as he was lowered to eternal rest. Deborah was the last to throw earth and her rose onto the coffin as the large crowd dispersed.

As time passed, there was more sad news for Deborah. It was her daughter, April in the UK, who telephoned with the news. Her retired ex-husband, Inspector Amadeus Rupert of the Metropolitan Police in London, had passed away peacefully at his castle in Cambridgeshire.

Deborah gave a wry smile at his title, "Lord Rupert of Beech-Tree Estate." She wondered if the title had been his wish; she doubted it very much. That was not how Amadeus Rupert had lived his life. He had no time for promotion or titles. He was a down-to-earth copper, and a good one. In retirement, he would have been sadly missed. Now one of the world's gems had gone.

Deborah and the girls flew to London for the funeral. There were many hugs from Colin, her son, and April, her daughter, before they set off for Cambridge.

The funeral service took place at the cathedral, followed by interment at the Beech-Tree Castle estate in Cambridge, where a mausoleum had been built to inter the Rupert family.

The journey back to the States on the QE2 seemed to take forever, and the trio was glad when the ship docked in New York. As planned, they did some shopping before flying down to Miami, where they were met by Geoff.

The years went by as usual, but with few events. The family had moved on. The country had moved on.

Marjory had remarried. Deborah didn't know how to take it at first, but Geoffrey told her in no uncertain terms that it was for the best. Geoffrey continued abruptly, "Marge and Johnny Roth will be made welcome here in Pine Grove Springs and at the log cabin in Idaho for the family get-together at Christmas." Deborah could only agree.

The winter brought cold weather that froze the eco-pond. The family was delighted and used the skating rink often, teaching the great-grandchildren to skate. There was much laughter and hilarity when the youngsters tumbled onto the ice and tried to get up.

Deborah and Geoff sat with their Scottish tartan travel rugs in their rocking chairs on the porch, listening to the joy coming from the ice rink.

"We've been very fortunate in our lives, Debbs. A lovely family of kids, grandkids, and great-grandkids. What more could we ask for?"

Deborah nodded, but her mind searched for the words to explain about their children—how she had deceived her devoted husband all those years.

"Geoffrey, there is something very important I must tell you about the children."

Geoff took a sip of his brandy and blew smoke rings into the air before speaking. He held up his hand. "I know what you're going to say, Debbs. I'm just as much to blame as you. However, before I continue, I want you to promise me that the children will never know the truth."

Deborah was about to speak.

"Let me finish, please." Geoff paused, puffing on his Havana cigar. "I've known from the first day I met you that I could never father children. This showed up in my medical all those years ago when I applied for the job with Boeing International. Therefore, when you told me you were pregnant, I knew the children weren't mine. I had a low sperm count. Infertile, barren, was how the medical examiner put it. This is where I must apologise for my deception over all those years that have slipped by us.

"I wanted children. Boeing International liked their workforce to have a settled relationship and a family life. Therefore, I went along with it until now." He hesitated. "I don't want to know who the father is, or was, but I have my suspicions. I hope we can put this behind us forever, Debs. You have your secrets, I have mine."

Deborah nodded her appreciation. "Let's go inside and enjoy the log fire while it lasts."

She took the empty glass from the man she had learned and grown to love. They walked into the log cabin and sat by the fire, talking.

The door opened, and one of the grandchildren spoke with excitement. "Grandpa, Grandma, it's starting to snow."

Geoff took the young boy onto his lap. He spoke softly. "The clouds over the Bitterroot Mountains have been growing darker every day. I think we're in for a heavy snowfall. If it snows heavily enough tonight, we'll build a snowman tomorrow. Now close the door gently on your way out."

He rose lethargically from the chair and took Deborah's spectacles from her nose. He placed them on the mantelpiece. "You'll not need those any longer, my dear heart."

Deborah's head fell forward as if in sleep, but it was sleep she would never awaken from. There seemed to be a hush that fell over the log cabin. The skaters on the eco-pond sounded miles away as Geoffrey Bunter went onto the porch to inform his family of Deborah's passing. Outside, the first flakes thickened and began to settle, and the world seemed to grow quieter with every soft drift of white.

After a crowded church service, Deborah Rupert Buntin was laid to rest beside her beloved son, Timmy. Geoffrey would eventually join them, and their spirits would fly above their eco-friendly log cabin in the forests and mountains of Idaho.

# The End

# Worlds Turn – Worlds Burn

# Chapter 13 - The Gathering Storm

The UK scientists met with heavy hearts at their hurriedly arranged meeting. They were preparing for the world's scientific convention to be held in Copenhagen in October of the same year, 2045. But there were much more important things to be discussed in their secret agenda. The world had become a very unstable place to live, despite the repeated threats of nuclear war that had kept Planet Earth at a so-called peace for one hundred years. It had now become obvious that the superpowers were expanding their race to reach other planets in the solar system, even though much of our own universe was uninhabitable and could not support life as we know it. Planet Earth was a jewel in the crown, a miracle that formed 13.5 billion years ago in outer space after the Big Bang. It created our star, our universe, which gave Planet Earth life over millions of years. If only those leaders could see that the nuclear war clock had stopped ticking.

When first formed, the nuclear clock threat sat at fifty-eight minutes. Now it had stopped, bringing us closer to Armageddon, the destruction of humanity, where rats would have superiority over decaying corpses. The poor souls who went to work daily were oblivious to the rising tensions in the Middle East again, a conflict that had continued since "Mad Mitch" of the Argyll & Sutherland Highlanders was removed as peacekeeper because some deemed that he was far too harsh and brutal with the Palestinian Arabs. This led to chaos as the Palestinians fought tit-for-tat wars with Israel, the promised land. In the Far East, where Vietnam had been fought over at a heavy cost of lives and money, the forced withdrawal of American peacekeepers created problems for those who did not, and never would, accept Communism. Rising tensions in Korea threatened regional stability. Riots erupted in cities and towns around the globe. The United States, Russia, Great Britain and China remained on permanent nuclear red alert. It was only a matter of time before somebody pressed the button.

However, it was not the threat of a nuclear warhead strike that caused this meeting to be held. Another rocket, with its capsule attached, had been sent through the stratosphere and ozone layer that protected our planet from the dangers of solar winds, to explore planets in another constellation filled with trillions of worlds, each supported by billions of their own stars. Every time one of those rockets was launched, another part of Earth's ozone layer disappeared. Now there were several holes in the ozone layer—small holes, but holes nevertheless. Many UK scientists blamed this for the catastrophic disaster that would follow should countries around the globe not cease their quest to find another planet like our own, capable of supporting life. Did they have a crystal ball that was pointing ever closer to nuclear war? That was what the media were told when this urgent gathering was discovered and hastily convened.

However, this was not the real reason for the meeting. The scientists had discovered something at the far reaches of our universe—something far more catastrophic than nuclear war, if that was possible. This was why the hurriedly arranged scientific meeting was taking place in a Berlin opera house, attended by media representatives and government officials from around the world. Planet Neptune, the ice-covered gas giant furthest from our Sun, had moved out of its orbit. The intense gravitational pull of the other planets had combined to cause this freak accident. Slowly but surely, the gas giant moved closer to Uranus, which in turn would drift nearer to Saturn with its rings. Mars was next in line for a collision. The moons of Neptune would be the first to be destroyed, and every other planet's moons that orbited would be obliterated when the domino-effect collisions began. Earth's scientists were working frantically to find a solution, but there was none. Nobody could hold back the gravitational pull of those planets. It was inevitable that there would be one almighty collision and explosion in space. How it would affect Planet Earth was anyone's guess. But life on our planet would never be the same again if we were to survive the debris that would send fragments of meteors from the destroyed planets hurtling towards us. Some would be the size of golf balls; others could be the size of a football pitch or larger. According to history, a large meteor from outer space killed the dinosaurs.

Now Earth would be bombarded with meteors—how many, nobody could tell—but the top scientists decided to keep this catastrophe secret. Not even kings, queens or presidents of countries around the world would be informed, in case it caused widespread panic and disorder. The scientists knew what would happen if governments around the globe learned of an inevitable catastrophe. Noah's Ark shelters, built and mothballed in the past when nuclear war had been averted at the negotiating table, would need to be hurriedly reopened and restocked with water, food and medicine. These Ark shelters were arranged for those deemed fit to repopulate—male and female humans vetted and approved for having children. Young married couples with two children, one of each sex, who had already been selected, would be given new Ark passes. But to do this effectively would require time, and that would mean the scientists disclosing to the world what was to come. It was a dilemma: if humanity was to have any chance of survival, then nuclear shelters would need to be used.

The question was asked: how long would it be before the first planetary collision took place? Conrad Wilson was no expert in universal physics. His field was biochemistry, though he had also earned a PhD in engineering at Glasgow University. Over the years, he had developed a friendship with a space scientist named Nina MacSween from Inverness. That was why Conrad Wilson was voted in as chairman of the scientific meetings and made responsible for the Noah's Ark projects throughout the UK. A decision had been made at the Copenhagen summit to keep the discovery secret until the scientists were certain of what would hit Planet Earth, when the strikes would occur and where. But with the Berlin meeting, that was about to change. One thing they all agreed on was that there would be several meteor strikes worldwide.

The scientists discussed the problem at length. Some argued that everyone should be left to choose their own destiny—whether to live or die in the blast or in the radiation fallout that would follow, with the nuclear winter certain to ensue. Others believed the world should be told of their discovery. Many said they would prepare their families for a quick and painless death by poison before the meteors fell, a choice billions of human beings would never have. Conrad Wilson, a Scot, chaired the Berlin meeting. It was now clear that Neptune's moons had moved considerably closer to their mother planet. The gravitational pull of the gas giant was drawing them in daily. One moon had already crashed onto the surface, causing a massive explosion and opening deep fissures across Neptune's crust. The scientists could only hope that none of the countries exploring our universe had yet become aware of Neptune's instability. They knew they were playing God, and whatever decision they made carried immense weight. The vote, split narrowly, was to keep it secret until they were sure of the trajectories. They told the world that the Copenhagen Scientific Summit was in everyone's best interest, but was it really? Now the scientists could finally reveal what was happening in our troubled universe, and a huge burden would be lifted from their shoulders.

The situation grew increasingly grave as the weeks and months passed. Neptune's moons were now destroyed, the gas giant moving ever closer to the first moon of Uranus. Debris filled the heavens. Questions were being asked by NASA in the United States as to why this had been kept secret by the world's scientists. The cat was out of the bag. Other superpowers began to monitor Neptune's movement and demanded answers. A world summit of major governments was quickly arranged to be held in Berlin. Every scientist who had voted to postpone disclosure was ordered to attend. Unhealthy arguments broke out among them. Who had said what at Copenhagen? Who was for, and who was against, keeping the discovery secret? Repercussions were sure to follow.

What had emerged from the scientific convention in Copenhagen had already reached the front pages of *The New York Times* and *The Washington Post*: **"World Scientists Cover Up Global Armageddon."** The story spread rapidly across newspapers and media outlets worldwide. Conrad Wilson tried to appeal for calm at the Berlin summit. Film crews and reporters filled every corner of the hall. Berlin itself had practically come to a standstill despite its wide boulevards and avenues. He recalled the barmaid at his favourite Scottish inn, tucked away in the Small Glen of the Grampian Hills, calling out her familiar evening refrain: "Time, ladies and gentlemen, please." This time, he left out the "time."

"I have beside me a respected planetary and cosmos scientist called Nina MacSween, who is based at the scientific offices in York. Nina can explain in graphic detail much better than I can, so please lend her your ear."

Nina MacSween stood up. "Before I begin, I would like to confess that I voted to keep this catastrophic event secret from the world. We have tried to predict what would happen if the world knew what was to come, and why we wanted it to be kept secret until nearer the time of collision. There is just the slightest chance that Neptune could slide past Uranus and its moons. If that happens, our universe can —and will —breathe a sigh of relief. We are still waiting on trajectory results. We are also trying to establish when the collision with Uranus will happen if the information we have at present is correct. However, we must expect the worst. If there is a collision, there will be a loud bang that no one has ever experienced before. This means that fragments of both planets will enter outer space and scatter in different directions. It will result in a heavy bombardment of meteors, such as our universe has experienced in the past. For an example of the number of strikes, you only need to look at the surface of our own moon. That gives you an indication of what could happen to our planet."

She was interrupted. "When will this take place? How soon can we expect a meteor shower?" The question caused a commotion throughout the opera house. It came from a reporter somewhere in the packed stalls, where journalists and government officials sat with bated breath.

"I'm not prepared to speculate about dates and times." Nina took a sip of water. "If your government officials want something to take back to your bosses, then I would suggest you disarm your nuclear warheads that are housed in your launching silos. I would also defuse any warheads you have in storage. This will minimise the risk of a complete nuclear wipeout of your country should a meteor fall within a twenty-five-mile radius. If it's any consolation, our universe will not be the only one affected. Other constellations will also feel the effect, and it should be noted that our universe will be altered beyond comprehension."

She paused to sip her water again. "We know there is something which was under observation in 1964 called 'Cygnus X-1'—'The Swan.' It took physicists Stephen Hawking and Kip Thorne to establish that it was a black hole on 3 March 2021. However, it was Karl Schwarzschild's solution to a black hole, published in 1915, that led to Albert Einstein's theory of relativity proving that black holes exist in the cosmos. The closest black hole to Earth is Gala BH 1, located 1,560 light-years away. It was discovered by the European Space Agency (ESA) in 2022. To cut this explanation short, black holes draw in everything from space debris to planets, moons, stars, and even light. In time, our cosmos will grow dark—nothing but darkness, because the black holes will have swallowed everything up."

She took another sip of water. "However, that is not going to happen for billions of years to come. The reason I'm telling you this is simple. We humans are on a course to Armageddon. If not by destruction of the ozone layer through rockets, then nuclear war will be inevitable. When we first discovered the power of the atom in 1945, superpowers built up an arsenal of destructive weapons. Back then, the nuclear clock ticked away from the sixty-minute hour. It was down to four seconds in the 1990s. Now there is no time left, because the clock has reached zero seconds and stopped ticking. I feel I must say this—humanity has a better chance of survival when this catastrophic event takes place than we would have in a nuclear war created by ourselves."

She gave a wry smile. "Go home, open and stock up your Noah's Arks with the necessities for human survival. For those people who have nowhere to go, then build what we know as an

Anderson Shelter in your back garden. These were constructed during the Second World War with great effect, giving protection from bomb blasts. They're easy and cheap to build. The deeper the shelter, the better your family's chance of survival. What will follow is a nuclear winter that could last for two years. You should bear that in mind and prepare. I want everybody across the world to take advice from your governments, and good luck to all."

Nina MacSween sat down with a heavy heart.

Conrad Wilson stood up quickly before questions could be raised. "A statement of our findings will be sent to your governments. For those in the audience who want questions answered, our two coordinators will remain on the podium to tell you more." He paused. "One thing I must say, which I think is important—countries with international and private space stations should start immediately to bring the human Martians back on board and set their space bus on course back to Mother Earth. That said, I now bring this emergency summit to a close."

He grabbed his briefcase and took Nina by the arm. They left by the backdoor stage entrance, only to be met by irate reporters and film crews. A police cordon helped them reach their waiting taxi.

"Let's get back to the hotel and pack our cases before this disaster hits all the front pages. Time is of the essence, Nina. No makeup and no fond goodbyes—just get back to the taxi as quick as possible. I've a feeling things are going to get very nasty when the world population finds out what's in store for them."

They taxied to the hotel and instructed the driver to wait, then made a quick dash to the airport to catch the first available flight to the UK. Nina flew to East Midlands Bradford, while Conrad caught a flight to Edinburgh. They arranged to meet at the city of

Edinburgh's science laboratories. Conrad told her to catch the first flight or train to Edinburgh as soon as she had collected her work and her Noah's Ark pass. Without it, she would be left out in the cold.

Nina was adamant that she would fly to Inverness first to meet her parents, then travel to Edinburgh as instructed. Conrad had his own family to care for and meetings with other scientists in the city to attend.

On the drive from Edinburgh Airport to their home in Charlotte Square, his wife, Cathrine, asked, "Are things really as bad as what the media are saying, Conrad? It doesn't seem possible that our universe will be badly affected—and as far out into space as the Orion Constellation? It hardly seems credible that if Neptune collides with Uranus, different constellations in the cosmos will also be affected."

"Yes, Cathrine, that is how desperate it has become. When we get home, I want you to pack a large trunk of clothes for you and the children. Don't hesitate, because if the collision comes sooner than expected, we have less than a week to get you and the children settled into Noah's Ark in Holyrood Park. That's why I urge you to be ready tonight. You have your Ark passes, so make sure you carry them with you and keep them safe."

"Mm, I've been giving this a great deal of thought, Conrad, and I'm not sure I want us to be imprisoned in the Ark for two years— perhaps more." She paused. "They say there's a possibility that Neptune will miss Uranus and drift harmlessly into space. If that's the case, then why all this urgency?"

Conrad raised his voice. "My colleague Nina MacSween did say there was that possibility. But all she was doing at the emergency summit was trying to prevent the tabloids and TV networks from revealing what's to come—rioting, looting, anarchy. Please believe me when I say it's only a matter of time before the truth comes to light. Then all hell will break loose in the city. So do as I ask—get you and the children ready by tonight."

Cathrine pulled the electric Range Rover into a parking space beside their bungalow. She placed a hand on Conrad's thigh and spoke softly as he prepared to move. "Please, my darling, as I've said, I've given this a great deal of thought. I know you have a lot of work to do with scientific meetings and the Ark. That's why I'm taking the children to my parents in the Outer Hebrides. I'll feel much safer in Harris than I will anywhere else. I'm not going to put pressure on you to come with us because of your scientific commitment and workload."

She wiped the tears from her cheeks before continuing. "Will we meet again? Well, it's now in the laps of the gods. One thing I do ask is that we go to bed and make love like the very first time we met at university."

Conrad smiled. "Only if you promise to be on your way to catch the ferry in Ullapool early tomorrow morning."

They packed a large trunk, had a light meal and got the children settled down for the night. They went to bed. Conrad knew it would be for the last time. It had been a passionate night of lovemaking and endearments swapped until the grey light of dawn broke, with heavy rain battering the bedroom window.

Conrad was up and showered. He dressed the children, then went to the bedroom and gently touched his wife. "Time to go, darling. I've made your breakfast and laid out the children's cereals."

Cathrine stretched, then groaned when she looked at the time—5:30 AM. "Come back to bed, Conrad, we've plenty of time."

"That's one thing we don't have, Cathrine. The enemy of time dictates what we must and mustn't do. Besides, you'll need all your time to catch the ferry." He walked back to the kitchen.

It was a tearful goodbye from both camps. Conrad handed her a small tin box that contained five cyanide pills wrapped in cotton wool.

"Don't allow you or the children to suffer, Cathrine. I've given you two extras for your parents. You know what to do if times get tough."

He waved as he watched the electric Range Rover drive away, the taillights fading into the rain.

"Don't allow you or the children to suffer, Cathrine. I've given you two extras for your parents. You know what to do if times get tough."

He waved as he watched the electric Range Rover drive away. There was no time for sentiment; he had important work to do. He cycled to the scientific laboratories, where he learned that Nina MacSween was on her way from Waverley train station. It gave him great relief to know she would be at the laboratories sooner than expected, having travelled overnight from York.

He jumped on his scooter and drove down to Holyrood Park. It was early morning, and the city was still quiet. He noticed that the electric fence was being erected, and that the crash bollards had been set in concrete to protect the perimeter. Two machine gun towers stood tall on either side of the fence. Notices had been posted with a clear message in several languages—a threat and a warning:

**"Anyone crossing beyond the perimeter fence will be shot."**

Soldiers were already guarding the work in progress. Conrad showed his pass and walked into the Ark, where a hive of activity was underway as supplies were being put in place. Fuel tanks were being filled to capacity.

He moved through each apartment block, checking that furniture had been positioned in every unit. The hospital and operating theatre were checked for equipment, followed by the crematorium and furnace for disposing of the dead within the Ark. A small factory for making furniture and a lathe stood ready for use. There was a gymnasium, a laundry to keep the women occupied, a small cinema for showing films, and a theatre for plays and pantomimes.

A training room had been set aside for firefighting and equipment storage. The weapons arsenal was safely locked in the armoury. Geiger counters for measuring radiation levels were placed next to the space suits, which hung on pegs by the loading bay beside the electric scooter and the small double bomb-proof door for easy access. This would be where Conrad Wilson would venture out in two years to take radiation readings.

Nothing was left to chance, right down to the central office where the day-to-day running of the Ark would take place. He spent most of the morning inspecting various parts of the structure, ensuring that everything necessary for human survival was ready. For a moment, he paused, realising that despite the chaos outside, this subterranean refuge might be mankind's last hope.

Satisfied with the inspection, he jumped back onto the electric scooter and made his way to the laboratories, where he found a weary-looking traveller. Nina MacSween sat at a desk, drinking strong black coffee.

"Everything is ship-shape at Noah's Ark. What about you—have you anything to report?"

"I have the trajectory reports," she said, her voice flat with exhaustion. "Collision will take place by Tuesday next week. Our colleagues are certain that at least a quarter of the planet Uranus will be sliced off at its northern pole. If that happens, there's a slight possibility that there won't be as much debris coming our way. However, they've informed us that more fissures of escaping gas have broken from Neptune's crust to its surface. There's now a serious threat of explosion that could blow Uranus to smithereens, and that would be a massive problem for the other planets in our universe—including us. More debris, bigger meteorites... We'll be lucky if our planet survives."

"Thanks for that analysis, Nina. There's nothing we can do but hope." He smiled faintly.

"I have some personal news." He threw the Ark passes on the desk. "My wife has taken the children to her parents on the Isle of Harris. That, sadly, is her prerogative. I tried to change her mind last night when we discussed the situation in bed, but her mind was made up."

He lifted the passes again and handed them to her. "Give them to a healthy family or friends. Cathrine has no need for them now."

He turned away from his colleague to hide the tears forming in his eyes. For the first time, the weight of what was coming pressed on him with unbearable force.

***

248

As the week drew closer to collision day, pandemonium broke out on the streets of Edinburgh and beyond. TV reports now showed what was happening in the real world: motorways and interstate freeways ground to a halt, as people desperate to escape the cities did so.

It had come sooner than expected—a loud bang at 6:43 PM registering 12.9 on the Richter scale, which measured earthquakes. A serious earthquake was usually recorded between six and eight on the scale, but this one shook Planet Earth to its very core. Buildings collapsed, water mains burst, and traffic came to a standstill amid countless collisions. Aircraft taking off and coming in to land careered off the runways and exploded into flames.

This was only the beginning of the devastation.

Conrad and Nina grabbed their scientific documents and tools. They jumped onto the electric scooter and, avoiding traffic, drove down Leith Walk and along the promenade of Portobello towards the Ark in Holyrood Park. Their passes were thoroughly scrutinised before they were allowed past the perimeter fence.

As they entered, Conrad's phone rang. It was Cathrine, her voice trembling yet steady. She told him they had arrived safely in Harris. The relief was overwhelming—for a fleeting moment, amid the chaos, he allowed himself to exhale.

# Chapter 14 - Sealing The Ark

Now the Ark began to fill with families who held passes. They were handed a document upon entry through the second bomb-blast door. It explained how to behave: there was zero tolerance of bad or obnoxious conduct.

No smoking and no alcohol were allowed inside the Ark. Any attempt to smuggle either would result in immediate confiscation.

Firefighting classes would be held each week. Women were encouraged to take up yoga and exercise, and there was also the prospect of a career in nursing. Various pieces of advice were provided on how to survive during their stay underground until the bomb-blast doors of Noah's Ark could be safely reopened. Scientific advice estimated this would take two years.

The scientists' committee sat in the conference boardroom, watching the monitors closely. Cameras on the abandoned space stations were transmitting images of Neptune creeping closer to its neighbour—an enormous sphere that made Uranus appear like a dwarf planet. The scientists grew nervous as they watched Neptune's immense shadow engulf Uranus.

The end was near. People made a last, desperate effort to enter the Ark legally. Entry had to be accelerated before the military on duty became the last to enter, just before the two bomb-blast doors were sealed shut.

Then it happened, just as some of the scientists had predicted.

The collision sent Uranus spinning out of its natural orbit, slicing a third of its surface into smithereens. Then came the almighty explosion as Neptune, the gas giant, ignited. It must have been a spark that triggered the explosion, unleashing catastrophic results. The blast blew Uranus and its moons deep into space. Space stations filming the event vanished into the dark void.

The last images observed by the scientists came from the Mars Observation Centre before the strength of the blast obliterated the research stations. The pictures were spectacular—showing the rings of Saturn disintegrating as the planet struggled to remain in orbit. How far Saturn had shifted was pure conjecture. It was the sacrifice of Uranus and Saturn that ultimately shielded Jupiter, Mars, Earth, Venus, and Mercury, although all would later suffer meteor strikes.

Carried by the force of the blast, Uranus generated solar winds capable of reaching speeds of up to three hundred miles per hour on Earth, and up to a thousand miles per second in space.

Because the solar system is in constant motion, the closest Uranus ever gets to Earth is 1.6 billion miles; the furthest is 1.98 billion miles (3.2 billion kilometres)—small distances by cosmic standards.

There were approximately 2.6, perhaps a maximum of 3.2, hours before the first meteorite would fall. The question was—where in the world would it strike?

The Ark committee had already assembled. They sat with stern faces as Nina MacSween addressed them.

"As you know, this extraordinary event was caused by a shift in planetary alignment. All the planets that had been in line have now moved in our universe. I'll name those planets for anyone who doesn't fully understand what has occurred." She paused and pointed at the wall chart.

"Starting with those nearest the Sun and moving outward: we have Mercury, Venus, Earth, Mars, Jupiter, Saturn, Uranus, and Neptune. This is the trajectory Neptune took on its destructive path. However, Neptune cannot be blamed entirely for this catastrophe. Certainly, it played a major role, but when Mars, Jupiter, Saturn, and Uranus moved out of alignment, the gravitational forces between them created a massive energy swing. Together, they pulled Neptune out of its safe orbit towards Uranus.

"There will be a decrease in the wind force after the first meteor strikes Earth. My colleagues and I estimate this will occur within 2.5 to 2.8 hours. This is because the Earth is caught between time zones relative to Uranus. The rest, I'm afraid, you already know. I should add that, with so much debris floating through the universe, there is every reason to believe meteor strikes will continue for years to come—perhaps five to ten years into the future."

One of the medical doctors tapped his fingers on the table.

"As we can see from the security cameras outside, the situation at the restricted area is dire. There are already casualties from crushing and gunfire, and some people have been electrocuted on the fences. My concern is that people with Ark passes are caught in this chaos and cannot reach the security zone. I suggest we keep the Ark open until the deadline of 3.2 hours, giving them every possible chance of survival."

Conrad shook his head. "We cannot risk the Ark's destruction with its doors wide open. The mechanical process of sealing them takes time—exactly four minutes and eight seconds for both bomb-blast doors to close and lock. I know this sounds harsh, but do you want to live, or do you want to die? Those extra minutes and seconds could decide your fate." He began pacing around the oval table.

"Let's take a vote. No abstentions, please. We'll start with three hours to closure. Those in favour, raise your hands." He counted. "Three."

He stopped. "Now, 2.8 hours to closure." He counted again. "Six."

"And 2.5 hours to closure." Another count. "Six."

He paused. "Has anyone had a change of heart?" The committee sat glum-faced; no hands were raised.

"Alright, ladies and gentlemen, I cast my vote in favour of the latter. Closure begins in 2.5 hours. We must consider the time it took to assemble and convene this meeting, so in reality, we are already around 2.7 or 2.8 hours from impact. That gives our decision a clear majority. I say this with a heavy heart, but those still outside had ample time to reach the Ark. Their delay may cost them their lives."

He took a breath and continued, his tone softening slightly. "I'll ask Commander Henderson and the security forces to get as many people with passes through as possible. I'll synchronise watches with every soldier to ensure they have a chance to enter before the bomb-blast doors shut. The warning bell will sound five minutes before closure—don't linger looking for friends or family. Get inside the shelter immediately. If there's no further business, please return to your allocated flats and await further instructions."

The committee filed silently out of the boardroom.

Conrad's decision had been the right one. As he looked out at the purple sky from the south-west entrance of Arthur's Seat, the unease was palpable. The distant screams from the electric fences and the rattle of gunfire from the watchtowers echoed through the air. The wind picked up, tossing street debris into swirling vortices.

He closed and secured the small bomb-proof door, then typed in the access code on the second one—known only to himself and Nina MacSween. He waited for the heavy bolts to slide into place before hurrying back into the Ark.

He reached the main bomb-blast doors just as the warning bell sounded. Chaos unfolded outside: soldiers fired and retreated in turn as desperate people surged forward. The fences collapsed under the sheer weight of bodies. Some climbed; others were shot or trampled to death. A few made it through just before the bell fell silent and the enormous outer door began to slide shut. Some were crushed as it sealed.

Moments later, the inner bomb-proof door began its slow descent.

Inside, panic subsided. The injured were catalogued and taken to the hospital while the committee reassigned the flats vacated by those who hadn't made it. On the monitors, people with passes waved them hopelessly at the security cameras, pleading for the doors to open.

A deafening bang shook the Ark to its foundations. All the cameras went black. Nina MacSween realised a meteor had struck within twenty-five miles. Anyone in that radius would have been vaporised. It must have been a large one to shake the volcanic rock of Arthur's Seat.

Like a ship after a storm, the carpenter was ordered to inspect the structure and report any damage to the committee.

Conrad noted the time and date: 2.9 hours after the Neptune explosion—21:50 on Tuesday, 5 November 2045. In the world above, it would have been Guy Fawkes Night, with fireworks lighting the sky.

There was much to do and countless meetings to arrange. It was time to settle into some semblance of life underground, though Conrad knew it would never truly be the same again.

He walked the crowded streets of the Ark, grateful that no one knew who he was—the man who had decided who would live and who would die.

# Chapter 15 - A New Order

He climbed the stairs to his single flat and collapsed onto the bed from sheer fatigue. It wasn't long before he drifted into an uneasy sleep, plagued by nightmares of people hanging on barbed wire fences. He woke in a sweat, waving his arms wildly.

He remembered seeing a similar scene in a film about the holocaust between 1941 and 1945—an extermination camp called Sobibor, where frail, shadow-like humans had attempted an escape. They had run at the barbed-wire electric fence only to be mown down by the guards. Those who managed to climb over had dashed for the forest, but most were killed by mines. The few who escaped were later captured and executed.

Conrad sat on the edge of his bed, trembling. The images were too vivid. He got up and went to the small kitchen to make tea. The exterminations he'd just dreamt of made him wonder whether there was truly any difference between then and now. He would take a lot of convincing.

He sat with his tea and a biscuit. Should he have gone with his wife and children to Harris in the Hebrides? How were they? How were the in-laws coping? The questions played endlessly in his mind. This was the first real chance he'd had to think about anyone else's position in this damned catastrophe.

He finished his tea and picked up a book, but couldn't concentrate. He went back to bed, tossing and turning until he dozed off again.

He woke with a start. The silence was unnatural—no sound of the dawn chorus, no chatter of children jumping onto the bed. It was 09:00 AM. Despite the restless night, he felt strangely refreshed.

After four cups of strong coffee and a slice of toast, he made his way down to the crowded street inside the Ark shelter. People stood around in a daze, aimless and hollow-eyed. It was something that needed addressing quickly before the committee faced a serious incident.

He was relieved to see most of the committee already gathered in the boardroom. When all were seated, he stood and spoke.

"My dear friends, I'm sure most of you had a restless night just like me, but it will pass as time goes by." He paused, scanning their tired faces. "I'm sure you've noticed the crowded streets. That is what we must address this morning. We must get the children back into classrooms for both primary and secondary education, Monday to Friday, the same as before. Then we must consider the adults.

"We have woodwork shops and engineering lathes that must be put to good use. Each of you has been appointed specific tasks, and I expect these facilities to be fully operational by Monday morning at 08:00. A six-hour working day with a fifteen-minute tea break. Apprenticeships should be encouraged.

"Next on the agenda is the laundry. The Ark laundry will be managed by eight women. Four other women will be appointed to keep the streets and flat closes clean. These tasks can rotate weekly. The same applies to the engineering shops, which will be swept daily by the apprentices. I want to make it perfectly clear from the outset—there will be no loitering or unemployment. We'll find something for everyone to do."

A knock at the door interrupted him. The carpenter entered.

"I've completed the sounding structures of the Ark as instructed, Mr Wilson. No apparent damage apart from broken china and glass cabinets in the flats. One of the cycling machines in the gym needs welding."

"Excellent, Sandy. Report to me if any other faults appear."

Conrad looked around the oval table.

"Well, I must confess, that's a load off my mind. Now, please let's consider other important work to maintain cleanliness in the shelter. Recycling is essential. This must be carried out by the residents themselves. Refuse collectors will take rubbish to the collection areas, where empty tins will be compressed into blocks. Paper will be recycled into papier mâché for children and adults to sculpt. Most other waste can be incinerated. However, there may come a time when we'll need to empty the rubbish store, which will require volunteers to exit via the rear bomb door and discard it into the large pit recently dug beside the seventh hole of the golf course."

He paused, then continued more solemnly.

"My next item on the agenda is something that everyone in the Ark must consider very carefully. As time passes, there will be those among us—perhaps even at this table—who feel trapped, believing the radiation levels and nuclear winter are over, and wish to leave the shelter. I personally have no objection, but our scientific body insists on a minimum of two years before any chance of relief outside.

"For the sake of democracy, I will provide Geiger counter readings to those who request to leave, so they can make an informed decision. However, the request must be submitted in writing so that a date and time can be arranged. It's important to note that no space suits will be supplied. No re-admission will be possible. When they go, they'll be on their own. Depending on our food and water situation, a small starter pack might be provided, but that is not guaranteed."

He took a sip from his spring water bottle.

"What I'm drinking now is an important commodity. We must conserve and treat it as a luxury. Always boil the water. The last thing we need is a cholera outbreak. That's why we've included water safety in our circular advice to every flat and pinned notices in the streets. I rely on all committee members to spread the word and inform residents that a weekly bulletin will be released each Sunday about life in Noah's Ark."

Conrad gave a wry smile.

"I would hope that if a family—especially one with children—runs out of something like nappies or baby food, a neighbour would help out, just like in the old days." He paused again, glancing at his notes.

"There are still a hundred and one things to organise. I'm sure suggestions will be made to the chair as time goes by. Please, never hesitate to speak if something's on your mind. That's what we're here for. Now, it's time for Nina to give us her opinion on the meteor strike."

Nina MacSween stood up.

"There isn't much information I can give you, except that the vibration we felt must have been close. I can only hazard a guess—perhaps Dunfermline, maybe Perth, or westward towards Falkirk or Stirling, depending on the meteor's size. But there's something positive: when the meteor struck, it would have reduced the solar wind speed considerably, down to a strong gale. So you Edinburgh folk won't notice much difference when we venture out in two years' time—assuming all goes well." She sat down quickly.

Conrad spoke again.

"We can be thankful that we took the decision to close the bomb-proof doors when we did. Otherwise, none of us would have survived the blast."

"Tell that to the ghosts and spirits of those who were cremated, Wilson."

Conrad noticed the anger in the doctor's eyes.

"I want to remind you, Doctor, that a democratic vote was taken at this table—one you voted against. I've heard rumours that you're unhappy with the way the committee is running things. I will, however, call a general election in the Ark to vote on whether the chair should be replaced once the shelter is running smoothly.

"Now, if I can turn your attention to page two, appendix five. This outlines behaviour within the Ark. You, as a professional man, must abide by the laws laid down by our judicial system and our high-court judge here in the Ark. Failure to do so could result in imprisonment, and further disregard for law and order could lead to expulsion from the Ark altogether. I hope it never comes to that."

Conrad wondered if he had gone too far with this radical man. Why was such a clever professional acting this way? Had he lost family, or was he simply an arrogant man who had slipped through the vetting system?

One thing was clear in Conrad's mind: this man could cause serious problems when it came to treating the sick and injured—problems that were bound to arise in time.

Doctor Morrison stood up abruptly and walked out, to the astonishment of the committee members.

"Let's put this incident behind us for now. The suggestions I've made are important. If there are any objections or additions, please speak up."

He waited patiently as the committee exchanged uncertain glances.

Finally, Nina MacSween stood and spoke with quiet authority.

"Get rid of the doctor from the committee, Mr Wilson. It's obvious he doesn't have the Ark's safety or welfare at heart. His position as Ark doctor should also be reviewed and voted on."

"Thank you for that, Miss MacSween. Let's give the doctor a chance to calm down. If a general election must be held, then I'll be the first to instigate it. Now, if there's no other business, we shall reconvene every Monday from now until the Ark doors are opened, unless otherwise advised."

Again, it was a slow exodus from the boardroom.

Nina MacSween remained behind. She whispered softly, "Get rid of the doctor, Conrad. He's trouble. I wouldn't be surprised if he takes it out on his patients. I can see problems ahead if he's allowed to continue holding surgeries. Why did you let him speak to you like that?"

"This is hypothetical, Nina. What proof do we have that he's a danger to the shelter? Just because there's a rumour about his displeasure with how we run things? That's his prerogative—so long as it doesn't come to physical blows."

"It might not come to that, Conrad, but I have a gut feeling he's up to no good. He's a menacing character—an activist. That's why you'd do well to get rid of him altogether."

"If he's as bad as you say, Nina, I'll have him watched. I've always believed in the old saying: 'Keep your friends close and your enemies closer.' Now let's get on with the work at hand. It's getting close to Christmas. I hope the children will be carol singing, and the adults have a pantomime arranged for the festivities."

"You're not serious, Conrad Wilson. I don't think the shelter will be in the mood for carol singing or any form of entertainment after what's happened."

"That's precisely why it's important to keep traditions alive— Christmas and every other festival. People need hope, Nina, or the fear will consume them."

Nina knew she was fighting a losing battle and said her goodbyes.

Conrad Wilson sat back and wondered what his wife was doing right now. Had a meteor fallen on Harris in the Western Hebrides? He knew it wouldn't need to hit the island directly—anywhere close would have been enough to wipe out life.

He locked the boardroom door and went down to the street, where there was commotion. He saw the doctor perched on a chair, held precariously by two men.

The doctor spotted him and pointed. "That's him! That's the man who killed your families! That's the man who closed the Ark doors early! Kill him—kill the evil swine!"

Conrad rushed through the angry mob and kicked the chair from under the doctor's feet. The two men tried to catch him but failed. The doctor crashed to the pavement and crawled into the crowd.

Conrad was more concerned for his own safety. Thinking quickly, he raised his hands in surrender. "My dear friends, you've been misinformed by someone who wants to destroy us all. Morrison has lost family and friends and wants revenge on the world!"

He watched as several known activists stepped forward. He took a step toward them.

"I should warn you—if I or any member of the committee are harmed, the military guard has orders to impose a curfew on the shelter. They also have permission to bring all followers of Doctor Morrison to justice. For some, that could mean a death sentence. Morrison and his gang will be found and dealt with accordingly. Some may be asked to leave the shelter—sorry, wrong phrase—some of you will be evicted without trial!"

Conrad was relieved to hear the heavy boots of the security forces approaching.

"Disperse before they arrive and make arrests! Go back home to your families, return to work—but do it quickly!"

The mob scattered as the soldiers rounded the corner. Conrad thanked them for their swift response.

Nina MacSween, having heard the commotion from her flat, appeared and appealed for calm. She approached the shaken chairman.

"Right, Conrad, time to hold an emergency meeting and deal with those who threaten the Ark's safety. The culprits will be on the video footage from Big Brother."

It was the first major disruption within the shelter, and Conrad felt a deep sadness. He expressed this at the emergency committee meeting that evening.

***

It was Nina MacSween who took the floor by surprise.

"I want Doctor Morrison found and evicted from the shelter. I also want the activists tried and punished—either with imprisonment or eviction." She took a sip of water.

"I now think it's time to impose a curfew. No group gatherings, no one on the streets after 18:00, and not before 07:00 unless under special circumstances."

She turned to face Conrad. "Mr Chairman, you had a lucky escape this afternoon. This must never happen again. I urge you to carry a gun for your protection, because after today's rumours—true or not—you'll be a target for those who lost loved ones. Many of them were in contact with family by mobile phone until the signal was lost. They saw the chaos, the shootings, the despair. Unless convinced it was for the common good, they'll hold a grudge. We must stand united against any threat to the stability of the shelter. That's why I'm pleading with you to carry a firearm. I rest my case."

Conrad addressed the committee. "Much as I admire Miss MacSween's concern for my safety, I don't believe now is the time for firearms. Perhaps that will come later. For now, we must focus on keeping the shelter running smoothly." He paused.

"I do agree with Nina that demonstrations like the one today cannot be tolerated. Therefore, I propose we implement a curfew and have armed guards patrol the shelter. As for Doctor Morrison, eviction is too harsh. He will stand trial, along with those who attempted to riot. Those in favour of the curfew, raise your hands."

It was carried unanimously.

"While I have you here, I'd like to share some good news. The food laboratories are now operational. By next year, we should have fresh vegetables and dairy produce. Also, each household will receive a turkey, chicken, or small roast beef joint for Christmas dinner. This will be reserved for special occasions only.

"Finally, radio broadcasts will run from 10:00 AM until 17:00 PM to prevent late-night disturbances. If there are no objections, we'll adjourn."

There was silence.

"Thank you for attending. We'll meet again as scheduled on Monday morning."

Over the following weeks, life in the shelter began to stabilise. Still, Conrad sensed an undercurrent of resentment. Some residents passed him in silence, offering no greeting. It didn't bother him much—he was simply relieved that the carol singing had gone ahead.

The Ark Operatic Society staged *Cinderella*. Though the performance was rough and the cast often needed prompting from the wings, it lifted spirits. Conrad received no thanks, but he didn't mind.

After Christmas and New Year, he raised the matter of leadership at the committee meeting, held over tea and shortbread. Every resident over sixteen received a voting card. Ballots were to be cast by the end of January 2046 at the theatre entrance.

Meanwhile, Conrad was summoned to appear in court as a witness at Doctor Morrison's trial. Morrison received three months' solitary confinement; the others were given formal warnings.

Then came the day of reckoning. Conrad stood with the other candidates whose names appeared on the ballot. His purple lapel badge symbolised peace and unity. The counting continued late into the night, and the result was broadcast the next morning, 1 February 2046.

A notice was pinned to the street board: Conrad Wilson had been defeated.

Nina MacSween was now chairwoman of the committee and leader of the Ark.

At the meeting where she was sworn in, many members—including Nina herself—felt the vote had gone the wrong way. She had only entered the race out of loyalty to Conrad, knowing what was coming. There were hugs, handshakes, and quiet commiserations before normal business resumed.

Conrad found it strange sitting at the side of the table instead of at its head. He hid his disappointment well and was the first to stand and congratulate Nina on her victory.

He had done his best, and that was enough. As he reflected on his tenure, a line came to mind from Abraham Lincoln, the American president who had fought to preserve the Union: *"Nearly all men can stand adversity, but if you want to test a man's character, give him power."*

And Conrad, more than anyone, knew how true that was.

"You can please some of the people some of the time, but you can't please all of the people all of the time." Conrad gave an ironic smile as he was told to pay attention.

That was how it was in the shelter over the coming months. Much of his earlier work was now paying dividends. The best results were the fresh dairy products and vegetables. The doctor, Dan Morrison, had learned his lesson and begun practising again, taking a share of the workload from his colleague.

It was strange how people who had cursed and ignored Conrad in the early days were now calling for a new election. They made it clear where they would put their crosses on the ballot paper. Conrad insisted they stick with the present committee and leader.

"It won't be long until we make a decision to venture out into the unknown."

This always brought calm to some agitated people. A clear plan, even a tentative one, steadied nerves.

The day soon came when a volunteer was required to step out into the unknown. Conrad volunteered without hesitation. He was quickly assisted into the space suit with an air purifier attached. The stun gun was placed in his right leg pouch. Then his helmet was secured.

He still remembered the security code for the first bomb-proof door, but it was Nina MacSween who typed it in. He lifted his hand in thanks before stepping into the area sealed by the outer door. He listened to the inner door lock before pressing the red button that operated the external mechanism. He slid back the four bolts of the outside door, allowing it to lift and move out of the grooves.

His Geiger counter responded immediately, showing high radiation levels. He switched on the searchlight. He was met by an alien sight: a deep, purple, clouded sky swirling in the solar wind, giving occasional glimpses of the aurora borealis. The colours were magnificent as they danced across the blasted landscape, only to vanish when the wind dropped.

Conrad stepped out of the shelter and walked northwards, looping round towards the large Ark doors he had been responsible for closing two years earlier. There was no electric fence, no security bollards; most important of all, there were no signs of life and no human corpses. The land looked lunar—windswept and desolate. His Geiger counter continued to register high readings.

He was disappointed. He had hoped the nuclear winter had blown away, but the dark clouds still blotted out the sun. Purple rain began to fall, discolouring his white suit and visor. He walked around Arthur's Seat until his SDU, the distress signal unit, began to sound. With fifteen minutes of oxygen left, he quickened his pace towards the small bomb-proof door.

When the inner door had sealed safely, he made for the drench showers, where his suit was scrubbed down. Assisted out of the suit, he dressed and went to the central office for debriefing. The committee sat with hands clasped and bated breath.

"I'm afraid I have some good and bad news for the people in the shelter." He paused. "The Geiger counter is still showing high radiation levels. We are still in the grip of a nuclear winter; the sun is partially blocked out. I say partially because there is movement in the purple sky that gave me a faint glimpse of the sun before the clouds hid it and darkness fell again.

"However, the strong solar wind has dropped, but purple rain is still falling." He paused once more. "When I walked around Arthur's Seat and the Ark, there was no sign of life. No human corpses. Everything was barren. Under the searchlight, I could just make out that the Parliament and Holyrood Palace had been destroyed; much of both appears to have been blown away in the meteor blast.

"The searchlight gave me a limited view, but we will encounter extensive destruction when we can eventually venture further afield."

A committee member asked, "When will that be possible, Mr Wilson?"

"I don't have a crystal ball. However, I suggest the chair monitors our situation more closely now that food is getting scarce. A monthly inspection of conditions outside would, at the very least, help us understand the grave position we're in."

Nina MacSween addressed the committee. "Well, ladies and gentlemen, there you have it. I won't disguise the fact that we have a crisis on our hands. I think Conrad's suggestion is sound, but personally, I'd prefer a two-week inspection cycle. What harm can it do?"

"It would draw attention to the fact that something is wrong," the fire chief replied. "Too many inspections would look desperate. Let's stick with Conrad's monthly inspections."

A vote was taken, and monthly inspections carried out.

"I don't think sharing every detail of our findings is a good idea," Nina added. "A short note of the good parts can go in the weekly bulletin. It would also be wise to keep quiet about dwindling food stocks. This will become obvious when weekly rations are reduced."

Life in the shelter continued much as before, but questions mounted about the lack of detailed information regarding Conrad Wilson's visit outside. At times, he was accosted in the street by angry families. Morale began to fray, and applications to leave increased.

The chairwoman told each applicant that their request would be considered. She was buying time. A circular went to every flat, explaining that they had lived safely in the shelter for over two years and that a few more weeks or months would make little difference. This message was repeated in the weekly bulletin and posted on the noticeboard.

Even so, some now demanded release. Fourteen people were given the date and time of Conrad's next monthly inspection. It was made clear, in bold red ink, that those who chose to exit could do so, but there would be no re-entry. Individuals still had time to change their minds.

Conrad was almost relieved to suit up for another reconnaissance. A large crowd gathered to watch. Nina called out the army security guard in case of disruption.

Conrad stepped into the gathering area, followed by eleven residents. All procedures completed, he slid back the securing bolts. The outer door sprang open. To his surprise, a blue sky greeted him. The Geiger counter showed only a faint reading, and a gentle breeze was blowing.

Everything was suddenly clearer. It was early morning; he could just make out sunrise touching the ruined buildings of the lower Old Town and what had once been the Royal Mile. He watched the group disperse with cautious enthusiasm. Instrument readings can improve before conditions are truly safe, he reminded himself; suits would still be mandatory for now.

He closed up and cycled the doors, to Nina's surprise. Removing his visor, he delivered the news.

"I must see this for myself, Conrad. Give me a minute while I get into a space suit."

Conrad nodded. While Nina changed, he charged the scooter batteries and wheeled it into the gathering area, ready to take it outside. With limited air supplies, any way to extend range safely was valuable.

Nina was apprehensive about riding in cumbersome gear, and she said so as the bolts were thrown back. Eventually, both mounted the scooter. They set off at a snail's pace and, once they reached the Portobello promenade, Conrad increased speed to 8 mph, dodging blocks of stone and timber.

They saw that the beach was strewn with debris and vehicles. There was even the fuselage of an aeroplane. Conrad surmised they had been blown out to sea in the blast and washed ashore by northward tidal waters. They passed two petrol stations and the remains of three partially destroyed supermarkets.

At Leith, the bottom of Leith Walk was impassable, so he turned towards the harbour. The sight was bleak: the Royal Yacht Britannia lay submerged on her side. As an engineer, Conrad's first thought was whether she could be refloated—something to investigate.

The new luxury flats at Leith Wharf had been destroyed, leaving only twisted steel and bare foundations. Most cruisers and yachts had either been washed away or blown across the marina concourse into a tangled pile. Beneath the wreckage, Conrad noticed a large three-masted yacht that had lost its masts but appeared intact. That, too, would merit investigation.

He turned the scooter back towards the promenade and the Ark. The scooter was parked in the loading bay before the two explorers re-entered the shelter.

There was much to tell. Nina took the drench shower first, followed by Conrad. Precautions remained strict: each was drenched and scrubbed. Then they met in the central office for debriefing.

It was Conrad who spoke first, forgetting his place, but his excitement overwhelmed him.

"There are three mangled supermarkets on the Portobello Promenade as far as Leith. I think there could be food stocks inside, and with a little care, we could begin to bring out tinned goods and anything else worth salvaging.

"There are also two petrol stations. How badly damaged I'm unsure, but it doesn't look as if they've been on fire. If that is the case, then this will give us fuel for any vehicles we can salvage. We noticed that in a builder's yard there was a bus, two diggers and a JCB with a bucket and shovel. They're on their side, but I'm sure we could jack them back into an upright position for use in clearing a road up to Princes Street and beyond. This is where I propose we build accommodation blocks. Personally, having lived in Charlotte Square, it is an ideal place to build a fortress."

He was interrupted. "Why on earth do we need a fortress? And if we do need such a building, why not use the castle?"

"The castle no longer exists, and who knows what obstructions we might face in clearing a roadway up to the top of Castle Mount, which would mean more work. However, I'm not discounting your suggestion, but I think that is something for the future." He paused.

"We must not get complacent. There are going to be other survivors of this holocaust from near and far. In whatever form, I reserve judgment. But food and drinking water would have been non-existent; that is another reason why we must get some form of fortification built as quickly as we can, and Charlotte Square is the ideal place."

Nina held up her hand to stop Conrad from continuing.

"Ladies and gentlemen, now there is a possibility that we can open the Ark shelter doors. I urge caution. Let's give it another two weeks before we inform the shelter of our find. This can be broadcast on the radio and in the weekly bulletin. I'm sure this will give those people some cheer." She paused.

"This means that on Monday, it will be the last committee meeting. However, there is something of great importance I must tell you." Nina hesitated.

"When we leave the shelter, each of us will probably go in search of families. However, I'm with Conrad in building a fortress in Charlotte Square. Everyone in the Ark will be told that they are welcome to join us. However, I want to make this clear. When we begin work in clearing the roads and building the fortress, my duties as chairwoman will no longer be required. Therefore, I propose we elect Conrad Wilson as President of our new project. He has carried us through thick and thin in this shelter despite all the backstabbing and bitchiness. I want the shelter to be aware of how his endeavours behind the scenes helped to keep the shelter running smoothly. Those who plan to join us on the Charlotte Square project will accept Conrad as their leader. If they don't conform to this, then they can seek safety elsewhere. Until Monday then."

Nina got up quickly and walked out of the boardroom. The committee sat in bewilderment.

Conrad and Nina made several trips to the builder's yard in the two weeks that were left before the Ark doors were opened to the public of the shelter. It was car jacks taken from the wreckage that righted each vehicle onto its four wheels and the digger onto its tank tracks. The batteries had been charged at the shelter, then installed in each vehicle. They were heavy-duty batteries, and that took time, but each vehicle was started up and left running, allowing the batteries to charge themselves.

Now they were ready to begin work on clearing Leith Walk and other obstacles in their way. Nina followed the bus without windows back to the front doors of the Ark in preparation for the people's departure.

The two weeks went by in the blink of an eye. The people had been supplied with food packs and water that emptied the food store to almost bare. Water was not a problem; there was still plenty fed from the small loch situated up on Arthur's Seat.

When Nina pressed the green buttons that opened the bomb-blast doors, there was an almighty cheer and weeping. Conrad felt like Abraham leading the Jews from Egyptian slavery towards the promised land. Only in this case, he was leading the first passengers towards the bus where they would be transported as far as Leith Walk. Others stood in the sunshine and walked away to the south and west, unaware that there could be problems further afield.

It was to be a long day for the bus driver. People were being bused regularly to the bottom of Leith Walk.

Conrad and some men entered the wreckage of the supermarkets. Shining their torches, they found shelves and stores of every tinned food imaginable. It was like entering an Aladdin's cave, where they also found clothing and bedding, cosmetics and sanitary items, including Dettol and soap, toothpaste and toilet rolls, and washing powder. The list of items was endless.

"When the bus returns, I'll get the burning gear and clear a decent entrance and exit. Then we'll stock up the shelter again. We can't be sure that the danger of meteor strikes is over. The only trouble we have now is the fact that we don't have a warning system."

In the days that followed, Conrad came across a gem. A Hathaway pump had been found among the rubble leading up to

Princes Street. This could be converted and used for pumping petrol and diesel from the service station storage tanks—something they would need for the future work to be carried out at the fortress and for the clearance of roads requiring machinery.

There was a feeling of optimism in the air. Those who toiled tirelessly each day, clearing the first road, Leith Walk, reached the carnage of the North British Hotel at the corner of the collapsed South Bridge. The works detail looked forlornly along Princes Street at more carnage from department stores that had been completely obliterated. The Princes Gardens were covered with wreckage of trams, diesel and electric trains, some still attached to the carriages. They looked down onto a non-existent Waverley train station.

Further along Princes Street, the Scott Monument was gone. The five-star Caledonian Hotel was a pile of rubble. They looked up to where the proud Edinburgh Castle once stood—the castle where many a military tattoo had enthralled home audiences and visitors from overseas. Some of the works at the party turned their heads away and resumed work.

Conrad arrived at the scene of devastation. He climbed over the rubble up to Charlotte Street, where the head of King George IV was lodged between two granite blocks. The short pink kilt and silk stockings of the statue had disappeared. He walked cautiously along to Charlotte Square to assess what had to be done.

Time would need to be spent in the shelter until the rebuilding programme could commence. He was sad to see the building where he and his family had spent many happy hours now in ruins. He stood in frustration, realising how much work would be needed, but got a pleasant surprise when he walked around what had once been a tree-lined square.

The First Minister of Scotland's residence walls were still standing. The roof had gone, but Conrad could see it would not take a great deal of effort to replace it. He now looked westward and could see that every building from the north, south, east, and west could be joined together. Not only would this turn the Square into a fortress, but it would give much-needed living space to anyone who sought refuge. Two towers with a heavy steel or wooden gate could be built on the eastern approach, making it the only entrance, and would complete the fortification.

His plans could be drawn up and implemented by the draughtsman. There was, however, a problem—the draughtsman had gone south-west to Dumfries to look for survivors of his family.

This hiccup wasn't beyond Conrad. He would spend his nights in the Ark shelter putting this together. He now met with the works foreman, Jack Dempster.

"Jack, I want you to get a clear road up and into Charlotte Square. Any building blocks or wood should be piled and kept— anything that we can use in the rebuilding and re-roofing of the Square."

He started the scooter and made his way down to Leith. He moved the digger from the builder's yard and drove it along the mile to the Leith Harbour wharf. Manoeuvring it into position, he started to clear the debris away from the large three-masted yacht.

The more he cleared, the more apparent it became that the bow and midship masts had snapped away from the decking. The canvas sails were still securely wrapped with rope to the mast that lay against the cabin roof. The stern mast had gone, but there might be a chance it could be found later among the debris. Two masts could still move this beautiful craft forward through any ocean.

# Chapter 16 - Ruins and Revelations

Conrad climbed aboard to assess the damage properly. As an engineer, he could see what would be needed: secure steel plates to the deck with four large bolts that would be attached to the mast plates and fixed with spring washers and four large nuts securing each plate. He would still have trouble finding what he needed.

He opened the half hatch and unsnapped the bottom half that led down to the galley, where he got the shock of his life. Two adult skeletons sat on the bench seat in a hugging pose. The next shock, which made his blood run cold, came when three large rats, as big as rabbits, leapt out and disappeared through the hatch, scurrying away. They were so big and fat they could hardly move.

Conrad explored the yacht with caution, but no more surprises awaited him. He managed to get the two skeletons into a part of the tattered sail. He tied the sail with ropes, then lowered the canvas body bag gently onto the concrete standing. Putting them on his shoulder, he walked to the edge of the quay and dropped the canvas containing the skeletons into the water. He considered saying a prayer, but couldn't find the words. He had no doubt that the North Sea currents would take them out to sea.

After fulfilling his crude and unsavoury burial, it was back to work. His biggest problem would be getting the yacht from the standing cradle it was perched on into the water without causing any damage.

There was a way if he welded four wheels onto the cradle, then towed it to the nearby slipway, or put it on two slings forward and aft and used the digger and JCB bucket. That would be fine on level ground, but the slope of the slipway could be catastrophic. He decided on the wheels as the best option.

He stood on the quay looking down at the submerged Royal Yacht *Britannia*. This would need balloons inflated with air—lots of them. He could rig up an inflator pump, but the balloons might pose a problem. The only thing he could think of was weather balloons, but where was he going to acquire them?

He decided to inspect the damage to *Britannia* first before anything was done, so he made a note to bring the welding equipment and diving gear, as well as four wheels of the same size. That would not be a problem; there were plenty of upturned vehicles on the beach.

It was time to make tracks back to the builder's yard with the digger, then scooter it back to Portobello and the shelter. He felt in a positive mood as he drove slowly along the promenade. He stopped and lifted his binoculars, scanning the North Sea in hope of seeing a ship—any ship—but alas, only the legs of the destroyed oil platforms were visible.

He started back towards the Ark shelter. He found Nina doing paperwork.

"It won't be long until the shelter is restocked. It'll take time for the vegetable seeds and dairy products to take hold. How is the clearance work getting on? Are you and the workmen any further forward?"

"The clearing and building work are in the hands of Jack Dempster's works party. We hope to start building by next week. You must come with me tomorrow to Charlotte Square and look at the Scottish First Minister's residence. I think we could have a roof put on and the building sealed by next week."

He was unsure whether to tell her about the yachting project, but went ahead—after all, she was a close friend.

"I've discovered a large yacht that was buried in debris, but I spent most of the day clearing it for personal use." He didn't go into any great detail but did say he needed four wheels to transport the yacht cradle to the slipway for launch.

"Please tell me, Conrad, why you're going through this personal charade when there is much more important work to be done?" Nina sounded grieved.

"It's simple, Nina. I must find out what has happened to my family. The only way I'm able to do that will be by sea. You saw what happened to the Royal Yacht, and it was sheltered and secured to the Leith quay."

Nina sat back and nodded.

"Is there much work needing to be done before it is seaworthy?"

"Not a lot—nothing I can't handle on my day off. However, I have a problem. I need four small wheels to weld onto the yacht cradle. The car jacks or trolley jacks can support the cradle while I'm welding the axle and wheels at the bow section. The same procedure would be carried out at the stern. Once I have the axle and wheels attached to the cradle, it would be a simple job to drag it to the slipway with the digger, point the yacht towards the water, and let it freewheel down into the basin, where work on the masts and other repairs can be carried out."

"You seem to have all this worked out, Conrad. I take it you're planning to leave us as soon as the yacht is seaworthy?"

"Not until I've fulfilled my duty here in the shelter and the building project. After that, I'll pass the reins to you. Jack will oversee the clearing and building work; the final say will come from you." He paused.

"I would rather you kept the yacht a secret, Nina. I don't want every Tom, Dick, and Harry pestering me for a crew place. I'll manage to handle the yacht on my own."

"No, you won't, Conrad Wilson, because I'm coming with you." She smiled.

"Have you checked the carnage on the Portobello beach? There's a beach buggy that's been washed ashore. What condition it's in, I have no idea—would that solve your wheel and axle problem?"

"That could be the very thing, Nina. Well spotted."

***

The next morning, they left the shelter with the gas acetylene bottles, welding rods, and burning gear. They drove the builder's Land Rover onto Portobello beach and over to the wrecked beach buggy.

Conrad began to burn the front axle welds that held it to the chassis. The two wheels dropped onto the sand. He did the same to the rear axle welds and watched with satisfaction as the wheels dropped into the shallow water.

"I think we'd better move, Nina—the tide's coming in. We'll move the wheels and axles further up the beach and remove the wheels from the axles. That'll make it easier when it comes to loading and unloading each item. We'll come back for the other sections later, after I've welded the axles and wheels onto the cradle. We'll need to stop at the builder's yard to get the hydraulic and car jacks."

They lifted the axle and two wheels onto the Land Rover and made their way off the beach and along the promenade to the builder's yard.

The two hydraulic jacks lifted the yacht cradle with ease, allowing Conrad to make the necessary welds. The wheels were put onto the axle, then each jack was lowered, allowing the wheels to take the weight of the yacht and cradle.

They drove back to the beach and retrieved the other axle and wheels. The same work was carried out at the cradle. Finally, the cradle sat perfectly level on the concrete.

Conrad attached a rope to the cradle and the digger bucket. The yacht cradle moved slowly towards the slipway, manoeuvred into position for launch with the digger taking the strain of the rope that held the cradle on the slope.

Nina stood with her camera. "Hold it, Conrad, I have something special for you."

She produced a bottle of champagne from the Land Rover. She handed Conrad the bottle and prepared to take pictures.

Conrad smashed the bottle of champagne against the bow.

"I name this yacht *Catherine Wilson*; may God bless her and all who sail in her."

The digger moved down the slipway slope, allowing the yacht to freewheel into the water and float free of its cradle. Nina climbed aboard. She tied a rope onto the bow cleat. It was an exhilarating moment for her. She took the rope and climbed onto the quay. *Catherine Wilson* was tied to a large securing ring while Conrad pulled the cradle from the water and parked it beside the twisted metal pile that had protected the yacht from damage.

He switched the digger engine off. Totally satisfied with his achievement, he walked back to the quay and boarded the *Catherine Wilson*. Nina had already begun cleaning the galley and polishing the woodwork in the lounge area. If she only knew about the skeletons hugged together and the rats, Conrad wondered if she would be so eager in her work surroundings.

However, he appreciated her enthusiasm, and she soon had the interior of the yacht looking spick and span. She was now spending more time assisting Conrad with rubbing down the wooden railings and painting with hard weather-seal wood stain. The yacht was looking like new. He had noticed that work had been carried out on de-fouling the hull. He was confident that the yacht was almost ready for sea.

The biggest job would be getting the masts installed onto the deck plates.

He had other tasks away from the yacht. Work had started on the rebuilding of Charlotte Square. The JCB had cleared a path along Princes Street. There was much to salvage from the destroyed department stores.

The workers had reached the ruins of the five-star Caledonian Hotel and had turned their attention to Johnston Terrace, where many of the buses would have parked on the nights of the Military

Tattoo. Now the terrace was impassable. Much of the Edinburgh Castle debris and large stone blocks were piled high against the cliff and roadway.

The large blocks could be moved gradually to Charlotte Square, though it would take time and a great deal of blood, sweat, and tears before a path could eventually reach the top of the Royal Mile. However, most of the castle stonework would make good foundation blocks for the proposed tenements and the two towers that would form the entrance to the Square.

The hours, days, weeks, and months rolled by. Charlotte Square was now completely enclosed and made into a fortress, with no windows on the first and second floors of the outside walls in case of attempted intrusion with ladders. This had been a well-thought-out plan and would prove advantageous in the future. The large oak door was now suspended in place. The tenement accommodation was complete. The water main was repaired, with all apparent destruction rectified. A water pump had been installed to lift the surplus water up to the holding tanks in each tenement block.

The stores were filled with food and clothing from the various shops that had been cleared of rubble. People with their furniture and possessions were moved from the shelter to the Square. Some were reluctant to move but were given an ultimatum: they could lose their slot if others who had gone to find family members returned with them. They were told in no uncertain terms that the Ark shelter was being closed and sealed for use in the future should it ever be needed.

Once again, there were those who moaned about the decision taken by the committee. The hours, days, weeks, and months passed by. Slowly but surely, the clearance work extended out towards the A8 and Edinburgh Airport.

The works party had no idea what was in store for them. Mile by mile, the road was cleared, enabling the works bus, which served as a canteen, to progress slowly in reverse. They had reached the airport slip road when, out of the blue, they were attacked by a group of what could only be described as screaming savages—twenty men and women with gaunt red eyes, long, greasy matted hair, some clad in Highland dress with tattooed and painted faces.

The works party raced for the bus, having to fight off the attackers. Two members were left behind as the bus pulled away, others holding on for dear life, jumping into the open boot that held the tea urn and lunch packs neatly stacked. Some leapt into the bucket of the JCB that followed the bus at full speed.

They were glad to reach the safety of the Square, where they explained the attack. Conrad put the security soldiers on red alert, and the armoury was opened to supply the men of the fortress with weapons.

It was three hours before the first of the savages arrived and demanded entry into the Square. Conrad stood at the window of the tower and tried to reason with their leader.

The reply was terse. "This is what will happen when we break down the door. It's your crowd of scientists that's responsible for what has happened to our city—our planet."

Two women walked towards the fortress carrying two heads stuck on poles, moving them up and down with glee. Conrad could only look at the bloody faces and eyes that seemed to have rolled back towards their foreheads. He recognised both heads of the young men immediately.

"What in heaven's name have you become?" he asked, close to tears.

This was the first sign of emotion he'd shown since his wife had left with the children nearly four years ago. He felt physically sick at the sight.

This was not what he wanted. This had gone beyond anarchy—it was human depravity at its worst. When more of the savages arrived, they fired arrows at the windows with their longbows. A futile effort to injure, but that was enough for the security captain. He pulled Conrad back from the window and shouted, "Disperse and go back to where you came from, or we'll fire!"

The delegated savages dived for cover, but they weren't finished. The JCB was started up and began to drive towards the fortress door. A soldier in the other tower shot the driver through the head, then took down another who attempted to reach the JCB that had hit the large granite block of the tower base. No damage was done, and the savages fled down towards Princes Street.

The order was given to stand down, but the doors remained closed until a search party—fully armed—searched behind piles of rubble with orders to shoot on sight. However, the savages must have realised they were beaten and retreated to wherever they had come from.

It was a lesson learned at a cost. The works party would henceforth be armed and accompanied by two professional soldiers. They would clear debris only within the city boundary. No more attempts would be made to find other living humans. Conrad was convinced that others out there would have turned savage, just like those he had witnessed.

He longed for the tranquillity of the Hebrides—for his wife and children. He was sick and tired of the unrest and whisperings within the fortress. Some said he should have negotiated more with the desperate humans at the door. Others whispered it was tantamount to murder.

They had forgotten about the two young heads removed from the women's poles and used as footballs, kicked down the slope onto Princes Street, where they were later recovered.

His mind was made up. Now was the time to make plans for his and Nina's departure on the yacht *Catherine Wilson*, which had been fully restored with masts and sails. Five-gallon diesel drums of fuel had been placed aft, and stocks of food and water barrels were aboard.

All that was needed now was a little self-assurance—and encouragement from Nina that she was ready. Two weeks after the terrible attack, he finally decided to go.

He went to her self-contained flat in the First Minister of Scotland's residence—something it would always be known as. Nina opened the door and gave him a hug.

"I've been expecting you, Conrad. Where have you been hiding?"

"From myself mostly, but no more hiding. I'm ready to sail off into the sunset. What about you?" He watched her go to the bedroom and return with a holdall.

"Does this answer your question? I've been ready for two weeks." She lifted the bag. "Let's get out of this hellhole. The place is gradually going down the tube, and I can see trouble ahead. Now's the time, Conrad."

They made their way quickly down to the yacht on the scooter. It was placed on board. They heard the Land Rover coming down Leith Walk. *Catherine Wilson*'s ropes were untied, and the engine was started up. The propeller went astern, and the yacht cleared the basin walls, heading out to sea.

Conrad saw five running figures approach the quay. Shots were fired, but the yacht was now in open water and out of range of the assassins' bullets. He knew this would have happened sooner or later—those who sought power would have had him executed.

He wound the midship sail into position and watched it billow in the breeze. Taking the helm, he set a course north towards Aberdeen and the Cromarty Firth.

Nina handed him a mug of drinking chocolate and a chocolate biscuit. She smiled.

"I think you must have ruffled a few feathers in the Ark and the fortress, Conrad Wilson. I wonder if I've made the right decision?"

"If not, then you still have time to swim back." For the first time in years, they laughed wholeheartedly together—all troubles behind them and a new adventure before them.

There were signs of life when they studied the River Forth through their field glasses—small fires burning on either side of the river. The proud Forth railway bridge that had stood for over a hundred and fifty years was now a tangled configuration of red steel and iron in the river. The recently constructed road bridge had disappeared completely.

*Catherine Wilson* continued northwards, bypassing the Firth of Tay and catching a glimpse of what was once the city of Dundee. Arbroath and Montrose appeared next; there was no sign of life.

When they reached the mouth of Aberdeen Harbour, a dilemma faced them. The harbour was littered with sunken ships—oil tankers and supply vessels that had once served the North Sea and Pentland Firth fields. They bypassed Peterhead and Fraserburgh.

After discussion, they decided to sail on before turning west along the Cromarty Firth to the Moray Firth and Inverness. The plan was to try to trace Nina's family.

However, the nearer they got to the city, the clearer it became that Inverness had taken a direct or close meteor hit. Not a building was standing. From the Moray Firth, it looked like a wasteland. The Black Isle Bridge had also collapsed. There was little point in going ashore.

The Geiger counter was sounding, indicating high levels of radiation in the air. That convinced them to discard the idea of landing.

Nina went below deck as Conrad set the sails, and the *Catherine Wilson* moved away from the mouth of the River Ness and the Caledonian Canal entrance—away from the obliterated city—north towards Wick and John o' Groats.

He could hear the sobs coming from below. He stood at the helm, wondering if this was the first time Nina had broken down. He let her get it out of her system. She was a strong character; she would recover in time.

But it took a while before she appeared, clutching two mugs of coffee.

Now was a good time, while the weather was calm, to teach her in detail how to trim the sails and to explain the magnetic compass. There was also the depth finder and the engine revolutions; this would be used when they teetered on the edge of the coastline. There were charts on board, but Conrad wasn't sure how to read them properly, so it was a game of chance when they went close to the shore to carry out an inspection. He made a mental note to practise with the chart symbols later.

He could read the barometer, which indicated a drop in pressure. Stormy weather was closing in and approaching fast.

They had passed Dunnet Head as the waves began to grow in the strengthening wind and rain. It was a race against time for what was hoped would be a sheltered harbour in the town of Thurso. Nina battled against the wind and rain to trim the sails as they approached the town. They were given a hero's welcome by the people standing on the pier as Conrad brought the *Catherine Wilson* alongside. One of them grabbed the bow rope while another secured the stern rope to a capstan. Conrad reached for the pistol and tucked it into his tunic. Nina did the same with the stun gun, just in case of any trouble. They had learned to be cautious after the scenario back on the Leith quay.

However, it proved that the dozen people who greeted them were friendly, each couple inviting them to spend the night at their house. Conrad obliged some by saying that Nina and he would be happy to spend time ashore until the storm abated.

It was good to sleep in a soft, feathered bed. The townsfolk were slightly surprised when Nina went to her guesthouse bed and Conrad to another after a singsong with spirits and wine. Fresh meat was on the dinner table. Nina had to ask how they managed to retain such pleasure; the householder was reluctant to answer. A brief glance between two locals suggested livestock had survived inland.

The twelve apostles, as Conrad named them, were gathered at the dinner table. There was a lot to talk about. Edinburgh and the Ark shelter took up most of the conversation, and why Nina and Conrad had set sail away from the bickering of the fortress. Finding Nina's parents and Conrad's family on the Isle of Harris was another topic. They spoke of the yacht journey, survival fires on the eastern coastline, the devastation of the capital and Inverness, the River Forth rail and road bridges, and the Tay railway and road bridge lying destroyed in the mouths of each river estuary. Aberdeen Harbour—just so much destruction.

Nina, in her infinite wisdom, drew a sketch of what had caused life on Earth to change so dramatically. The locals were dumbfounded when she explained the collision of the planets.

They spent three nights in the town before being given an enthusiastic send-off with fresh food and water. There was a rubber dinghy with oars attached to the stern rail—something he and Nina had thought of. They continued to wave enthusiastically until the harbour of Thurso disappeared.

Conrad had left a warning note for his landlord. It was short and to the point:

"Arm yourselves against marauding, starving humans. Nina and I were attacked by a group that we think have turned into cannibals. Not everybody is as friendly as your townsfolk."

A course was set for Strathy Point, then onwards to Loch Eriboll, where they dropped anchor and had a complete rest. Conrad had read somewhere that this was the loch that the battlecruiser HMS *Hood* had sailed from to encounter the German battleship *Bismarck*. HMS *Hood* was struck with several shells from different ships, like the *Prinz Eugen*, but it was construed that it was the *Bismarck* that sent her to the bottom of the Denmark Strait on 24 May 1941; only three of her crew survived. Conrad thought it strange that no list of crew members serving aboard the great ship could be accounted for.

His thoughts changed when he saw naked Nina dive into the freezing waters of the loch for a swim. She swam underwater to the yacht and hauled herself aboard like a dried, shrivelled prune. She stood for a moment, giving Conrad a good look at her body, before going below to dry and get into warm clothes.

"That's what I needed, Conrad. I feel cleansed from top to toe."

She smiled as Conrad weighed anchor and set sail. Their next course would be for Cape Wrath, then a short crossing to the Outer Hebrides—Lewis and Harris. The sea was choppy as they rounded the Wrath into the Minch.

Conrad was feeling optimistic after seeing the folk of Thurso. He was sure that his family would have made it through the turmoil of the mainland meteor strikes, but when they pulled into Stornoway Harbour, there was no welcome from the islanders. Conrad noticed that many of the buildings were destroyed; most were charred relics of what they had once been. Nina pointed at a dog tearing a toy doll to shreds. But the closer they got to the harbour, the doll turned out to be a baby in the mouth of the rabid dog.

# Chapter 17 - Orders, Unrest, and Elections

Conrad puffed out his cheeks at the sight. He reached for the rifle but was too late; the dog disappeared with its prize meat into the rubble.

His mind was filled with despair as he brought the "Cathrine Wilson" alongside the quay.

Fully armed, they made their way up to a small hill overlooking the town. They surveyed the burnt debris as far as their field glasses could see.

It was Nina who spotted the three fierce-looking dogs, saliva dripping from their mouths, come bounding up the hill towards them. She gave a short burst of fire with the machine gun, and each animal rolled over with loud yelps and growls.

"Let's get back to the yacht, Conrad, there's nothing for us here."

"We could try to salvage something from the town. There's bound to be something we could use, Nina."

She just shook her head. "This damage is different from the outlying meteor blasts we've seen. This is burning on a grand scale."

"Can you explain yourself in more detail? I'm very interested in your theory."

Nina started off down the hill. Conrad trotted after her.

"Well, Nina, explain yourself."

She stopped suddenly and looked into his eyes.

"This landscape reminds me of the atomic bombs that were dropped on the cities of Hiroshima and Nagasaki in Japan. I think this damage has been caused by a nuclear explosion, and the only place that springs to mind is the rocket range on the Isle of Benbecula, where nuclear warheads were stored in the event of a nuclear war.

"The government said the rocket range was for carrying out rocket tests, but we scientists know different." She hesitated before continuing. "I don't wish to alarm you, but if you recall my lecture at the emergency meeting in Berlin, I told governments with atomic rockets and warheads to disarm them and use the launching silos as nuclear shelters. If this advice was not carried out, then it would be as I iterated—a small meteor strike close to the warhead storage could result in Armageddon for those living nearby. The poor folk would have two disasters to contend with, and it's doubtful if anybody within a twenty-five-mile radius, as the crow flies, will have survived."

Nina set off again, only this time she was running towards the yacht. She stood by the bow rail as Conrad appeared.

"Ready to cast off when you are, Captain." She saluted.

Conrad rubbed his cheek. "There are two things I can't understand, Nina. The first is when we arrived—the dog with the baby in its jaws, a baby with flesh, not a skeleton. The second is the rabid dogs on the hill. If they survived, is it not possible that some of the townsfolk could also have survived? Don't you think we're being a little hasty in our assumption that there is no life in Stornoway? Why don't we do a little exploring before we leave?"

"Check the Geiger counter, Conrad; it has the highest reading since we exited the shelter. However, I'm prepared to wait while you exercise your whim. Then we can set sail for Harris… Is that not our aim?" She paused. "I don't want to sound inhuman, Conrad, but any survivors of the nuclear fallout will be dead or dying. We must be practical and careful if we are to avoid heavy intake of radiation. Those dead and dying people, like others we will encounter on this Western Isles trip, will have suffered radiation burns and sickness. Now tell me what you want to do."

"You're right, Nina. Let's have a coffee before we set sail. The small port of Tarbert in Harris is less than an hour's sail, where I'll find my answers once and for all. I'm prepared for the worst now I've seen what has happened here."

They sat with their coffee, discussing their plans and what to do if Conrad didn't find his family.

Nina spoke frankly. "We've been lucky so far. Getting fresh water and supplies in Thurso has helped us immensely, but the further south we go, everything will be contaminated within the twenty-five-mile radius of the Benbecula rocket range. We'll need to check how far south we could get before clearing the radiation belt. We don't know if any other meteors have fallen on the Inner and Outer Hebridean Islands. My proposal is, after we've traced your family's circumstances, we head back to Thurso, where we can hopefully replenish our water and food stocks. There is little point in going any further south. Besides, I'm fed up eating fish." She smiled, then cleared the coffee mugs to the galley.

They set sail for the Isle of Harris.

***

The Tarbert harbour pier was clear. The hotel had been burnt and was practically demolished. The houses and savings bank above

294

the pier were also just a pile of charred debris. Conrad leapt ashore and secured the "Cathrine Wilson."

He unloaded the scooter onto the quay and explained why he was using it.

"There are very few cars on these islands. Most of the work would have been done the old-fashioned way—horses and carts, with hard graft. There will be no rows of houses to block our path. It's mostly farms and crofts that litter this part of the island. Anything that's in our way, we can move."

Fully armed, they drove to the top of the hill and looked across the Minch to the mountains of Skye in the Inner Hebrides. It really was a magnificent view: white fluffy clouds, blue clear water. In another time, another world, you could believe you were on holiday. But there was always the grim reality when they climbed onto the scooter and made their way across the island to the croft where his wife was born.

He was an optimist and believed they would have survived, no matter what was thrown at them. They walked around the croft, calling out the names of his family. There was silence. He opened the croft door, and Conrad was paralysed with grief. The skeletal figures of his wife and two children lay on the floor. There was no sign of his in-laws; however, Nina discovered their skeletal bodies in the crude Anderson shelter in the back garden. The bones had obviously been gnawed by rats. The vermin lay a short distance from the shelter but intact, which made her wonder what had gone on here.

She went into the croft and soon discovered the truth. She lifted the sobbing engineer to his feet and whispered, "They didn't suffer because they were in the shelter with her parents when the meteor struck and the nuclear warheads exploded. I think they survived but were later overcome by radiation sickness; you can still see traces of dried piles of vomit on the floor." Nina put an arm around him.

"The glass vessels on the floor are the cyanide capsules you gave them, so I believe they met a quick and dignified end—the children first, her parents next, and finally Cathrine."

She took him out of the nightmare. "Let's find a spade and give them a Christian burial."

They found the spades in the burnt ruins of what was once the garden shed and set about digging two graves.

Mr and Mrs MacSween were placed in one. Cathrine, with her two children, was placed in the other. When the children were laid to rest beside their mother, the love of his life, Conrad wanted to die. He even considered standing at the edge of the grave and biting down on his cyanide capsule.

It was Nina who brought him to his senses as she began filling in the parents' grave. "We need to get back to the yacht before nightfall, so let's get the burials finished, with a silent prayer."

Conrad stepped back from the graveside and began shovelling earth onto the skeletal remains. He felt a wave of remorse, wishing he had been with his family at the time of their demise. It was too late for regret. He bent down and kissed the grass on top of both graves. He said nothing as he made his way to the scooter.

Nina appeared with two small crosses and patted them into the grave ground. They set off on a journey back to the "Cathrine Wilson" in deep sadness.

The decision was made to berth overnight and set off for what they called home the next morning. They talked about the time it had taken them to reach this point—eight months, three weeks, and four days.

Nina heard her friend breaking his heart. She was tempted to climb into his bed and comfort him but thought it would be too soon for Conrad, who had just buried his family. The gentle rocking of the yacht finally put her to sleep.

It was Conrad who was in the galley preparing breakfast. Nina came behind him and gave him a hug.

"Feeling any better this morning?"

"I'll feel better when we set sail away from Harris. I was bothered with ghostly memories, so after breakfast we'll be on our way."

Nina understood his reasoning. She wanted to be clear of the burned-out Hebridean Islands but sat at the breakfast bar in silence.

Instead of taking the angled route across the Minch to Cape Wrath, they sailed eastwards towards Uig on the Isle of Skye, where the red and black Cuillin mountains came into view. They studied the coast for any sign of life, but it was just like Lewis and Harris; the town was a burnt-out shell.

They turned north, bypassing the island of Raasay, then weighed anchor at the Summer Isles. Once again, Nina enjoyed her naked swim.

"One of these days you're going to contract hypothermia, Nina." He handed her the towel.

The "Cathrine Wilson" was battling against heavy weather and making little headway in the stormy waters of the Minch. After hard work trimming the sails, then hoisting them to reap the benefit of the wind that had changed direction and dropped to a breeze, the yacht was carried up to Cape Wrath and the Pentland Firth.

They decided to bypass Loch Eriboll while the weather was favourable. They considered pulling into Loch Tongue, but they were making good progress, so it was all hands on deck until they finally reached the town of Thurso.

Conrad commented that there was a research and development nuclear-powered reactor built in 1955 at Dounreay, close to the town, and closed in 1994 when it was taken offline, thus ending a generation of nuclear-powered energy—9,250 GWh in all. He went on to say that the closing of Dounreay had been an economic disaster for the town and the region of Caithness, putting 1,250 employees and 700 contractors on the dole.

Nina wondered where he got his information from.

"As a physicist, I was indirectly involved in the clean-up operation that is still ongoing—or I should say was ongoing—because of the present climate we live in. After closing the complex site, it had a thirty-year decommissioning, clean-up, and demolition project, but the site won't be completely decontaminated until the year 2323."

He drew the yacht close to the pier while Nina put in place the protective rubber bouncers. There was an uneasy silence surrounding the harbour. The only sound was the waves breaking against the pier. There was no welcoming party as before, and the two scientists expressed alarm.

"What in hell's name has happened here, Nina? Get the firearms just in case."

Nina raced below to the weapons cupboard. They walked tentatively and at the ready towards the town and came upon the first victim lying in her own dried vomit.

"Radiation, Nina… You can see how the vermin have been busy."

He switched on the Geiger counter. The reading was low.

"Is it possible that the contaminated ground at Dounreay could have caused this, Conrad?"

"No, not possible on such a scale to end human life. This, I imagine, was caused by a great deal of radiation in the atmosphere at some time. It brings us back to the scenario of which way the wind blows. Her death could have been caused by radiation from anywhere on the planet—even new meteor strikes outside the twenty-five-mile radius. Otherwise, she would have been burnt to ash and would not be lying here. A strike close to home would have blown her ashes to kingdom come and destroyed the town." He paused, scanning the horizon. "I think we should tread carefully, Nina. It's possible that dogs have survived, and remember what we encountered on the Isle of Lewis. Therefore, I suggest we go as far as the train station to confirm what we've just found. We'll get bottles of water and any food we can salvage and carry, then get back to the yacht tout de suite."

"Do you think we should bury her, Conrad? It's so sad to leave her lying like this."

"Be sensible, Nina. We can't go burying every corpse we come across. It's hard to explain, but let's leave her to the weather and the vermin. That way, the rats will meet their end like they did on Harris."

They walked to the railway station, viewing several bodies on the way. Nina felt relieved when they reached the safety of the "Cathrine Wilson."

They set the sails and left the dead town of Thurso behind. The yacht was travelling along the Pentland Firth at a steady speed.

They pulled into John O' Groats for a rest. It was much the same as Thurso—gnawed bodies lay around, some in their own vomit; others, who had tried to get some relief, were floating in the harbour.

It was now abundantly clear to the two scientists that things were serious. It didn't take a meteor strike to wipe out a town or a place. Once again, the Geiger counter reading was low. Now they were faced with a decision on which way to go.

Over a hot meal, they talked it over. It was Nina who spoke sternly.

"I think we should go back to Edinburgh and seek shelter in the Ark—the fortress. No matter where we go, the radiation is going to follow us, and I'd rather be in the shelter if another meteor strikes close to home."

"Are you mad, Nina? Think of the send-off we got when we first set out on our journey."

"Okay, you decide what you're going to do, but you can drop me off in Inverness. I'll search for my parents among the rubble."

"That would be a suicide mission, and you know it, Nina. We've come through a lot together. I'm not going to help you throw your life away, so Edinburgh it is."

"I'm trying to find an answer to our dilemma, Conrad. That's why I suggested the Ark shelter as our best option." There was no more said on the subject.

Next morning, they plotted a course diagonally across the Cromarty Firth—not a place to be in a yacht when the northern and western gales got up. The waves crashed over the bow, drenching the "Cathrine Wilson" in salt water.

All hatches were closed. The pair struggled to trim the mainsail, allowing the bow sail to take the brunt of the weather, which still gave them propulsion towards the North Sea coast at Fraserburgh.

For the first time in the expedition, Nina was terrified. There had been other storms and gales, but this was different, as the yacht plunged into twenty-foot wave troughs, then rose to the wave apex before plunging back into the depths. She clung to the safety line, aware of how easily the sea could claim them both.

They were lucky to have the safety lines attached to the port railing, giving them a lifeline should either one be washed overboard. Conrad had also taken the precaution of securing each of them to the central mast fixing. The storm lasted two hours, and by the end, they were both physically seasick.

As they turned south towards the Firth of Tay, they scanned the shoreline for any sign of life. Fires that they had seen on the outward journey were no longer visible. The blue sky revealed meteorites traversing across space like Halley's Comet in the past. Some small fragments of debris from space could be seen burning up as they entered the Earth's atmosphere.

The scientists were convinced that they hadn't yet witnessed the worst of what was happening. With no communication to other parts of the world, they were at a dead end trying to figure out what the future would be for planet Earth. Their diaries did not make good reading. All they could do was continue towards Edinburgh's fortress—the Ark shelter.

A careful study was made of the east coast and marked into the yacht's log. Each day's report was the same: "Good, favourable weather. No sign of life."

They reached the mouth of the River Tay and eventually the Firth of Forth. Once again, there were no fires burning at night. Looking up the River Forth was like staring into desolation row—empty, lifeless, silent.

Conrad looked at his diary, then hurried up on deck where Nina was at the tiller wheel. He looked up into the heavens. The stars still shone—stars whose light had left them a million years ago and was only now reaching the planet. It showed the vastness of the cosmos, with billions of stars and trillions of planets. The Milky Way arched overhead, a ghostly reminder of what was eternal. Conrad studied the sky.

"I noticed this when we sailed from Harris, but now I have to ask," he hesitated, "where's the moon? According to my diary, we should be looking at a full moon."

"Don't forget your diary is out of date," Nina said with a smile.

"It matters not, Nina. The ancient Egyptians and desert tribes could plan their lunar calendars a year in advance, as could the Aztecs and Incas in South America."

"Let's just concentrate on getting home—if that's how we can describe it, Conrad. We'll be ready for whatever the heathens can throw at us."

She gave him one of her wry smiles. They had been away for nearly two years. Surely some form of government stability would have been restored inside the fortress. They didn't worry about the Ark shelter. It had been sealed by the combination security codes which Nina and Conrad both held in their heads.

After a long and arduous journey, the sails were trimmed and secured. Nina used the engine to berth the "Cathrine Wilson" yacht in the Leith basin. Conrad tipped the rubber protection buoys over the side, then climbed the ladder to the quayside to secure the yacht.

There was something different about the place. There was no sign of the digger that had launched the yacht. He couldn't put his finger on it just yet, but his intuition told him something wasn't quite right. He put a fresh magazine into his machine gun, then pulled the scooter onto the quay.

"You stay here, Nina. I'm going to have a look around. If I'm not back by nightfall, take the yacht out of the basin for protection, and please don't hesitate to shoot anyone approaching the yacht."

"Does that mean you as well, Conrad?" She paused. "Just be careful. I don't want to be alive without you."

Conrad started the scooter and took off towards Leith Walk. It was much the same as he and Nina had left it two years before. He reached the top of Leith Walk and drove into Princes Street. There was a surprise in store—the Royal Botanic Garden had been cleared of debris. An attempt had been made to re-erect the Scott Monument further along Princes Street. But apart from that, there was an uneasy silence—a silence so intense it would have deafened the unsuspecting and unprotected eardrums. Conrad had expected to hear some form of work going on at this time of day.

He switched off the scooter and stood listening for a bird song. That was something else missing from the sky. He had blamed the weather conditions for the lack of seabirds, but now there were doubts in his mind. The city felt like an abandoned stage after a performance—the set still standing, but all the actors gone.

He walked cautiously up to the fortress in Charlotte Square. Things weren't right. The large oak doors swung lazily on their hinges. Had the fortress been invaded and an attempt made to destroy it altogether? That thought seemed ridiculous because surely, if the fortress had been invaded, the attackers would either take it over or burn it to the ground.

Conrad removed the gun from his shoulder holster. He walked carefully around the square when he spotted the bodies in the wood garden. He crouched on one knee in a defensive position before venturing into the trees. He turned each body over, looking for tell-tale signs of radiation sickness. Men, women, and children had been shot through the head—some in the chest, others in the back, as if they had been running away from something.

There was no sign of mutilation like the commune heathens from the airport had displayed, with workers' heads on poles and promises of revenge if they ever reached the fortress. But that hadn't happened—the security gates had not been forced. Had somebody gone mad? It was one possible explanation for this massacre.

Conrad turned his attention to the tenements, starting with the one nearest the gates. He searched every flat. The ones that were locked, he forced open, only to find them empty. In the second close, he found a dead soldier in the stairwell and another on the stairs. He stepped over the body and climbed to the third floor, where he discovered a dozen bodies, some in a state of undress, shot at close range by an automatic weapon. They had all been sprayed with bullets, reaching the top floor while attempting to escape.

In the third close, some victims were on the stairs, others in their flats—and, like the second, they had been shot at close range. Conrad concluded this had been an execution carried out by a professional. There were two soldiers unaccounted for.

He had seen enough. He walked across the square to what was once the First Minister of Scotland's residence, now converted into four flats. He and Nina had occupied two. In the other two, he found the dead bodies of neighbours and their families. A dead soldier lay across the entrance door of a flat. Conrad noticed that the soldiers he had found were unarmed. There was still one who was unaccounted for.

He searched every part of the fortress. The armoury was empty. The food stores were empty. What had happened here?

He walked down to the scooter. He had planned to visit the Ark shelter, but the light was fading, so he made his way back to the yacht, where Nina was waiting patiently for his return. She had a meal ready for him.

Over dinner, Conrad explained the devastation he had found.

"We'll take separate watches during the night—four hours on, four hours off—then we'll drive to the Ark shelter tomorrow. We need to find out if anyone escaped the fortress carnage and made their way to the shelter hoping to gain entry. But they would have found it securely locked. It's only you and I who have the security code for opening the entrance and exit door at the rear."

Conrad took the first watch, 20:00 to midnight. He looked up at the stars and wondered what damage had been done to the cosmos. He took the second watch from 04:00 to 08:00.

He woke Nina with a gentle shake and a cup of coffee. After breakfast, they set off fully armed for the shelter.

They noticed a bus had been driven against the Ark shelter door. Conrad instructed Nina to stay back but keep alert. He walked towards the bus and stepped up into the aisle. The driver was dead, riddled with multiple wounds. The carnage inside the bus was horrific—men, women, and children massacred where they sat.

Conrad made his way off the bus, signalling for Nina to follow him.

"Did you find anybody alive, Conrad?"

He didn't expand on what he had found. "Nobody, and nothing that concerns us. Let's make our way to the rear where we can enter by the safety area."

Another shock awaited them. The loading ramp's bomb-proof door had been detached from its holdings, burnt off by a nearby acetylene gas torch. The digger had done the rest of the damage. Bit by bit, it had clawed away the bomb-proof concrete inner door. The Ark shelter had been breached, and a large gaping hole meant whoever had carried out this dastardly deed could still be alive and inside.

They stepped into the breach with pistols at the ready, using their LED pencil torches. Conrad flicked the generator switch up and down—nothing happened. Either the generator was out of fuel, or the batteries were dead.

A likely reason was that all the lights in the Ark shelter had been left on, putting greater demand on the generator. Without fuel top-ups, it would eventually have run dry and ceased to function.

# Chapter 18 - Blue Sky, New Plans

Eventually, the heavy-duty batteries would have gone flat, bringing darkness throughout. They checked the storerooms and found them stripped bare of any food. The armoury had also been emptied.

Step by cautious step, they searched each of the apartments—the central office where they had once sat with members to discuss the future running of the shelter. They ended their search at the gymnasium and operating theatre. It was like the story of the ship that drifted aimlessly, the "Mary Celeste"—everything intact aboard, tables set for a meal, but no crew.

They took care to ensure every electrical appliance and switch had been turned off in each apartment.

When they finally stepped outside through the breach, Conrad spoke earnestly.

"I think our first task is to take the five-gallon diesel cans from the yacht and top up the generator supply here at the shelter. We'll start up the generator using the heavy-duty batteries from the bus. Leave the generators running while we go to the filling station on the promenade and hope the foot pump and diesel outlet are still available. If so, we'll spend the day doing that until the generator's holding tank has plenty of diesel in it for future use—or until daylight begins to wane."

They set about their tasks with gusto, using the battle-hardened electric scooter that had served them so well.

That night, they sat discussing what could possibly have gone wrong in what had once been a reasonably safe environment like the fortress.

Conrad gave his theory of events.

"Let's start at the very beginning, when we experienced disruption in the shelter. There was still a deep anger against those making the decisions, especially against me—and that's why I called an election. I now move on to the clearance of roads and the building of the fortress. This took away some of the unrest. People were involved again and had a sense of pride. They had a daily task to perform.

"Now I come to the question—who wielded out punishment for small misdemeanours that could have been sorted at board level?"

"Jack Dempster, the works foreman?" Nina asked quickly.

Conrad shook his head. "Duncan Henderson—the Commander of the security soldiers, Nina. He was known always to carry a swagger stick with him. There were no reports of the beatings because people were afraid of repercussions from him. But it was Jack Dempster who reported him to me because the beatings were affecting his works programme. I think that's the reason I started planning our escape. I know I was being watched. I believe it was Duncan Henderson and his gang who were firing at us the day we set sail from the Leith quay." He paused.

"So, when we departed, the Commander took charge and control of the fortress. Those that didn't conform and obey his coup and despotic regime were singled out and shot. I think what I'm about to say next has a bearing on the security soldiers. Did they start to revolt against the murder of innocent families? I think so. Had they considered the situation that they and their families might be next? The Commander couldn't risk a coup when he took command; therefore, he had them shot. I'm trying to figure out how he managed that, and the assumption I've come up with is this." Conrad hesitated.

"The Commander was responsible for handing out the weapons. Each soldier would have been handed a rifle and given a specific task of rounding up the disobedient, but the bullets had been removed from the rifles, and Duncan Henderson shot them without any resistance. It was he who would have carried out the executions in each close. He would have taken the rifles, which were still an important commodity, back to the armoury and locked them away.

"Now he had the residents of the fortress at his mercy. But our despot hadn't finished. I think he drove out to the airport commune and offered them a peace treaty—an entry into the fortress; food, water, medical supplies; and, most important, ammunition. The commune would have been in dire straits had they not accepted this saviour's offer."

Conrad gave a wry smile. "Now the Commander has a problem. With so many mouths to feed, and food stocks running low, he set about gaining entrance to the Ark shelter, where there were adequate supplies to feed the hungry mouths. He knew it would be impossible to break down the bomb-proof doors at the front, so he began dismantling the loading-bay entrance. Over a period, they clawed at the loading-platform doors until they finally gained entrance. That began a downward spiral that we witnessed today. It has now become clear that Henderson knew nothing of the supermarkets on the promenade."

Nina spoke softly. "Is Duncan Henderson alive today? If he is, I'll shoot him myself."

Conrad rose and held her fondly by the shoulders. He gave her an endearing shake. "My, what a 'she-devil' I have in my midst. How lucky I am that she's on my side."

They both gave a stifled laugh.

"I wouldn't worry too much about the Commander. If he and the others have joined the airport commune, they'll have met their match. It won't be long before someone sticks a knife in him. Let's have an early night; we have a lot to do tomorrow." He paused. "Before we retire, I want to suggest a different expedition. I was wondering what has happened to our friends south of the border. So, if we travel down the east coast of England to the English Channel, then along the south coast to the Isles of Scilly, into the Celtic Sea, calling to explore Dublin, then travel up the Irish Sea, the Isle of Man, and Belfast—it wouldn't take long to travel from there up and into the Firth of Clyde and the River Clyde, just to see if the city of Glasgow has survived."

"That's a long sea journey, and there is no guarantee that we'll be able to scavenge for food and water. Therefore, I'm prepared to go to our limit, which would be Scarborough in East Yorkshire."

Conrad was disappointed. They had taken risks before and won through, but the decision had to be unanimous. He trudged wearily to his cabin and fell asleep fully dressed.

Next morning, they were up early to get as much done as possible before setting sail for the English coast. The Ark shelter batteries were now fully charged. The digger and JCB batteries were charged, and the machines were ready to go to work. Nina checked the side entrance door by typing in the codes. The doors opened lethargically after being stuck in the same position for so long. She didn't close them with the codes but left them in the manual operating control-lever position so that they could be opened manually. She didn't want to witness any more damage when they returned from their next expedition, should any survivors stumble across the Ark shelter. Their problem would be finding food to sustain them. Water wasn't a problem—the Ark shelter supply came from the small loch up on Arthur's Seat above the shelter. Nina had always intended to climb to the summit to inspect the city of Edinburgh from the heights; she put it on her to-do list when they got back.

Conrad had manoeuvred the steel bomb-proof door into position with the digger and began to weld a seam down both edges. Nina explained that the coded doors were working as normal. She went on to say she had left them for manual operation.

"Is that a good idea, Nina? What happens if the commune and the Commander come back? We need to be sure that the Ark shelter is secure."

Nina shrugged her shoulders. "They would only find another way into the Ark shelter like before; besides, that is not what the Noah's Ark shelter was built for."

Conrad knew it would be a waste of breath disagreeing any further.

After all lights were switched off and the time clock that controlled the street lights unplugged, the generator was shut down, and the small bomb-proof doors were firmly closed behind them. They stopped to fill the five-gallon jerrycans. Conrad made another trip to the filling station for the second diesel jerrycan. Finally, the jerrycans and the scooter were lowered onto the "Cathrine Wilson" in preparation for their next adventure.

The sun was rising when they set sail for the border with England. When they turned south, bypassing Dunbar then Berwick-upon-Tweed, there was a stiff breeze that billowed both sails. The yacht was travelling through the calm waters of the North Sea at a considerable speed.

They reached Newcastle on the River Tyne sooner than expected. There was a strange purple fog that engulfed the river and the city.

"That is really weird, Conrad," Nina said, raising her binoculars again. "Let's get out of here and head for Scarborough."

Conrad scanned the fog that blanketed the city of Newcastle. There was a telling sign that something was wrong. The Angel of the North was missing from the hill above the city. He should have been able to see the top of the bridge that spanned the River Tyne. Once again, nothing was visible. He was disappointed.

Nina had already begun to hoist the mainsail and advised Conrad to take the helm. "This is not a good environment to be in."

He reached for the Geiger counter. It read excessive radiation levels, bordering on the dangerous bleeping signal. He raced to the bow and hoisted the sail. The "Cathrine Wilson" departed from the mouth of the River Tyne. Nina was relieved that the wind was blowing favourably.

They bypassed Hartlepool and Whitby and reached Robin Hood's Bay, where they dropped anchor. They would proceed south to Scarborough the following morning.

It was a beautiful morning with a beautiful setting. Robin Hood's Bay was a small curved sandy cove with a lush green embankment and what had once been thatched hamlets above a cave. They had breakfast on deck.

Conrad lifted his binoculars and tested the air with the Geiger counter, relieved it registered zero. It was the first time he had encountered this. He scanned the shoreline around the cove and stopped suddenly.

"What have you seen, Conrad?" Nina said with interest.

He handed her the binoculars. "The cave, Nina—take a look at the cave."

There was no doubt in her mind—a human being. The first live human they had encountered since they had arrived at Thurso on their way to the Outer Hebrides. They both stood on the deck waving their arms with excitement. The figure at the cave entrance gestured in the same manner.

They left their breakfast, fetched the outboard motor from below, then boarded the rubber rescue dinghy with haste. Conrad pulled the rope to start the outboard. It spluttered into life and the dinghy moved towards the shore where the lonely figure stood.

Nina couldn't contain herself. She jumped into the water and waded ashore, taking the stranger's hand and shaking it with joy.

Introductions were made, then they walked up to the cave entrance and sat on the sand. They talked and talked until Nina put a question to him.

"How many have survived, Johnny?" Nina asked quickly.

"My wife and I were the only survivors from the hamlets. Many people survived the initial blast that destroyed the village. It was the purple haze cloud that came in from the south that killed each villager off, I assumed with radiation sickness and typhoid fever. The purple rain that fell from the clouds wasn't boiled; the people ignored the warning and paid the price. They dropped like ten-pin bowling skittles until they were finally wiped out. However, luck was on our side. We were out fishing when the purple mist came in from the south and descended across the landscape. It was truly weird. Just like a blanket, it moved very slowly northwards, but by that time the damage was done. We spent the night and all the next day drifting in the boat, watching the thick purple haze move in slow motion."

"That would be the mist-like fog we saw on the Tyne, Johnny. We have a Geiger counter that registers radiation levels, which showed dangerously high levels in the river estuary, so we set sail immediately from the River Tyne estuary."

"Did you shower or gargle after you left the area? They say it helps to keep the body clear of radiation. Personally, I don't believe a word of it."

Conrad could see the concern in Nina's face. "Where is your wife now, Johnny?"

"Thora died of natural causes three months ago. She's buried on the ridge above the cave. That way she is always with me."

*Conrad and Nina exchanged a brief, respectful silence—the first quiet acknowledgement that hope and loss were now inseparable companions. They both understood the need to move carefully, test the air often, and treat any water before use.*

"And the fishing boat?"

"Taken by some villagers hoping to escape the devastation that surrounded them. I never saw either of them again."

"What about food and water… Do you struggle with that?"

Johnny hesitated. Was this pair of scavengers ready to kill him and take his supply line? He was candid with his answer. "There are still some crops that grow in the field—potatoes and turnips mostly. I wash them thoroughly in the North Sea salt water before boiling them. I also walk as far as York and Scarborough, hoping to find what's left in the destroyed supermarkets."

"That's our next destination," Nina said, interrupting the conversation.

"You're wasting your time, Nina. The town was destroyed by a meteor that landed in Bridlington. Then came the purple mist. The only survivors and beneficiaries are the rats—thousands of the blighters as big as kittens."

Nina shivered. "We have a nuclear shelter in Edinburgh if you wish to join us."

Johnny smiled, then opened his arms. "And leave all this luxury behind? No fear, thanks. Besides, Thora would be left on her own. I can't allow that to happen."

Nina appreciated his loyalty. "A change of plan, Conrad. You've heard what Johnny has said about Scarborough, so what's the point of going there? Can I suggest we set sail for home instead?"

Conrad nodded in agreement.

Johnny stood up. "Both of you have made a wise decision. Who knows what the future holds in store for us? The meteors still fill the night sky. Where will the next one land? And now it's time to pay Thora a visit."

Conrad was quick to ask a question. "Your position out here makes it an ideal place to view the stars at night, but have you seen our moon? I've searched the night skies for months with no results."

The old man looked sad. "You'll never see another moon, Conrad. The lunar surface was pounded so badly it just gave up and disintegrated into small fragments that were blown away into outer space. I would imagine some larger fragments landed here on Earth, but most parts just burnt away when they entered Earth's stratosphere."

Johnny walked them down to the water's edge and helped push the dinghy from the shore. When they reached the yacht, they could see Johnny standing on the ridge, waving furiously. There were tears in Nina's eyes as they hoisted the mainsail. Would she ever again encounter a living human being? She doubted that very much.

Now it was back to work. The journey north was slow as the "Cathrine Wilson" yacht battled against the currents of the North Sea. The wind had swung round to the northwest. That made it harder for the sails to fill and propel the yacht forward. It meant constant trimming and hoisting the bow sail. Sometimes the engine propeller was used to assist a dormant mainsail. It took some careful work to conserve enough fuel to glide into the Leith harbour basin. On the way north, every opportunity was taken to scan the coastline for any sign of life. They had been given false hope by the appearance of Johnny, the Yorkshire survivor.

It had been a hard and arduous journey to the place they called home. The Leith basin berth was just as they had left it. Their prime objective would be the Ark shelter, to find out if it had been vandalised.

After a good night's sleep, they set out after breakfast for the shelter, taking an empty jerrycan with them to refill at the filling station. After a quick inspection of the outer doors, which were intact, they stepped inside the Ark shelter and switched on the generator, then poured another five gallons of diesel into the holding tank. The street lighting was switched on manually. Armed and ready, they walked up one side of the street, searching each flat, and down the other side. Everything was as they had left it before sailing southwards.

There was a sound of relief in Nina's voice as she made her way to the toilet block. After a short time, she appeared ashen-faced. She avoided answering Conrad's question if she was all right. They shut down the street lighting and generator, once again closing the west-side small door that could be opened manually. The five-gallon jerrycan was refilled and taken to the yacht.

They now had time to deliberate on their journey south, the discovery of a living soul, and restoring the yacht's supplies.

"What now, Nina? Where will our endeavours take us? I thought of Scandinavia—Norway, Sweden—the world's our oyster." He smiled.

"Why do you make out that our damned position isn't serious, as if nothing has happened?"

Conrad wondered what had become of Nina. Her moods had changed since leaving Robin Hood's Bay. It was not her style to be touchy. She had always acted responsibly and met each challenge with gusto. She would talk things over with him, as he did with her, but something was bothering her, and now was the time to sort it out.

He placed an arm around her shoulders. "Right, my dear friend and companion. It's time to tell your old sparring partner what's wrong—why the mood swings?"

She turned to face him. "I suppose it's just a matter of time before you find out the cause of my moods."

She stepped back from him and lifted her sweatshirt. "This is what's wrong, Conrad."

He couldn't believe his eyes. On both sides of her stomach were purple and black bulbous swellings. She lifted the garment over her brassiere to her shoulders. It revealed bulbous swellings on her chest and below her oxters.

"This is a sure sign that I've contracted radiation. I was feeling sick when we were at the Ark shelter. It's just a matter of time before the sickness takes hold, so I'm afraid I'll have to give Scandinavia a miss."

Conrad had to sit. He was close to breaking down but held back the tears in his glazed eyes. He was struck dumb. There were so many things he wanted to say to the woman who had been his soulmate since his wife and children had gone to her parents on the Isle of Harris. It was Nina who had given him the strength to carry on when he had wanted to give up.

She sat down beside him. "I'm sorry if I've been a pain these last few days, but now you know the reason." She got up quickly and asked, "What would you say to a corned beef candlelight meal?" She smiled.

Conrad wasn't listening. He was examining the small bulbous swellings on his own torso. He felt for the swellings in his armpits.

There were signs, but not as advanced as Nina's. He stood up and ventured to the galley kitchen.

"You sit and rest, Nina. I'll make the dinner."

"Don't you dare treat me like an invalid, Conrad Wilson. If it pleases you, we'll both make the dinner."

They sat down to a corned beef candlelight meal, with wine and sliced tinned pears and custard for afters. Coffee and mints made them sit back and relax as another bottle of red was opened. They talked quite candidly about where they had contracted the radiation.

"Definitely at the River Tyne estuary," Nina said confidently. "I had a gut feeling that something was wrong when we witnessed the purple fog that engulfed the city of Newcastle, and we have nobody to blame but ourselves." She gave another wry smile.

Conrad agreed. "What now, Nina—do you want me to take you back to Inverness? Say the word and we'll set sail tomorrow morning."

"I don't think we'll have the time to do that, Conrad—then we also have you to consider. We've been together through thick and thin. If I can suggest something while we finish our wine." She took a large swallow before continuing. "I don't think it'll be too long before our radiation starts to take hold and make us vomit. I can feel churning in my stomach and lungs, and before you say it, this is not the wine." She smiled.

"Our lives are coming to an end, my friend—probably I'll go first—so this is what I want you to do." She finished her wine, then topped up their glasses. "Put me into deep freeze in the Ark shelter until you play catch-up, then take us both out to sea, where we can easily be put over the side of the 'Cathrine Wilson' that has served our cause so well. Please tell me what you're thinking. You always were the quiet one."

"What I'm thinking is close to your suggestion, with a slight twist. Why not set sail into the North Sea together and end it there when I open the seacocks to the sea? We have our cyanide poison vessels to make things easier. When you've decided to end your life, I'll take the precaution of shooting you, before I crunch on my cyanide vessel, then quickly turn the gun on myself."

Nina gave a stifled laugh. "You always were one for dramatics, Conrad Wilson—but yes, that is an excellent idea."

They finished the bottle of red before going to their cabins.

Next morning, Conrad was busy on the quayside. He had taken the long thick rope they had used when they launched the yacht two years before. He couldn't help hearing Nina's suffering as she retched and vomited loudly over the side of the yacht. His own bulbous boils had swelled during the night, and he was beginning to feel the pains in his stomach and chest as the radiation took effect on his immune system.

He threw the thick rope with a loop onto the yacht and climbed aboard.

"You're not planning to hang me from the yardarm, Conrad?"

"No, but I have a purpose for it, so have patience."

The yacht was put astern then turned to face the open North Sea. Conrad steered towards one of the oil-platform legs. He tied the rope to the bollard fixing on the bow, then wrapped it and secured it with several reef knots. He brought the "Cathrine Wilson" alongside the leg.

The tide was high enough to lasso the rope onto the leg. He watched as the rope slid down below the water level. Nina watched in amazement. She understood the purpose: it was to secure the yacht to the leg, which would act as a capstan and keep the "Cathrine Wilson" in one place when she sank to the seabed.

She watched him put what supplies they had aboard into the rubber dinghy, then untie it from the stern. They watched as the dinghy floated away.

"I've kept a bottle of champagne, dear Conrad," she said, attempting to stifle a vomit.

"Why not, dear heart—we deserve it."

They went below and began to drink to a future—an unknown future. Conrad couldn't get to a sink or toilet quickly enough. He retched and vomited time after time onto the floor.

"Never mind, Conrad. You've done well today. We'll leave that mess for the sea to clean up, but now I think it's time." She took his champagne flute and threw it into the false fireplace.

Nina opened all the portholes and hatches as Conrad went down to the bilges of the yacht and opened the seacocks. They met in the galley and hugged each other tightly. She took his trembling hand and led him to her bedroom.

They lay down together and reached for their cyanide poison vessels. Conrad checked the revolver for bullets again.

Now they were ready. Conrad took her hand in his. Nina kissed him gently on the cheek, then placed the glass vessel into her mouth. She looked at him one last time before biting down on the cyanide poison. She was dead in seconds.

Conrad hugged her close, then shot her in the temple. He had to be quick before the flooding water reached the cabin. He bit down on the glass vessel, then fired at his temple.

The "Cathrine Wilson" yacht had now completed her last mission successfully as she sank serenely to the ocean's depths, firmly secured to the leg on the ocean floor. The two friends would be together for eternity.

# The End